# A Will of IRON

LINDA BEUTLER

Oysterville, WA

This is a work of fiction. Names, characters, places, and incidents are products of the author's imagination or are used fictitiously. Any resemblance to actual events or persons, living or dead, is entirely coincidental.

A WILL OF IRON

 For information: P.O. Box 34, Oysterville WA 98641

ISBN: 978-1-936009-44-2

Cover design by Zorylee Diaz-Lupitou
Layout by Ellen Pickels

# PROLOGUE

*7 April 1812*

*This has been a most trying evening. Mama continues furious that Darcy has gone away again without extending an offer of marriage. I say, bless him. She goes on and on, and I do wish she would invite the vicarage guests to dinner to ease the strain on me as she does not yammer quite so much in company. Or perhaps the presence of others makes it easier for me to ignore her. Selfish, Anne!*

*After feeling achy and fatigued all afternoon, I now have an increasingly sharp pain. It seems to be inside of me behind my right hip. I pray it is naught to do with the baby. I excused myself from Mama early, and Mrs. J is preparing a draught for me.*

*Oh, how Mama pines for my cousins, but I confess I was glad to see the back of them. Darcy and Alex interrupted my study of Elizabeth Bennet, and I shall be happy to return to sketching her character. What an interesting young woman she is. How might she develop if given a chance to marry well or possessed of the funds to assure her independence? Throughout the day, I considered her appearance Sunday evening and grow convinced she does not view marriage as her destiny. That she exercises some hold over Darcy is fascinating. I do so long for him to settle and find happiness. It may as well be her as anyone. That there appears no affection on her side is odd, as surely she must know he is eligible and coveted. We cannot accuse her of courting his money; I shall say that.*

*Darcy's life has been one of duty with little enough pleasure. Circumstances have wrung the capacity for joy out of him, poor man. He was my favourite cousin when we were children, but grief and duty have ruined him. He was certainly more out of spirits than ever when he left here, and I did not learn more of what might have transpired between him and Miss Bennet.*

*If the morning finds the pain decreased, I shall drive to the vicarage and perhaps convince EB to join me in the phaeton for a little tour. I do think I would like her to know there is more to me than she might surmise. Our odious vicar will no doubt see this as a sensational act, but what do I care now? Soon I shall have need of a friend made of sturdier stuff than dear, simple Mrs. J is. Although my actions court disgrace, it is my own selfish release I seek, and Miss Bennet might be a better companion to me—more astute certainly and capable of unconventional thought. And, in return, I am able to set her wages very high indeed.*

*Perhaps I shall give EB a little gift tomorrow, something she could sell if her circumstances ever come to that necessity. Knowing what I have already arranged, one might deem it foreshadowing, but I pray it is not. Here is Mrs. J with my tea and draught. —A de B*

# CHAPTER 1
## A Death at Rosings

*Wednesday, 8 April 1812, Rosings*

Lady Catherine de Bourgh stood at the foot of her daughter's bed looking at the lifeless body. She could still hear in her mind the frenzied, incoherent wailing of Mrs. Jenkinson, Anne's companion, when she had entered her ladyship's bedchamber just after dawn. It would take days to erase the sound from her memory, but erase it she would.

"Daft woman," Lady Catherine muttered. That the woman would burst into Lady Catherine's room without first allowing the maid to awaken her ladyship properly and that Mrs. Jenkinson's first coherent words involved begging—no, *beseeching*—that she not be blamed for Anne's death were not to be borne. She dismissed Mrs. Jenkinson summarily.

Lesser maids were now assisting Mrs. Jenkinson's removal, and the larger footmen would see the harmless, tiny, twittering woman off the grounds of Rosings Park. They would help her catch the post coach to London, and Lady Catherine would *not* provide a character.

With a sigh, she shook her head. It was a revelation after nurturing and abetting her daughter's hypochondria for over twenty years—since Anne had caught a stubborn cold at the age of four and learnt to manipulate her mother with exaggerated or altogether imaginary ailments—that there actually might have been something seriously wrong. Perhaps the arrival of the doctor would solve the mystery. For now, Lady Catherine ordered the body not be touched and turned away to dress more carefully than she had earlier in the haste of panic.

She stopped before crossing the hall to her own suite, turning a grim eye in appraisal of the painting of Fitzwilliam Darcy next to Anne's door. "Fie, Nephew…I shall have you understand she died of a broken heart, I am sure." A movement outside the windows at the end of the hall caught her eye. She looked at her pocket watch. It was ten o'clock, and William Collins, the vicar, was making his way to Rosings from the Hunsford parish house, crunching along the gravel as he did most every morning. *I could set my clocks by him. Well. This morning he can wait until the doctor arrives and I am more formally attired.*

"Albertine!" Lady Catherine called with unnecessary stridency. Her maid was already standing in the dressing room with arms extended to begin removing the morning dress and replace it with a mourning gown and black veil.

"*Oui, madame*?" Albertine was a Yorkshire woman through and through —born Bertha Donald—but it pleased Lady Catherine to pretend she had a French maid. In her heart, she never trusted the French, an intuition she boasted of in the present political atmosphere—"I was right, you see," she often said—still, it was the fashion to have a French maid. Since Bertha was not opposed to learning a few words of what Lady Catherine thought a quite slovenly language, everyone was appeased.

"Unpack all of my widow's weeds from when dear Sir Lewis died. I cannot imagine my figure has altered much in these fifteen years. After the doctor has gone and I have written to the family and the Archbishop of Canterbury, we shall try to salvage what we can. We must send some of the old gowns to Mrs. Collins to wear. For now, this gown I bought when old Mr. Darcy died will do." She was soon waiting to receive the physician in a gown fitting her much like a sausage casing.

William Collins was not a clever man, nor was he astute. He was not adept at anything in particular although he was verbose. He was a passable gardener through diligence rather than intuitive skill. But for all of that, even *he* could sense the situation was far from well at Rosings. The usually loquacious footman, who would relate the latest gossip along with speculation as to her ladyship's current mood and chat until his mistress's arrival necessitated his return to feigned taciturnity, was not present. The housekeeper, a dour woman, led him to the small drawing room where Lady Catherine usually received him. He sat alone for *quite* some time.

By the head of the bed stood the impatiently waiting physician of the inert Anne de Bourgh. He looked up, amused, as Lady Catherine bustled into the room, her panting bosom straining at the buttons of a black bombazine and satin pelisse covering a black lace and mesh gown over a white petticoat. She stopped on the opposite side of the bed and, for one quiet moment, observed the ashen face of Anne in her final repose.

The physician cleared his throat. "Ahem, your ladyship. Might we have the curtains opened? Making my examination with natural light would be most efficacious."

Lady Catherine waved a hand, and the two chambermaids flung back the draperies, admitting the pale spring sun. Even this displeased Lady Catherine as the loss of her daughter was at last beginning to weigh on her. She would have found a polite drizzle more suitable.

"Well?" asked Lady Catherine.

"With your assistance, ma'am." The physician took a handful of counterpane and waited for Lady Catherine to do the same. Together they drew down the bedclothes that covered the corpse.

"Ah!" gasped Lady Catherine.

"Oh, my!" echoed the doctor. The lower half of Anne's torso down to her knees was covered in blood, still rather brightly red, having been covered and kept warm by the last heat from her feverish body.

Anne de Bourgh died wearing a heavy, white flannel nightgown, and it was soaked in various hues of red that faded to a quite unfortunate shade of pink at the stain's outer reaches.

For all her appearance of strength, Lady Catherine turned away and motioned to her maid for a chamber pot in which to vomit; however, her acute nausea did not go quite that far, as much as she felt it could.

"Would your ladyship take something to calm your stomach and nerves?" The physician was quick to place the needs of the living over those of the dead.

Lady Catherine shed a raven feather from her black lace cap as she violently shook her head until she could murmur, "No. No, thank you." She motioned for Albertine to bring a chair, and she sank into it.

The physician watched her carefully. "Do you feel well enough to answer a few questions, your ladyship?"

Lady Catherine settled her wits and returned to form. "Of course I do."

"These will be indelicate questions, madam." The physician cast a doubtful eye upon the chambermaids and returned his gaze to Lady Catherine.

"What indelicacy would bother Anne now? Pray, ask your questions, Dr. Roberts."

"Were her courses difficult for her?"

It occurred to Lady Catherine that she had no notion whether her daughter's monthly bleeding was regular, difficult, scant, or voluminous. "Candid as my dear daughter was about her physical limitations and ailments—although she was always so very brave—had her monthlies been unusual in any way, I can only assume she would have been forthcoming."

The physician merely nodded, thinking it odd that the mother of the neighbourhood's most wealthy virgin had no knowledge of her daughter's particulars. He looked at the three other occupants of the room, the lady's maid and two chambermaids, and lowered his voice. "She was not with child?"

Lady Catherine stood, levitated by righteous outrage. Wild-eyed, she motioned for her maid to approach and snatched the fan from her hands. Oscillating it as vigorously as possible, she hissed, "No, sir, she most certainly was not!"

Again, the doctor glanced about the room. "Lady Catherine, may I ask after Mrs. Jenkinson? I find it highly unusual for so intimate a companion to be absent from her mistress's side. Has she been made unwell by these circumstances?"

With her indignation firmly on exhibit, Lady Catherine explained her utterly justifiable release of Mrs. Jenkinson from her employment.

"Madam, you make my task a great deal more difficult. How am I to ascertain a cause of death when the person most likely to have last seen Miss de Bourgh alive is banished from the house?" The physician shook his head with disapprobation. "Do you suspect anything untoward?"

"I most certainly do not," came the mortified reply.

The physician turned and sniffed the tumbler sitting near the bed. It smelt of brandy and elderberry cordial. There was an empty vial of laudanum, but the teacup smelt of nothing stronger than chamomile.

"And what of Paulette, Miss de Bourgh's maid?"

"Ah, well. She is presently making an inventory of my daughter's jewels. Mrs. Jenkinson might have wished to take a souvenir to which she was not entitled."

The physician stifled his chuckle. He knew Lady Catherine well enough to find her typically ridiculous in considering petty theft a greater insult than the possible accidental poisoning of her daughter.

"May I speak to Paulette, please?"

The doctor covered the body. Albertine stepped into the next chamber, Anne's sitting room, and returned with Paulette, a younger but otherwise similar person to Mrs. Jenkinson: small, frail, nearly feeble-minded, skittish, and timid. The little maid hailed from one of the poorer districts of London and, like Albertine, received a French name. Paulette approached with lowered eyes.

"You need not fear, Paulette; Miss Anne is covered," the physician began. "I would ask you to speak of Miss Anne's recent health. Were her courses regular?"

The maid glanced at Lady Catherine fearfully. "Answer him, Paulette," came the order.

"Yes'm." Paulette faced the doctor. "She has not bled since after Christmas, sir. I remember 'cause her time came Christmas mornin', and she was sore put out. Went around mutterin' for days."

"What? Why was I not told of this?" Lady Catherine adopted the tone of an imperious despot.

The little maid lowered her head and responded with a barely audible, "It was to be a secret, ma'am."

And with that, the curiosity of the physician was fully engaged. "With your permission, your ladyship, I believe I must make a physical examination of your daughter's body."

Lady Catherine looked at him stupidly. She was most displeased.

"I must beg your leave to touch her, Lady Catherine."

She frowned and narrowed her eyes. She surveyed the maids. "Paulette, Albertine, stay with me. You two"—she pursed her lips at the chambermaids—"go!"

The chambermaids did not require a second instruction.

Upon finishing his examination—made more lengthy by the unsurprising, repeated fainting of Paulette—the physician requested the maids leave the room. When he and Lady Catherine were alone, he drew himself to his full height, if slightly bent with a back infirmity, and said, "I believe your daughter died from complications *primigravida*."

Lady Catherine tried to appear sage. "Yes, I have warned her of that many times."

The doctor lowered his eyes and sighed to suppress outright laughter. "Let me remind you, ma'am, *primigravida* refers to a first…um. Hmmm. I *do* believe your daughter"—he dropped his voice—"was with child."

Lady Catherine's eyes flew open. The colour drained from her face then returned in full force, and she made every effort to chase the doctor from the premises.

It was of no concern to him that a caterwauling Lady Catherine hurriedly escorted him from the house. He hied to Hunsford village where he sought Mrs. Spiggotson, the midwife. He had learnt more of female complaints from her than from any *medicinae liber.*

*1 July 1811*

*And so starts another half-year of my ramblings in these blank pages. Long, or so it is to be hoped, in the far-off future, someone will come upon these ravings and sputterings and think what a strange life I had been forced to live and what a thoroughly odd woman I was to accept this lot with so little outward complaint. I accept the disapprobation of the future with a wink. Perhaps this year something will happen. Perhaps this year I shall find an escape that does not involve making an unhappy marriage. I have come into my inheritance and now have both the means and the wit to contrive something.*

*…And so, indeed, it already has! Merely two hours after writing that first of a half-year's daily paragraphs, my cousins, Darcy and Georgiana, followed later by Alexander, arrived with more than their usual bustle and fanfare. Little G is soggy with tears. Darcy tries with little success to control a towering rage in her presence. Only Alex, for all his military bombast and tendency to morbid metaphor, shows the silly chit any compassion. It seems Little G has been interrupted in a scheme to elope with a highly unsuitable person, and has been unceremoniously deposited here whilst her guardians decide whether anything more must be done to secure her reputation. Mama is true to form, insisting too loudly for the necessary secrecy. One could set a clock by the manner and punctuality of her comments. As ever, I cloak myself in disinterestedness and ennui and shall choose my moment after Darcy and*

*Alex have gone to listen to Little G's tale as no one else will and try to help her if I am able. Of course, advice to the lovelorn is not my long suit. I know nothing of such matters. —A de B*

*3 July 1811*

*Little G's saga gains in the telling, and each day brings a new revelation. It seems the unsuitable suitor was George Wickham, son of Uncle Darcy's steward, John Wickham. His plan was to compromise her and gain access to her 30,000£, leaving her ruined and shamed, taking a nick out of the Darcy family's old escutcheon. He sounds an interesting sort to be so blinded by the need for revenge, but revenge for what? That his father was not George Darcy? It must be quite a thing, the drive to release one's envy. Had Mama been a man, would she have been such a one, jealous of the good fortune of a friend?*

*I do vaguely recall George Wickham when at Pemberley as a child, but Mama would have kept me well away from such a playmate. I believe he is slightly younger than Darcy, perhaps a year older than I.*

*But I cannot wish the man on Little G. I have not spoken to her yet. She is to be with us a month, so there is time to offer her comfort and the warning due one who may inherit an even more vast estate than Rosings if her brother does not find a suitable wife. I pray daily for Darcy to marry. Anyone will do as long as it is not I. —A de B*

# CHAPTER 2
## Into Safekeeping

*Wednesday, 8 April 1812, the village of Hunsford*

Mrs. Jenkinson stood primly, wearing a worried expression. She shifted from one foot to the other, preferring to stand guard over her two small cases rather than occupy a bench. It was a relief it was not a market day, and no one was in the lane that she knew well enough to have to explain anything. It would be over four hours until the post coach would pass through, carrying her away from the village and anyone who ought to know the truth.

It was a surprise, then, when Mrs. Charlotte Collins and Miss Elizabeth Bennet emerged from a cottage where the vicar's wife was paying a sick-room call. Mrs. Jenkinson was clearly alarmed to encounter them, but the dithering woman realised her opportunity.

"Oh, Mrs. Collins! Miss Bennet! This is a terrible day…terrible!"

"Mrs. Jenkinson! Why are you here?" asked Elizabeth.

Charlotte noted the luggage and reached the likeliest conclusion. "Have you been let go?"

"She is dead, Mrs. Collins! Miss Anne died in the night, and Lady Catherine has put me out." Mrs. Jenkinson burst into tears. Distressed, Elizabeth and Charlotte gathered around her with words of sympathy. When Mrs. Jenkinson could collect herself, she murmured, "And I know the truth, Mrs. Collins. I have the proof of why she died, and I do not know what to do. Lady Catherine would not want to admit the truth or have it known, but Miss Anne would."

"Whatever do you mean?" Elizabeth asked with a touch of exasperation.

"Miss Anne kept a journal. I was able to conceal the most recent two volumes, or the truth would be hidden and probably destroyed. Her ladyship would never let it out if she knew."

"What is your situation, Mrs. Jenkinson?" asked Charlotte. "What is your destination?" She was inclined to behave charitably towards Mrs. Jenkinson, to say nothing of how piqued her curiosity had become. She met Elizabeth's eye, silently requesting her friend's patience. Elizabeth nodded. Her interest was also raised.

"Her ladyship has put me out," Mrs. Jenkinson whined, "with a ticket to London and the wages she owed. She will not give me a recommendation… all because I awoke her rather than allow her maid to do so. And her daughter lying *dead*!" Mrs Jenkinson sniffed but did not allow herself to be overcome.

Knowing her husband to be at Rosings, Charlotte met Elizabeth's eye again, now with a look of instant decision. "Lizzy, help me with Mrs. Jenkinson's cases, and we shall return to the vicarage. She will wait with us, and we shall determine what is to be done."

"Oh, no, Mrs. Collins! What would your husband say?" Mrs. Jenkinson was a simple woman, but even a person more possessed by foolishness than she would have observed that no one and nothing came before William Collins's devotion to his patroness.

"He will not know of it. It is half past ten, and he is at Rosings. Under the circumstances, he will no doubt stay longer than his usual hour."

Mrs. Jenkinson nodded. "Oh, of course…such a steady man."

Elizabeth and Charlotte each took a case and followed Mrs. Jenkinson the quarter-mile to the vicarage.

Charlotte called for the tea service as she entered her house, and the three women settled into Mr. Collins's book room, which afforded them the best view of the road. They sat quietly until after the hot water was brought. As soon as the servant withdrew and Charlotte set about making and pouring the tea, Mrs. Jenkinson turned to the smaller of her two cases and drew forth two black-bound books. She sat with them upon her lap, tapping them idly and ignoring her tea.

Elizabeth leaned forward. "Mrs. Jenkinson, are you unwell?"

"Who could be well on a day such as this?" She looked at Elizabeth and then at Charlotte and seemed to come to a decision. She held the two books towards Charlotte. "Take these, Mrs. Collins."

Charlotte reached for them just as Mrs. Jenkinson leaned back, withdrawing the books to her bosom. "They contain Miss Anne's heartfelt dreams, thoughts, and desires, or so she said." Mrs. Jenkinson drew herself up straight and proud. "I, of course, have not read them—not one word—though Miss Anne did often tell me what she had written or asked me to remind her of something she wanted to write lest she forget." Mrs. Jenkinson realised she had withheld the books and proffered them again, this time towards Elizabeth. "You should read them too, Miss Bennet. You might not have known it, but she thought highly of you."

As Elizabeth reached for them, Mrs. Jenkinson absently pulled the books back to her lap, folding her hands over them. "It would be safer if you both knew the contents. Yes, you should both read them."

Hiding a smile, Elizabeth said, "Indeed, Mrs. Jenkinson, I understand you felt more for Miss de Bourgh than mere companionship, and if it gives you comfort that Mrs. Collins and I read her words, then we shall certainly do so."

"She was a remarkable young lady in spite of her mother," Mrs. Jenkinson whispered and then looked rather shocked to have admitted such a thing.

Charlotte leaned forward, placing a hand on Mrs. Jenkinson's atop the books. "We shall keep them in my sitting room. My husband never enters it without my permission if that is a concern."

Mrs. Jenkinson emitted a small bleating sound that, combined with a faint smile, seemed to indicate happiness. "Thank you for your kindness, Mrs. Collins and Miss Bennet. You have been unfailingly civil to me, gracious and thoughtful." She at last lifted the books from her lap and allowed them to be taken.

After sipping her tea, Mrs. Jenkinson added, "Miss Anne is in good hands now. I fear what she has written may be shocking, but you are women of sense and may understand her better than I. Thank you for relieving me of this burden."

Charlotte cleared her throat. "Mrs. Jenkinson, you said Lady Catherine will not give you a reference, but I could do so, should you need it. I am only her vicar's wife, but a recommendation from me may be of some service to you.

"Regarding these journals, it may be necessary to consult you about specifics contained in them. I am going to give you my egg money, and I wish you to stay at The Bell in Bromley for a fortnight before you proceed to London. I would like to know I could reach you or send the curricle for you if your presence is required to answer some question arising from Miss de Bourgh's writings."

Mrs. Jenkinson's eyes grew wide. "I could never impose upon you, Mrs. Collins. I could afford a week or at least five days. The Bell is a respectable inn, and I can pay my own way with my wages."

"My father has given me a generous amount for my visit here, Mrs. Jenkinson," said Elizabeth, "and I have spent hardly a farthing. Charlotte and I shall see you to a fortnight at The Bell. My intuition begs the three of us remain in close connection."

Mrs. Jenkinson sighed. "Oh, my, such generosity. I hardly know what to say. I *would* like to stay near to hear of the funeral and know she is safe in the ground. Whatever her ladyship might feel towards me, Miss Anne was most kind. The least I can do is to place these words of truth into your protection."

Two hours later, with Mr. Collins not yet returned from Rosings and Mrs. Jenkinson increasingly afraid that he would, Charlotte bid the footman to load Mrs. Jenkinson's cases into the curricle and to meet the three ladies at the post junction whilst they journeyed there on foot. When the coach to Bromley appeared, Charlotte negotiated a reduced fare, insisting Mrs. Jenkinson retain the difference, and bid her to write upon her arrival using the name Mrs. Jenkins, which none doubted would be sufficient to put Mr. Collins off the scent.

"But how will you know a Mrs. Jenkins at The Bell?" fretted Mrs Jenkinson as her cases were loaded onto the coach.

"Never mind that," Charlotte whispered conspiratorially. "My husband is not the type to question my actions—he is not suspicious—and he is often at Rosings when the post arrives."

*Which must make wifely dissemblance extremely easy...yes, Charlotte manages my cousin very well indeed,* Elizabeth mused.

After the coach departed, Charlotte and Elizabeth hastily returned to the vicarage and Charlotte's sitting room. They called for a fresh tea service and firmly shut the door.

Mr. Collins still sat, forgotten but patient, in the small sitting room at Rosings Park.

Once settled with blackcurrant scones and tea, Elizabeth and

Charlotte began reading Anne de Bourgh's journals, at first randomly and aloud to each other. Elizabeth had the older volume from July through December of the previous year, and Charlotte read snippets from the volume begun in January 1812, but she was concerned by what she read for Elizabeth's maidenly sensibilities.

It was instantly apparent to Charlotte that Anne was with child at the time of her death, and some manner of complication had caused her decline. Elizabeth found the passage that explained Anne's motivation for getting herself into an interesting condition, and the reasoning was confusing to both of them as Elizabeth recited the words. *"The material question is how to remove myself from my mother's sphere,"* Elizabeth read. *"She would hound me to the ends of the earth, I am convinced, unless I am somehow able to make myself a pariah to her…to do something so beyond the boundaries of civil society that disowning me would be preferable to keeping me near.*

*"I am amazed to learn the immensity of the wealth I have inherited. Papa was indeed a generous man, but my life would be far better were he still walking amongst us. I would rather have him for another lucid hour than to own all of his riches. Other than the estate itself, where Mama is to remain until her death unless I marry, his capital is all mine along with the de Bourgh jewels, which Mama has yet to relinquish. That is neither here nor there, for where would I wear them?*

*"But if I can make myself abhorrent to her, I am now easily able to purchase my own establishment and be independent. And how best to do it? Short of committing a crime—for I would not go to prison to obtain freedom—causing a scandal is the only choice. Even allowing myself to be compromised will not suffice since a marriage could be managed and the affair hidden under a cloak of propriety. No, the only option is to get myself with child: the child of a man thoroughly odious, wholly without merit, and having no standing in the world. I know only one such man, and although he lurks about this neighbourhood to find access to my fair young cousin, she is not the only heiress herein, and his ambition can surely be bought by my much greater and more immediately accessible fortune. If he seeks to insult Darcy, perhaps the ruin of his assumed betrothed might serve as well, if not better, than destroying the sister.*

*"Only through negotiation shall I learn the cost of begetting a child and what I must pay for secrecy."*

Elizabeth's voice had dropped to a whisper as she finished. Unshed tears stung her eyes. "Oh, Charlotte…she has paid with her *life*."

The two friends stared at each other in exhausted and wondering silence.

*Meanwhile, at Rosings*

Shortly after his arrival, Mr. Collins heard a to-do at the entrance of Rosings Park and stood, facing the hall doors. Thus, he saw the local doctor pass the sitting room at a rapid pace with servants fluttering around him taking his hat, gloves, and coat.

After some moments, as the noise diminished to herald the return of hushed silence, Mr. Collins sat down. He surmised Miss de Bourgh must be much more ill than usual for the doctor to be called, and if his assumption was correct, the reason Lady Catherine had kept him waiting was in deference to the needs of her daughter. He was not a man to be rankled by the inconsideration of his patroness, but he did begin to wonder if he should depart. He sat wondering for a very long time.

No little time later, the doctor passed the sitting room door in much the same rush as he had arrived. This time, Lady Catherine's imperious voice followed the man, chasing him from the house.

"You will tell no one of your suspicions, you thundering lack-wit. With child! I have never heard of such a thing. If news of your supposition reaches me through any other persons, I shall know you have most grievously breeched my trust. Do I make myself understood?"

The doctor pulled up short and rounded on the mistress of Rosings Park. "The front doors are open, madam, and *your* voice is raised, not mine!"

Lady Catherine and the doctor looked into the open doors of the small sitting room to see Mr. Collins standing there with wide eyes and his fingers clasping his lips lest he emit some untoward sound. Mr. Collins bowed to them.

"Oh!" Lady Catherine screeched and, before a footman could do it for her, slammed the sitting room doors with great vigour.

The doctor could no longer withhold his laughter and hastily quitted the house.

Silence returned to its rightful place, and Mr. Collins sat, more profoundly confused than ever before—which was a vast deal. Was one of the maids of fallen morals? Mr. Collins fretted and shook his head. Lady Catherine would blame him, most assuredly, for not keeping a sufficiently watchful eye upon his flock. And of course she would be justified, for the low as well as the high-born deserved his spiritual guidance. But how could he be chided for sparing all possible attention for his noble patroness?

IT WAS ANOTHER THREE QUARTERS OF AN HOUR BEFORE THE SITTING ROOM doors opened and Lady Catherine swept in wearing an ill-fitting black gown. With an elaborate attempt at dignified grief—and a persuadable audience upon which to practice—she sat next to Mr. Collins on the settee and drew him down next to her, although not too close. She tugged a lace black-edged handkerchief from her wrist with a loud sniffle.

"I hope you have surmised this to be a day of great tragedy, William," she said, feigning more sadness than she felt. She reckoned the use of her vicar's Christian name was warranted to impress upon him the gravity of the situation.

"Indeed I have, your ladyship, and I desire you to know my sympathies flow to you as the Thames flows to the Channel. If I may be so bold to ask, what is the nature of the tragedy?"

After a sufficiently dramatic pause, Lady Catherine announced, "Anne... my dear Anne, died in her sleep last night. We found her this morning."

In his shock, Mr. Collins slid onto one knee on the floor in front of her, taking her hands and instead finding he was enclosing the soggy handkerchief in his stumpy fingers. He felt tears sting his eyes. "I am bereft. England has been deprived..."

"Yes, yes...of its finest jewel," Lady Catherine huffed. "Sit up, sir."

Absently using her handkerchief to wipe his eyes, Mr. Collins hoisted his ample buttocks onto the settee. "If it pleases your ladyship, would you permit me to arrange for a little service for your honourable and noble self, and the ladies Miss de Bourgh counted as friends... my wife, Mrs. Jenkinson? I would gladly do so, as ladies must not attend the funeral."

Lady Catherine dropped all pretences and returned to her usual officious manner as she stripped her handkerchief from Mr. Collins's hand and pulled a dryer specimen from her pocket. She had forgotten how exhausting it was to appear grief stricken. "Nonsense. I have written an express to the Archbishop of Canterbury. You are not even a year in your office; thus, if there is to be a gathering for the ladies, he will preside. Do try not to fawn upon the man over much whilst he is at Rosings, Mr. Collins. It would vex me greatly. And it will do you no good in any case as your life-long career will not be in the church, not once you become a landed gentleman."

Mr. Collins stared at his benefactress. He gradually determined that she must suffer an unusual form of grief to speak of another death yet to come, perhaps many years away, with such nonchalance. Most grieving mothers with whom his position necessitated he condole bore their trials much differently. Lady Catherine seemed at times—for this was not the first instance of its mention—that she rather hoped his cousin Mr. Thomas Bennet of Longbourn would die soon, so Mr. Collins would inherit the modest estate.

Lady Catherine continued, "But we will, of course, invite the neighbourhood to visit Rosings after the funeral. I have written to all my family to attend. It is a shame my nephews have only just gone away. Better they had stayed..." Her voice drifted off.

Lady Catherine stood a moment before idly wandering to the window. A goshawk had flown from the trees, drawing her attention as she silently mused. *If Darcy is the father, I shall kill him...* The hawk startled a trio of pigeons, and as Lady Catherine watched excitedly, the bird of prey grasped the slowest and settled momentarily onto the ground. "I should have been an accomplished falconer, had I ever sought to learn..."

A movement in the outer hall caught Mr. Collins's eye, and he stared as the doctor, so violently ushered from the house not an hour earlier, scuttled past the sitting room with Mrs. Spiggotson, the midwife, trailing behind. She was regarding her surroundings with unguarded astonishment. The doctor met the eyes of the vicar and placed a finger to his lips, begging for discretion.

"Excuse me, Lady Catherine, but..." Mr. Collins began, for he would never be a party to any deception of his patroness.

"Would that I had been born a goshawk," Lady Catherine muttered aloud. "The females are near to double the size of the males."

Her tone sent a nervous shiver down Mr. Collins's spine, and he forgot the doctor and midwife. "I am certain your ladyship would have been the strongest, bravest bird in all the land."

Lady Catherine's only response was an irritated shake of her shoulders as if to settle her feathers. "Yes, well..."

She turned back to Mr. Collins, and her eyes narrowed in a way that made him flustered for it accentuated her Roman nose.

"We must ask your pretty cousin, Miss Bennet, to stay for the funeral. I would not have any but gentlewomen wait upon the Archbishop and my brother, the earl, and his countess. I think we can trust Miss Bennet in such a circumstance, for all her bold opinions."

From over Lady Catherine's shoulder, the hawk arose from the ground with a visibly bleeding pigeon in its talons. It was a frightful sight, rendering Mr. Collins all astonishment that his splendid benefactress could wish to embody so alarming a creature.

"And Mrs. Collins with her. They will serve the coffee and tea. They know their place and will be silent." Lady Catherine punctuated her plan with a nod.

A footman entered the room and cleared his throat.

"Yes?" Lady Catherine drawled at the servant.

"Mr. Andrew Steventon to see you, ma'am."

Lady Catherine thought for a moment, trying to place the name.

"He is a local attorney, your ladyship," Mr. Collins prompted.

"I know very well who he is," she fussed. "Oh, send him in."

Mr. Collins noticed that the little attorney with birdlike eyes viewed the interior of Rosings much as the midwife had. The clergyman's tut-tut was barely audible. He felt the lower orders should at least make the attempt to appear more accustomed to fine surroundings, though he quite understood the tendency to be overwhelmed when faced with the great chimney-piece and so many glazed windows. He had only recently learnt there were seventy-five steps, exactly seventy-five, in the grand staircase and of the finest travertine marble. If given a moment, he would recall the name of the Italian village from whence it was quarried.

"Steventon!" Lady Catherine pronounced. "State your business."

"It has come to my attention, your ladyship, that Miss de Bourgh has passed."

Lady Catherine rolled her eyes. Who but the doctor would have spread the news? What more might this odious man know? "Have you come to express your condolences?"

The little man seemed confident. "Indeed, ma'am. I am sorry to lose so pleasing a client, always amiable. But I am come to inform you that Miss de Bourgh left us with the expression of her final wishes. I had the honour of preparing her Last Will and Testament some three months ago, although it was her wont to alter it rather constantly. Her codicils have codicils..." He chuckled but what was found humorous by the lawyer did not incite amusement in his present company.

For once, it was Lady Catherine's lot to stare in astonishment.

Steventon continued, "With all due haste I shall assemble the several parties benefiting from Miss de Bourgh's largess as mistress of Rosings Park and her father's only heir."

Mr. Collins quaked at Lady Catherine's mounting rage.

"And who might those beneficiaries be?" Lady Catherine's voice was a low threatening hiss.

"I am not at liberty to divulge the particulars, but her principal heir is Colonel Alexander Fitzwilliam. Mr. and Miss Darcy are mentioned. She has also been quite generous to Mrs. Elspeth Jenkinson, Mrs. Charlotte Collins, and Miss Elizabeth Bennet."

"Miss Elizabeth Bennet?" Lady Catherine shrieked. She swept her wide-eyed visage on Mr. Collins. "And your *wife*? My dear Anne cannot have been in her right mind!" Lady Catherine turned and fled the room, still emitting frantic sounds that could only rarely be recognised as words of the King's English. The lawyer followed her.

Upon a moment's consideration, it struck Mr. Collins that the only time he had previously heard such a noise, it had emanated in similar amplitude and duration from Mrs. Bennet when Miss Elizabeth had refused his offer of marriage.

Unsure whether he had been dismissed, Mr. Collins sat again for some minutes. At last, he ventured a look at his tin pocket watch, decided Mrs. Collins would be wondering at his long absence, and quietly took himself home.

*20 February 1812*

*For joy! I am now quite certain I am with child. It is over ten days since my courses ought to have commenced, perhaps nearer a fortnight. I did not bleed in January at all. My bosom is tender, and I cannot bear a corset. Also, I have been unwell most mornings since the first of the month. In this cold weather, I wear many shawls and keep apart from my mother, thus she has not noticed my discomfort. I am so full of mirth and hope, I cannot complain.*

*I sent Paulette to Mrs. Spiggotson with a note outlining my ailments, and she has confirmed that I am likely "a setting hen," as she so charmingly stated it. She has suggested we meet in a fortnight at the cottage where I had my assignations with Mr. C, and she will examine me.*

*My delight knows no bounds. Never did I dream I would derive such liberation of spirit from a thing women before me have done since time beyond measure. By this month next year, I shall be a Mama myself and an independent woman living in a distant place, as far from Rosings Park as it is possible to be and still be a good English woman on fertile English soil. I shall style myself a widow with a husband lost in the war. Yes, it will all be well worked-out.*

*My release is at hand! —A de B*

# CHAPTER 3
## Cooing to Broken Hearts

*Wednesday, 8 April 1812, London, Darcy House*

"I used to rule the world, Alex, or at least I thought I did," Fitzwilliam Darcy mused as he stared into the courtyard of his London residence.

His languid posture as he leaned against the window frame was uncharacteristic, but so had his manner been since arriving in London from Rosings.

Colonel Alexander Fitzwilliam did not respond immediately, unsure how to deal with his despondent cousin. Darcy's present dejection was unprecedented. He could be either affable and intelligent or high-handed and haughty, even lapsing into the dictatorial, but to see him easing into the early afternoon unshaven and unshod was an entirely novel circumstance.

Finally the colonel spoke. "Your heart has been broken, Darcy, quite savaged. I understand, but I daresay, life must go on. Certainly, you should be sad, but you must maintain decorum. Georgie will be here soon, and you ought to think how your appearance will affect her. She has never seen you thus."

Darcy kicked absently at the baseboard with his bare foot. "*I* have never seen me thus. I have never before been found wanting by someone whose good opinion I value so highly. The past year has taught me that I govern nothing, certainly not the actions of men, and I know nothing of women's hearts—not my sister's and most decidedly not Miss Elizabeth…" Darcy's throat tightened before he could say "Bennet."

The colonel stood abruptly. "You have been rejected by one of the best marriage prospects—if you overlook her want of fortune—that either of us has seen in several years. I therefore give you leave to wallow in self-pity for two more days, which will be one week from when you brought this tragedy upon yourself. At the end of two days, I expect to see improvement." He spoke as if explaining regulations to a raw recruit. "Shall I write to my mother and ask her to keep Georgiana one more week?"

Darcy turned to his cousin. "A week? Only a week? Who am I, Charles Bingley?" Darcy instantly regretted the words. Bingley deserved a better friend than he had been through the winter. What was it *she* said, that he exposed Mr. Bingley to the world's derision for indecision and caprice? *Not a friend at all.*

"No." Darcy shook his head. "I must write to Bingley. I should have written straight away. The injustice I have done him may be repaired; he needs to know."

Darcy turned and looked towards his desk, but it seemed an insurmountable distance, and he instead leaned his head against the smooth wood moulding around the window.

The colonel cleared his throat. "Darcy, what of your sister?" He tried to sound gentle even though he did not feel gentleness was deserved. When no answer came, his tone became sarcastic. "You remember? A tall, pretty, shy sort of girl?"

Darcy glared. "Do not write to your mother. Let Georgiana come this afternoon from Matlock House as arranged. She will provide a distraction."

"But did you not say you have written to her about Miss Elizabeth?"

Darcy looked even more distressed but said only, "Georgie may be more easily put off by a harsh glare than you are, Alex." He sighed. "How many times must I repeat the story of my folly? You, Georgiana, probably Bingley..."

"Why Bingley?"

"How else am I to explain the depths of my lunacy? My hypocrisy? My 'selfish disdain for the feelings of others'?"

"'Selfish disdain for the feelings of others?' Did *she* say so?"

"Oh yes, she most certainly did."

"Then she does not know you, Darcy. She does not know your goodness."

"Oh, she knows me very well, Cousin. Better than anyone. It would be vain to deny it. Other than my dealings with Wickham, everything she said of me is true. The last night at Rosings, I came to admit—after the anger had somewhat lessened—how I must have always appeared to her, and further consideration of her words gave me ample evidence of their justice. Would that I had been so circumspect *before* proposing. She apologised if her spirited behaviour led me on, but my own pride undid me. She gave many signs of disapprobation; I simply would not believe them.

"And the letter I wrote… I said more than I ought, especially about Bingley and Miss Bennet. How arrogant of me to attempt to defend myself while not knowing the heart of her sister. I moved the two of them around as if they were as insensible as chessmen."

The colonel aimed a sigh of disgust at his cousin and looked at his pocket watch. "Here is my suggestion: if your sister is indeed to join us this afternoon, you must get thee to a valet. Have a good soak, shave, and get yourself up smart for Georgiana's arrival. I shall stay with you one more night so you do not have to face Georgie's questions alone, but that is as far as I am prepared to go. My leave is over at the end of this se'nnight. Cooing to your broken heart—a wound largely self-inflicted—is not how I intend to spend it."

"You are all things benevolent, Alex." Darcy turned a practiced glare at his cousin, unwilling to admit aloud that he was right. "Although my advancing beard could be seen as a demonstration of my virility, the effect is not appropriate for Georgie."

"And you stink. I have smelt much worse, but you do not reek of a gentleman."

"Yes, yes, certainly…" Darcy muttered his way out of the study.

Colonel Fitzwilliam settled himself at a large table covered with a folio containing maps of France that, given the current military actions, kept him as well entertained as a romantic novel would have suited Georgiana.

After a fleeting hour, a footman entered the study and looked about in confusion before clearing his throat.

"Yes, may I help?" the colonel asked.

"I am sorry, sir. I understood Mr. Darcy to be with you. I am bid to inform you and the master that Miss Darcy has arrived, and will join you in the drawing room in half an hour."

"Thank you," the colonel responded as he returned his gaze to the maps.

A few minutes later, Colonel Fitzwilliam was wondering whether it was time to dip into his cousin's excellent brandy when another discreet knock was heard at the study door. The colonel found he was half hoping that orders had arrived to return to his regiment posthaste.

Darcy's perfect butler, Mr. Simpson, entered. He held a letter. "An express, sir. It is addressed to both you and my master from Rosings Park."

"Thank you, Simpson; you may go," Darcy said as he entered the room behind the butler. He took the missive from the salver, and Simpson's exit was confirmed by the door clicking shut. "From our blasted aunt." Darcy sat at his desk and read the letter while his cousin watched, awaiting a thorough report. When Darcy's face paled, and his hand holding the letter thumped slack upon the desk, the colonel stood and moved directly to him.

He noticed, upon taking up the letter with no resistance from Darcy, that the sealing wax was black—an announcement of death. He read the terrible news. "Poor, poor Anne," the colonel muttered. "I suppose we must return as precipitously as we came away?"

Looking pained, Darcy stood. "Yes, and Georgiana must accompany us. The entire family will gather. Let us tell her, and the three of us can share this distress." For the briefest moment, his mind neglected an obvious fact.

The cousins started out the door with the colonel beginning to think of wording an express to General Willis requesting bereavement leave.

Darcy moaned, "Oh, God," and halted in his steps as apprehension swept over him.

"Darcy?" The colonel turned.

Darcy pinched the bridge of his nose. "*She* will still be there…she was not to come away until this Friday. I am bound to see her."

"Elizabeth Bennet?"

Darcy nodded.

"I cannot imagine we shall spend much time in the company of the Hunsford crowd. Surely, our aunt will require better for Anne than the prattling of William Collins. Nothing less than the Archbishop of Canterbury will do. You know Lady Catherine; she will not want the Fitzwilliam aristocracy polluted by the vicar Collins."

Darcy winced. "No, I would wager not." He shook off his trepidation and returned to the more dutiful dismay of relating the death of Anne de Bourgh to Georgiana.

*7 July 1811*

*Mama has outdone herself. Even within Little G's hearing, her verbal blows rain down on Darcy constantly, and worse now that Alex has had to return to his duties. How Darcy bears it, I do not know. Mama insists he propose to me, thinking this will stabilise a home for Little G, who by all appearances is quite contrite. Poor Darcy is due to leave tomorrow. Little G will stay until August, and we are all in search of a more thoroughly researched companion for her. Once a lady is hired, Little G and said companion will travel to Pemberley. Darcy is expecting guests—some people named Bingley. Mama sniffs that they are nouveau riche, as though the de Bourghs were not. She hates the French but loves employing their insults. —A de B*

*23 July 1811*

*I think we have found a companion for Little G. Mama is crowing with the credit of it, but it is, as usual, undeserved praise, as she only knew someone who knew someone, when in truth, Darcy found notice of the woman from a gentleman at his club whom Mama knew only distantly. The lady was here yesterday, a Mrs. Annesley, and we all liked her, not that my opinion was required. Darcy and Alex interviewed her, and Darcy had previously contacted her references. She is a widow of perhaps thirty-five years of age who lost the three children she bore her husband one after the other to a fever, and then lost the man himself. Life may have beaten a lesser woman, but Mrs. Annesley is intelligent and without complaint. Once my cousins had completed their interview, they allowed my mother a share of the conversation, and nothing Mama said discomfited the lady in the least. This I witnessed for myself as Mama insisted, "Anne and I shall observe her and give you our opinion." She never asked what I thought, but had she, I would have said I found the woman quite pleasingly observant.*

*Little G is much changed. She is loath to play any instrument except that in Mrs. Jenkinson's room, and she seems to have developed a horror of performing. Perhaps it is only a horror of my mother; one could not fault her for that. What is it about music that renders my mother such a fool? I notice Little G wearing childish clothes, and she does not walk out as she used to. The summer flowers in the cutting garden are at their height, but she will not go abroad, even with me. She has not spoken of her experience with Wickham but she did confide to me that she never liked Mrs. Younge,*

*Wickham's accomplice, and she wishes she had the courage to have said so to Alex, who would have been more sympathetic than her brother. G believes she has bitterly disappointed Darcy. I daresay she has, though Darcy will not hear of it. Wickham had her believing he was in constant convivial correspondence with Darcy and there was no schism in their childhood friendship. Poor Little G. It is thus proved that it is possible to know too little of the world and to be made weak by cosseting—as if the example I embody is not proof enough. She is not a spoilt child…far from it. For all her physical and material advantages, she persists in a profound shyness and modesty. This is manifested more now than ever.*

*G will remain with us for perhaps ten more days. Mrs. Annesley will join the family here as soon as she has settled her affairs in London where she lives with a brother. They will remain for another five days or a week and then proceed to Pemberley to stay through August and September. Once the heat of summer breaks, Little G will return to town and await the pleasure of her brother and Alex. I do agree with Mama to this extent: the girl needs distractions. More music lessons, more drawing…anything to restore her confidence.*

*I do admit to some envy. How I would love to trade Mrs. Jenkinson for Mrs. Annesley. Mrs. J is a dear old thing but has little wit. Mrs. Annesley is clever. I am unkind, but I come by it honestly, do I not? —A de B*

# CHAPTER 4
## *Suspicions Confirmed*

*Thursday, 9 April 1812, the Hunsford vicarage*

It was a calm afternoon, and having taken a small meal with Charlotte and her cousin upon his return from Rosings, Elizabeth fled from his repeated recitation of the plans for the arrival of the Archbishop of Canterbury and of Lady Catherine's "so very noble"—but probably more akin to sullen—grief. The journals of Anne de Bourgh awaited her, and the reading of them was rapidly becoming an irresistible pastime.

Deciding a bench in the flower garden sufficiently private, Elizabeth alit there with the second volume. She opened it randomly to 28 January 1812.

*Oh, Mama… She is at me to write to Darcy to extend the de facto invitation for Easter. He hardly needs such a letter. It is a tradition of many years standing, and he wrote at the New Year to confirm that Alex was granted permission from General Bailey to join us. Mama states that Darcy would read some deeper romantic reason in my taking the interest. Nothing changes; she is ever urging me to encourage him. I laugh to myself; he would know my writing could only be done under duress. He would be rightfully certain she had stood over me with a cat-o'-nine-tails since nothing short of that would induce me!*

*How he has changed since taking on Pemberley and further still by this trouble with Little G. Such a charming boy he was. I looked to him then as the example of affability and cleverness. He was most pleased with the arrival of*

*Georgiana. I recall how ready he was to love the little mite. My last memories of Lady Anne were her smiles as she sat on a chaise watching Darcy carry the wiggling infant with such tender care. As his mother began fading away, so did his withdrawal from joy. I shall never forget his countenance when we arrived for the funeral. He stood so solemnly next to his shattered father, better able than Uncle Darcy to keep up the appearance of greeting us properly, and it was to Darcy's fingers, not her father's, that a tiny Little G did cling, giggling and barely walking. The pain in Darcy's eyes was heartrending. There he was, just turned thirteen, forever altered. I shall never forget it.*

*At his father's funeral, little had changed except his age. He wore his self-confidence as a shield, and I never saw him cry although the elderly Kympton vicar said Darcy's grief had touched him as he had ne'er seen such in so young a man. As the years passed after Uncle's death, Darcy did seem to lighten, and after our private confessions—lack of more than familial feeling on his side, and for my part, knowing I could never be happy in so cold and remote a county as Derbyshire with an equally cold and remote spouse—we were easier with each other even as Mama became more determined and ridiculous. Once apprised of my feelings, Darcy took her hectoring with better grace. When I came into the de Bourgh fortune last year, he encouraged me during his Easter visit to restore the London house and keep myself in the city. But London is a sickly place. I never feel anything but poorly there.*

*I suppose it is his nature that everything changed for the worse after Ramsgate. The pain of yet another of life's betrayals was plain enough for any to see, but Mama could not see—would not see. Her ceaseless prattle must have grated more than ever, or might have were Darcy not completely occupied by the guilt tearing his nerves to shreds. Then there was the further burden of preventing Alex from doing anything that might disgrace his uniform. Had Little G's virtue been truly lost, I think neither Darcy nor I nor any in the Fitzwilliam family could have succeeded in preventing a duel—or outright murder. It is for the best that Mama is obsessed that the business remain undiscovered.*

*Lives there such a woman who could ease the spirits of Fitzwilliam Darcy, who could unearth the affable boy he was and reveal the amiable man? He and I are of one mind in that he must marry. Certainly, each new Season presents him with ample selection. There are many ladies with connections sufficient to tempt him; certainly, some of those might be tolerably handsome enough for his manly needs, yet he remains above the marriage market, so Alex writes. Neither of us can imagine what keeps him from a great alliance and the getting of heirs. He is not the sort to allow grief to keep him from his duty.*

*Could it be he seeks a love match and awaits a lady to ignite his passionate regard? I can hardly believe it. —A de B*

A shiver of presentiment travelled the length of Elizabeth's spine. "*Lives there such a woman…to ignite his passionate regard. …Tolerably handsome enough for his manly needs.*" It was only the sound of a carriage on the road and the slamming of the vicarage side door that distracted her from a sad headache.

The Darcy carriage slowed unexpectedly as Mr. Collins bowed deeply before it. From her seat beneath the sheltering but not yet blooming hollyhocks, Elizabeth could hear Darcy speak. She expected some ungracious reply to her cousin's obsequious welcome, but the subdued quality of Darcy's voice gave her heart a mighty squeeze.

"Greetings to you, Mr. Collins. Let me thank you for the consolation I know you have so generously *and abundantly* offered to my aunt."

There was only the vaguest whisper of irony in Darcy's comment. Elizabeth could not believe her ears and adjusted her posture to peek at the road from amongst the leafy stems. She saw her cousin draw breath.

"I look forward to a longer conversation with you, sir," Darcy said, silencing the vicar, "but for now, pray excuse me as I must offer her my own sympathy and regret straightaway. Good day, Mr. Collins. I trust we shall meet again soon."

"G-good day, Mr. Darcy," was all her cousin could stammer as he bowed before the carriage rolled away.

Her observation could not completely restore Elizabeth to her former dislike of Darcy, or anything near it. She felt a sinking sensation. There had been no doubt she would see him again, but with Anne de Bourgh's insight and the forlorn gentlemanly tone of his voice, she found within herself naught but forbearance and a desire to comfort. But her primary urge was to return the journal to Charlotte's sitting room and repair to her bedroom to engage herself in a letter she had hidden there. *"Lives there such a woman…?"*

"Apparently not," she absently murmured aloud. She had an ill-formed sense of having failed at something. It was a decidedly foreign sensation and most unpleasant.

Darcy stood before the front doors of Rosings and steeled himself for what he knew was to follow. Affixed above the carved heading stones was the de Bourgh funerary hatchment created for his uncle, who had died some sixteen years previously before the birth of Georgiana. Darcy removed his hat at the sight of it. Lower down were two smaller versions hastily rendered to announce the demise of the de Bourgh heiress, one on each door and each surrounded by a wreath of raven feathers. Darcy shivered in disgust. He knew he was about to learn, amongst other unpleasantness, how many birds had died to supply the gruesome embellishment to the more suitable marks of mourning.

Upon entering the house, he nodded to the footman to open the door to Rosings' largest drawing room. He expected harsh words delivered with a resonating magnitude, and was therefore taken unaware by the narrowed studying eyes of his aunt accompanied by silence. After some moments, she languidly held up a hand, which he bowed over. Still silent, she flicked a finger at the chair upon which she wished him to sit.

"Nephew, you did not spend the winter holidays in London? You came into Kent? How many times?" Lady Catherine questioned him accusingly. "You left my niece alone and unguarded in London to carry on your assignations here? No wonder Georgiana fell victim to near ruination in Ramsgate; she has not had proper guidance."

Darcy's head tilted with a frown. "I never left London, as you must know from your brother. Georgiana and I were seen at many festivities, and were rather constantly at Matlock House. Where do your questions tend?" Never had his aunt seemed more indirect and ridiculous, and not just a little menacing. Was this some strange manifestation of grief?

"You may choose to be circuitous, Nephew, but I shall be direct since you are the cause of Anne's death."

Darcy was on his feet. "I am *what*?" He realised the implied threat in his stance and turned to pacing.

Lady Catherine mistook Darcy's confusion for some admission of guilt. "It was your dalliances, your incautious pursuit of your own pleasure that brought her end."

"Of what can you possibly be speaking? I cannot take your meaning except that you accuse me in the vaguest yet most insulting manner possible." He spat the words out slowly, trying to keep from having his wits become as addled as his aunt's were.

"However insincere you may choose to be, you will not find *me* so."

Darcy could only stare.

"Selfish boy. This is not to be borne."

"Of what does your ladyship accuse me? I am at a total loss."

"Yes..." Lady Catherine's eyes narrowed again. "What gentleman would admit to the arts and allurements you must have used to have your way?"

"My *way*?" Darcy's countenance was severe.

"It makes no sense to me, Nephew, why you would despoil your cousin before settling a betrothal and making it known."

"Madam, have you been taking strong spirits? Did the doctor suggest you drink laudanum?" He began to gain some apprehension of her indictment though it had precious little logic.

"Why not simply arrange for a speedy engagement, affix a date, and *then* proceed?"

Darcy stopped, agape. As his aunt seemed about to speak again, he held up a staying hand and sent her a fierce glare. "You accuse me of seducing my cousin? A lady I have not seen since last July?" He came near to laughing, and so turned to the window to gather his aplomb, muttering, "Even *I* do not presume to be as virile as that—"

He was surprised to receive a slap of his aunt's fan to the back of his head.

"Obstinate, headstrong boy!" She reared back to smite him again. "I am ashamed of you!"

Darcy easily caught her wrist and twisted her towards her favourite chair. "Dearest Aunt... We shall have no more of this conversing at cross-purposes. Why ever would you accuse me of defiling my cousin? *Was* she so misused?"

Lady Catherine was breathing heavily. She rang the servants' bell at her elbow and said nothing to Darcy until it was answered and tea requested. When the footman withdrew, the lady spoke again. "Will you promise me that you never entered into an illicit affair with her?"

"A gentleman does not reveal himself, but she is gone and must be made blameless. I never laid a hand upon my cousin or attempted to lure her into any misbehaviour. She and I had agreed between us that we were not suited."

"Aha! Were you not alone with her to conduct such a conversation? If you were sensible of your own good, you would confess everything."

"There is nothing to confess except our foreknowledge that we would have made you deeply distressed by conspiring never to marry one other. And Mrs. Jenkinson was present."

"That bloody, bloody woman..." she muttered.

"Lady Catherine!" For all her tantrums, Darcy had never before heard his aunt curse.

A gasp and the upheaval of a tea tray made it clear the entering footman had heard it all. As if this were not turmoil enough, the butler appeared and glared at the scrambling footman before announcing, "Dr. Roberts, your ladyship."

The physician entered the room, but he was brought up short by the presence of Mr. Darcy. "Excuse me, Lady Catherine. Should I return at a later time?"

Lady Catherine glared down at him. "No, my nephew ought to hear what you have to say since this may all be his fault."

Darcy grimly shook his head at the floor.

The physician seemed uncertain. "I believed you would not allow it, but I returned yesterday with Mrs. Spiggotson..."

"And she is...?" Lady Catherine asked.

"The best of the local midwives, your ladyship."

Darcy's head came up abruptly.

Lady Catherine's fury was felt by all in the room, but none more so than by the physician, for she boxed his ears. "You odious charlatan! What can it say for the reputation of this house that you would bring such a creature here?"

The physician ignored the question, rubbing the sides of his head before explaining, "It was my estimation that a more knowledgeable person than I should examine your departed daughter, and she confirmed my fears. Your daughter died from complications of being with child. We believe Miss de Bourgh to have conceived in January. Mrs. Spiggotson suspects the babe was not seated properly in the womb. No doubt your daughter died in great pain and distress, unless Mrs. Jenkinson dosed her with sufficient strong spirits, which I believe she would have done."

Darcy was struck dumb. He stared as his aunt chased the doctor from the house, his awe giving way to curiosity.

*Poor dear Anne…Who was the father? Who has so wantonly seduced her? She had mentioned no one to me but perhaps to Alex? Would she confide in him rather than me?*

"See what you have done with your wilful selfishness?" Lady Catherine panted as she returned.

Darcy turned to her, speaking in the coldest possible manner. "Do please stop being ridiculous. I have been nowhere near Kent since leaving you in late July. Do attempt *some* rational thought. Have there been strange men about the Park or in Hunsford? Could she have been"—he paused at the discomfiting thought he was about to suggest—"forced?"

Lady Catherine turned away muttering, "We must presume Mrs. Jenkinson knows, and she is now gone. The doctor knows, and this 'Spigot' person, and perhaps even Anne's little lawyer." She glanced at Darcy. "If it was not you who has done this, how do we preserve her reputation? *My* reputation? What of the family?"

Darcy drew in a heavy breath before responding. "This is your first concern? *Reputations?* Your daughter has died amidst great pain and suffering. Why are you not prostrate with grief?"

"She is dead, Nephew. My tears will not return her. And now I learn she died in a disgraceful condition. What have I to mourn?"

Darcy stared unblinking.

Under his steady displeasure, Lady Catherine merely shrugged. "I have written the Archbishop and hope to have an express from him soon." She sighed loudly and strode to the window, musing, "Pity we have not more time for the arrangements."

"You would chide her for dying in April rather than December?" Darcy asked, growing more disgusted as the minutes passed.

"How many carriages were in your father's cortege?" she asked abruptly.

"Ten."

"What? Only ten? I seem to recall there being very many more!"

"No, only ten. It was but three miles from Kympton to the family vault at Pemberley. We did not wish for the cortège to meet itself coming and going." Darcy spoke solemnly, reminded of the painful loss.

Lady Catherine's eyes narrowed. "Pity there is not time to have the mutes from Pemberley sent down. The stable master claims we have enough for only five carriages, each with four horses, though it is likely the Archbishop will supply his own. I want no vulgar clip-clopping and no clinking bridles."

Darcy looked doubtfully at his aunt. "What need have you for carriages? The men will walk the distance to the de Bourgh crypt in the churchyard. There is no need of more than two, or three at most, as the mourners will return here after the burial."

"Your father was the master of a great estate, and yet the neighbourhood could muster only ten carriages? We had many more for Sir Lewis. Now *there* was a man of consequence, of influence… But you would be too young to remember."

Darcy turned away to hide the rolling of his eyes. *My father always said my uncle's influence arose from threats of forcing men to dine with my aunt at Rosings if they were disagreeable in some matter of politics…*

"Anne was his heiress. She will have at least as many carriages as her father." Lady Catherine spoke with authority.

Darcy tried to remember the funeral of Sir Lewis de Bourgh, and was not at all sure he was made to attend. *No…of course… My mother was ill from a miscarriage.*

"Lady Catherine, surely you recall there were no Darcys at my uncle's funeral. My dear mother, your sister, was not well."

Lady Catherine muttered, "Most ill-timed, that…" She wandered out of the room.

Darcy shook his head in disbelief. His mother's misfortune was ill-timed? "Old she-devil…" he muttered in return. He stood by the windows with his hands behind his back, gazing along the vista from a sweeping lawn to the fields of sheep. As he watched, the figure of a young woman moved into the scene, walking along the hidden watercourse that comprised the Rosings ha-ha. His chest tightened.

Elizabeth Bennet did not look towards the house, but Darcy knew her all the same. She was a hundred yards away, but her shape and saunter, the tilt of her head, and the sweep of her arms as she bent to embrace a clump of wild spring vetch were all forever etched upon his heart. *Better I see her again from here.* For a few moments, he watched in a kind of enchantment before his worries intruded. *Did she read the letter? Did I say enough? Will it save her from Wickham?* She wandered away into the trees, and Darcy felt himself breathe again. *I have seen her, and I do not appear to love her any less than I did seven days ago. Yet I know myself better, and her too. I must see her happily settled, if not with me, perhaps with Alex; they appear to have been friendly from the start. I shall speak to him when he arrives.*

*Friday, 10 April 1812, Rosings Park*

Colonel Fitzwilliam and Georgiana Darcy arrived late in the morning, and they were immediately ushered into the small summer breakfast parlour for a light luncheon as Lady Catherine knew the colonel did not care to stop at The Bell to break the trip. She disapproved of his habit even more when he was accompanying Georgiana. Lady Catherine considered her niece nearly as delicate as Anne had been, though any other observer would have laughed at the notion of the tall, well-formed Georgiana being sickly. She was shy but by no means frail.

Lady Catherine approved of Georgiana's black lace gown over a white petticoat and the colonel's dark frock coat. At least he had spared them his red regimentals.

The arrival of an express from the Archbishop of Canterbury drew Lady Catherine from the room. Not moments later, the butler entered with three missives on a salver. "Sirs, Miss Darcy, these are from the local attorney, Mr. Steventon, for each of you."

Darcy's was opened and read first, and although addressed specifically, each letter proved to be comprised of the same language. They were summoned to the reading of the Last Will and Testament of Miss Anne de Bourgh on the morning of Tuesday next.

"The clerk awaits a response," the butler stated when he saw all of the letters had been opened.

Darcy glanced at the colonel who nodded.

"We shall be there as directed," Darcy confirmed.

As the butler turned to leave, the return of Lady Catherine was announced by the increasing loudness of her caterwauling.

"This is not to be borne! We cannot have a rotting body in the house. I must send another express at once. What care I if a royal infant wants christening? 'Tis merely a cousin. Darcy!" She turned into the room. "Join me in writing to hasten Anne's service, else the Archbishop will not arrive until

Monday! Is not His Grace some distant relation of yours on the Manners side, your father's mother?"

She stopped abruptly at the disapproving faces of her younger family members. The men realised their breach of manners and jumped to their feet, and Georgiana seemed atremble where she sat. "And another thing… Are any of you aware of Anne keeping journals?" She cast a hard eye about the room. The belligerence of her voice did not inspire answers, either positive or negative, from her audience. "The most recent volumes are missing. I have set the servants to a thorough search of the house, including *your* rooms."

She swept from the room, leaving startled silence in her wake.

# CHAPTER 5
## A Funeral

*Monday, 13 April 1812*

Waiting for an opening in the hectic calendar of Charles Manners-Sutton, The Most Reverend and Right Honourable Lord Archbishop of Canterbury, caused two days of delay in the funeral of Anne de Bourgh. To save attracting rats and sending odd smells afloat in Rosings, Lady Catherine agreed to have the body spend its last night outside the family crypt below stairs in the Hunsford church, where it was the duty of Mr. Collins to guard it from peril. It was excessively chilly there, and Lady Catherine reminded Mr. Collins, "A cool mind is a clear mind." Her expression was wry; she had amused herself.

Early the following morning, Anne was fitted into her eternity box and carried outside to the lych-gates awaiting the pall bearers: Mr. Fitzwilliam Darcy; Colonel Alexander Fitzwilliam; Theodore Fitzwilliam, the Earl of Matlock (Colonel Fitzwilliam's father); James Fitzwilliam, the Viscount Scofbridge (the colonel's elder brother and the earl's heir); Kenneth Sapwater, Lord Dirthbevridge (elder brother of Regina, Countess of Matlock), and Sir Everett Sapwater (Lord Dirthbevridge's eldest son).

The tolling of the bells warned Elizabeth and Charlotte that it was time to proceed to Rosings, and there they busied themselves with preparations as the funeral took place. Bells tolled again as Anne de Bourgh made her final journey to the family crypt, a conspicuous affair with ornate hawk heads at the corners rendered from a rather sickly green marble.

As was the custom in the best families, the women relations did not attend the funeral. Lady Catherine kept to her rooms. She did not care for Regina, her sister by marriage, and thought her name pretentious. What had her parents been thinking? Only the final tolling of the bells indicating the menfolk and the unwieldy number of carriages were processing to Rosings brought the two ladies from their chambers to wait silently in the receiving room.

Over an hour later, Darcy entered the receiving room behind the Archbishop. The shoulder feast was finished, but the sexes had not parted company. Lady Catherine had been adamant—for how else could she be? —that only family attend the meal, but the Archbishop had outflanked her by making invitations of his own. Thus had Mr. Collins been allowed at the table, though he nearly fell asleep in his lamb ragout. The townspeople were allowed in for coffee or tea.

Darcy glanced across to where Elizabeth stood at the coffee service, wearing a dove grey gown of mourning that did not imply familial grief, but it was a respectful colour befitting a family friend. She caught his gaze and nodded with genteel solemnity. He returned the gesture, and their eyes locked together. He would have shifted his notice to the slow entrance of Lady Catherine leaning heavily upon her brother the earl's arm, but Elizabeth raised her brows as if to maintain Darcy's attention.

"Are you well?" She mouthed the words silently, carefully, making sure he understood. Elizabeth was quite certain Darcy would never again allow himself to be drawn into private conversation with her. She did not know how to acknowledge his letter. Her harsh words in response to his proposal seemed petty indeed when weighed against this loss. She would not like him to think her uncivil. Some force from her heart compelled her to seek his attention, if only to learn whether he would grant it or cut her in a manner unnoticed by anyone but her.

Darcy blinked slowly, and mimed the word, "sad." He was surprised that she would care about his emotions in the face of his insults to her and her family, but he knew she was capable of kindness, just as he was certain he did not deserve it. Yet here they were—together again—and to his astonishment, rather than fleeing, she sought his attention.

The corners of her mouth pulled into her cheeks in a tight mirthless smile of recognition, and she nodded, still meeting his eyes. Mourners were passing Darcy as he stood rather in their way, and he was forced to break his contact with Elizabeth's compassionate eyes and knowing weary smile.

The congregation of mourners turned to face the Archbishop of Canterbury as he cleared his throat to read a simple statement of loss written by Lady Catherine and edited, rather heavily as it happened, by His Grace.

Instead of listening, Darcy stared at Elizabeth, admiring her profile. *Sad does not begin to describe how I feel. Although I love you, Elizabeth Bennet, I misjudged you, confounded by my passion and my unfounded pride. You reveal yourself at every turn to be a truly good woman. Even though you despise me, you ask after my welfare. Am I always to be humbled by you?*

Darcy looked to the colonel sitting with family in the best seats nearest the fire. His cousin was *not* stealing glances at the lady he was likely to court when the events of the funeral and meetings with lawyers and financiers were complete. Whilst in mourning, the courtship would be subdued, but surely, Alexander would take the present opportunity to introduce Elizabeth to his parents. An initial polite overture would make the necessaries less awkward when it came time for the colonel to announce his betrothal.

The earl stood and walked to Darcy. They patted each other's shoulders, for they had previously managed no time for familial affection. Darcy turned his back towards the serving table. He hoped he might avoid the painful distraction of Elizabeth's eyes. The two men spoke words of quiet commiseration. After a few moments, the colonel joined them.

Elizabeth served coffee to several clergymen, underlings of the Archbishop with whom she was not acquainted. The earl observed her around Darcy's shoulder. "Tell me, Son," he addressed Colonel Fitzwilliam, "I do not believe I have met the lady serving coffee. One of the village women, is she? She looks more refined than Hunsford could produce. Quite a prettyish sort of girl."

The colonel barely flicked his eyes in Elizabeth's direction but he could surmise of whom his father spoke. He hesitated.

Darcy felt all of the awkwardness of his cousin's hesitance although he did not understand it. He cleared his throat with a glance at the colonel and produced the requested information.

"Her father has"—Darcy paused, stopping before blurting "*a small estate,*" fully and painfully knowledgeable of the acuity of Elizabeth Bennet's hearing —"an estate, Longbourn, in Hertfordshire. She is the second eldest daughter. I paid calls upon them whilst staying in the neighbourhood last autumn.

This lady is the particular friend of Mrs. Collins, the wife of Hunsford's vicar, whom you see there pouring out tea. They were neighbours before Mrs. Collins married."

Elizabeth heard it all—the pause in Darcy's description when he might have disparaged the size or importance of Longbourn—and was amazed at the turn of his speech. He admitted to an acquaintance with her family. She would not have believed it of him had she not heard it for herself.

"Hmm!" The earl's voice dropped. "She pours an elegant cup of coffee. Lovely hands. A handsome person. Perhaps a second daughter for a second son?" His elbow knocked his son's. "Eh?" He then included Darcy in his speculations. "Well, which of you will introduce me?"

"Hardly the time, Father." The colonel looked uncomfortable and glanced warily over his father's shoulder at Lady Catherine.

Darcy stood looking at his uncle and cousin. *What is wrong with Alex? Why does he not seize this opportunity? His father would smooth the path if he likes her.* Darcy turned slightly, observing Elizabeth more indirectly than with his usual unswerving stare. She was standing alone, pairing additional coffee cups and saucers to keep busy.

"Miss Bennet?" Darcy heard himself say, and he took a step towards her, his uncle following with alacrity. "If I may?"

The earl smiled and nodded. The colonel shifted his weight.

"Uncle, may I present Miss Elizabeth Bennet of Longbourn? Miss Elizabeth, this is my uncle, the Earl of Matlock. He is Colonel Fitzwilliam's father."

Elizabeth executed a graceful curtsey, and the earl bowed over her hand. "Thank you, Darcy, for effecting an introduction. And thank *you*, Miss Bennet, for assisting my family today."

"You are most welcome, my lord. Lady Catherine has been an attentive hostess on several occasions during my visit in Hunsford, and I am pleased to do whatever I am able in this time of sorrow." Elizabeth met the earl's eyes with sincerity.

The earl lowered his voice. "*Attentive*, Miss Bennet? Yes, you *are* good to be judicious where other words might be more accurate." His eyes crinkled at the corners—eyes as used to smiling and being pleased as Lady Catherine's were to frowning and finding fault.

Elizabeth smiled in return but maintained a diplomatic silence, save for the expressive raising of an eyebrow.

"Are you taking coffee, Brother?" Lady Catherine's voice cut through the room like a cold rapier. "Pour it out, Miss Bennet. Do not stand there idle."

Elizabeth turned away from Lady Catherine to hide a wider smile as all three men rolled their eyes.

"I shall take coffee, Miss Bennet. Alexander, fetch a cup of tea for your mother," the earl suggested. The colonel moved away to speak to Mrs. Collins.

"How long do you stay in Kent, my lord?" Elizabeth asked as she handed the earl his cup.

"Not long. We have obligations that require our return to London tomorrow. My wife is not comfortable here in any case. My sister considers that I married beneath myself—no matter the wedding was thirty-five years and two fine sons ago—she never lets us forget."

Elizabeth shook her head ruefully. She was not in the least surprised to hear of Lady Catherine being rude and ridiculous to a sister by marriage, even one who would precede her in the Fitzwilliam family order. "You are quite candid, my lord!"

"Your eyes inspire candour, Miss Bennet, do they not, nephew?" The earl turned to Darcy, only to see him lower his formerly appreciative gaze from this engaging young lady to study the pattern in the carpet.

"They do," Darcy murmured.

Elizabeth subtly gripped the table, feeling the colour rise in her cheeks.

Darcy saw her delicate white knuckles tighten at the table's edge, and wondered what it meant. He dared not return his eyes to her face. Surely, she was not daunted by the introduction to a nobleman.

The colonel returned with a cup of tea. The earl took a last quick glance from Darcy to Elizabeth and looked at his son. "Interesting, Alexander," he muttered aloud and turned to sit with his sister. His son and nephew followed suit.

As the mourning guests began to leave, Lady Catherine arose from her seat intending to dismiss Elizabeth and Charlotte from their duties. Darcy did not see his aunt following him across the room as he was returning his uncle's cup.

"Thank you, Mr. Darcy, for introducing me to your uncle," Elizabeth said quietly.

"You are most welcome, Miss Bennet. He requested an introduction." Darcy searched her eyes for a moment of understanding.

"It was kind of you, sir."

"You *introduced* her to your uncle?" Lady Catherine's voice held a shrill edge of fatigue. It was tiring for her to maintain politeness whilst the Archbishop was in her home. "You forget yourself, Darcy!"

Darcy was also worn thin by the emotion of the day's events and by being in the same room with Elizabeth for two hours even though fifty other people milled about. "Lady Catherine, you must certainly know Miss Bennet well enough to apprehend she would not presume upon such an introduction, especially one made during a time of mourning."

Lady Catherine eyed her nephew and sniffed, "Hmm...well." She turned to Charlotte. "Mrs. Collins, you and Miss Bennet are excused with my thanks." She swept away, calling loudly for her maid.

Darcy's annoyed features followed his aunt as she quitted the room. "My aunt is quite tired, I think. I must apologise if she has embarrassed you."

The light danced in Elizabeth's eyes. "Mr. Darcy, I have been here upwards of six weeks. Your aunt shows a remarkable consistency of character and temperament. She has been no worse today than any other. Do not make yourself uneasy."

Darcy made an acknowledging shake of his head. "Yes, I am not surprised you have taken her measure."

"She was too easily drawn out, whereas I did not understand another member of your family half so well as I should have." She looked down quickly, hoping he would not mistake her meaning.

Darcy's eyes searched Elizabeth's downturned face but saw only a slow blush spread over her smooth cheeks. "If the person to whom you refer had been more forthcoming, if his manners were more civil or even amiable, perhaps you would have had an easier task of sketching his character." Darcy handed the coffee cup to her rather than setting it upon the table, and as he had hoped, their fingers touched as Elizabeth took hold of the saucer.

The cup and saucer rattled in Elizabeth's hand until she set them down. "Thank you, Mr. Darcy," she said solemnly, her eyes full of understanding.

It was her seriousness that convinced Darcy she knew he had been speaking of himself when repeating the words she had once spoken, and she was not thanking him merely for returning an errant cup of coffee.

WITH RELIEF AT THE END OF THE FUNERAL GATHERING CAME AN ACCOMpanying fatigue. Although in something of a mood to chide Alexander for appearing inept in not introducing Elizabeth to the earl, Darcy decided the matter could wait for another time. He neither knew nor cared where his cousin had gone. Instead, Darcy hid in the Rosings library and did not fight the drowsiness creeping upon him as he nursed a small portion of brandy before the fire.

A gentle hand lay upon his shoulder, and he glanced up, staring in recognition. Elizabeth Bennet was leaning over him with a slight smile on her lips and sparkles in her fire-lit eyes.

He smiled in return and sat straighter. "Miss Elizabeth..." He started to rise but pressure from her delicate hand and a shake of her head stilled him.

"Do not inconvenience yourself, Mr. Darcy. I have simply come to thank you for the service you rendered me today. It was kind of you to introduce me to your uncle—most kind indeed as well as unnecessary and undeserved."

He started to speak, but he was silenced by the brush of her fingertips upon his forehead moving aside a wayward curl. This was followed by the softest kiss, placed where the curl had been. *Forgiven! I am forgiven!* He raised his hand to hers, still upon his shoulder. She grasped his, moved in front of him, and sat upon his thighs, looking intently into his face. She was blushing, and Darcy felt his colour rise with hers.

"You need not thank me for what was merely civil behaviour, Miss Bennet," he breathed.

"On the contrary, Mr. Darcy. I am not in the least insensible to the awkwardness of our situation. You have done me a kindness, and now I would be consoled by returning the favour to you."

Darcy was entranced as she lifted his hand to her lips. Suddenly he was aware of what she was wearing. Gone was the mourning grey; in its place was the evening dress she had worn on Easter when she had played the pianoforte for them. It would take only the nodding forward of his head to nuzzle the downy full flesh at her neckline.

Elizabeth shifted her weight in his lap. Her hand released his and rested calmly upon the fall of his trousers. His manly organ expanded rapidly beneath her hand, concerning him lest she should feel it. He was hoarse as he asked, "A favour to me?"

"What would you have of me, sir?" Her eyes were merry as she pondered. "A kiss?" She quickly brought her sweet lips to his and just as quickly pulled away. "A touch?" With her other hand, she plucked up one of Darcy's and guided his warm fingers along the neckline of her bodice. The action raised her divine fragrance. "A caress?" The hand upon his trousers began to manipulate him, tentatively at first, then gaining confidence as she felt his response. "What will best soothe you, Mr. Darcy?"

At the risk of sounding greedy, his inclination was to request more of all three, but his words escaped in an inarticulate moan.

Elizabeth leaned into him, pinning his hand—which she had abandoned with two of his fingers hooked at her neckline—between them, filling his palm with her fluttering breast. Her lips were at his ear. "We shall not discompose my gown, sir, nor shall we raise my skirts. However, what we might do to *your* clothes is another matter entirely."

He chuckled and attempted to prepare a saucy retort, only to groan instead as her fingers nimbly worked the buttons that would free him to her tender ministrations.

"Fitzwilliam?"

Darcy's eyes flew open as the hand on his shoulder increased its violence to awaken him.

"Brother, are you unwell?"

His glance darted to Georgiana's concerned countenance. After an addled moment, he shook his head.

Having successfully gained his attention, Georgiana huffed into the chair that was the match of the one occupied by Darcy. "Do I understand correctly, Brother, that the young lady serving coffee is *the* Elizabeth Bennet of whom you have written?"

Darcy stared at his sister blankly for several moments, vastly disconcerted. She looked at him expectantly, and he was relieved to see that she was unaware of his condition as he had dozed. He straightened himself and met her gaze.

"Yes. Mrs. Collins is her particular friend, and Miss Bennet has been a guest at the vicarage for some weeks. She was due to leave Friday last, but our family's events and her inclusion in Anne's will have lengthened her stay."

"But that is a lucky thing, is it not, that you will see more of her? She seems a pleasant sort of girl."

"*Lucky* that our cousin Anne is dead? Perhaps 'lucky' is not the word you want, my dear." Darcy gave his sister a rueful glance.

Georgiana pulled a face. "I know that look, and I do not mean to be irreverent, merely honest. In any case, I should very much like to meet her."

Darcy smiled more to himself than to his sister. "I shall introduce you when the opportunity presents itself."

Georgiana blew out a sigh and laughed lightly. "Oh, good. I am relieved."

"Why should you be?"

"When I was out walking this morning, I met a *very* pretty, dark-haired lady running through the beech grove like a gazelle. Her exercise brought her colour up; she has a lovely complexion. My being there discomposed her at first, but she laughed in a most pleasing and friendly way, and I thought from your description that she must be Miss Bennet. You will be proud of me. I screwed my courage to the sticking place and introduced myself. We spoke only a few words, but I thought we got on frightfully well."

Darcy's eyes closed. *Happy thought...Georgie has met Elizabeth without my leave and now quotes Lady Macbeth.* He opened his eyes; Georgiana was still sitting forward in her chair, looking pleased.

"I hope you were not indiscreet," Darcy sighed.

Georgiana appeared offended. "I most certainly was *not* indiscreet. At most, I might have seemed curious, but I assure you, she would never suspect that I hope at some future time, sooner rather than later *if you please*" —her words became pointed—"to commence calling her 'sister.' I should like it *very* well."

Darcy rolled his eyes and groaned. Georgiana laughed at him and skipped from the room.

Charlotte cast a sidelong glance at her friend as they returned to the vicarage. They had covered more than half the distance without speaking a word. "You are quiet, Lizzy."

"I am in a state of wonderment at Mr. Darcy."

"I saw that he spoke to you and introduced his uncle. I hope you are flattered. He once again singles you out."

"I *would* be flattered if I could comprehend him. I cannot do justice to his kindness. Nor am I sure he would be best pleased to know that I chanced upon his sister this morning in the grove, and she introduced herself. She was not at all what I expected. Even though she caught me running, she seemed forbearing and still sought to be known to me. She was not proud but was all things amiable."

Charlotte smiled to herself. Darcy continued to admire her friend, and Elizabeth had now met the sister—another hurdle leapt successfully. The impediments to his offering for Elizabeth were gone, dead amidst a scandal of Anne's making though few yet knew of it. Other than being in mourning, everything ought to progress nicely now. She sighed, feeling quite satisfied.

Charlotte believed her friend much better suited to Fitzwilliam Darcy than to Colonel Fitzwilliam. Why she held so fast to this opinion, she did not choose to ponder.

*8 March 1812*

*I made sure our quadrille table was superlatively stupid, that I might observe EB's behaviour when above her company in intellect if not in rank.*

*It was with great interest that I watched when she was informed that Rosings expects a visit from my cousin Fitzwilliam Darcy. I overheard her say to Mrs. Collins, with great expression in her eyes, she might be amused to see how he is received here, assuming to have the hopelessness of a certain Miss Bingley's designs on Darcy confirmed by observing his behaviour to me! It soon became known to Mama that all of the ladies of the Hunsford vicarage had already been frequently seen by Cousin Darcy when he lately stayed in their neighbourhood. Mama was not at all pleased.*

*In sum, it appears to me that EB does not like Darcy but is prepared to be entertained by observing him, and the rumour is abroad that he and I are betrothed. How very bothersome. —A de B*

*30 March 1812*

*Like bees to honey, Darcy and Alex cannot resist EB. It would seem that Alex defers to Darcy though she seems more at ease and laughs comfortably with Alex. It takes no skill at observation to see Alex likes her very much, yet he holds back in a way so as to make me think there is some conspiracy betwixt my cousins. The men have made their pact, but I do not see that EB might approve of their decision. When Alex talks to her, he is self-conscious; he knows Darcy watches.*

*Yes, Darcy is the more intriguing study. I watched him as best I could when the Hunsford party visited but without much success. He certainly looked at her a great deal, but the expression of that look was disputable. It was an earnest steadfast gaze, but I could not detect much admiration in it, and sometimes it appeared to be nothing but absence of mind. But who would not be rendered insensate by my mother's ceaseless prattle dominating all more refreshing opinions?*

*It is all too interesting. I wish I felt better. It is my condition, certainly, that preoccupies my thoughts and renders me less astute than is my wont. When next we are all together, which I believe will be Thursday evening, I must make a better effort to concentrate. Which cousin is assuming a right to her, and is it the one she prefers? I think one of the men will have to show more regard than he might truly feel in order to secure her. She must be left in no doubt if she is to be won. Please, Darcy…if you have warned Alex off, stop standing around staring and say something flattering. —A de B*

# CHAPTER 6
## A Will of Iron

*Tuesday, 14 April 1812*

Over the period of half an hour, those summoned by Andrew Steventon, Esquire to his humble law offices in Hunsford had arrived, and all were seated. Georgiana Darcy entered first, accompanied by her brother and cousin. The colonel had a dual reason to be in attendance as both guardian to Miss Darcy and a beneficiary in his own right.

The colonel and Georgiana were surprised to see Elizabeth Bennet arrive next. She was welcomed most civilly by Mr. Steventon's clerk and seated near a window. Elizabeth stood nervously from time to time, looking out onto the main road.

"May I ask whom you expect, Miss Bennet?" queried the colonel.

Elizabeth turned to respond. "Mrs. Collins, sir. She is waiting at the vicarage for another person, and both will be conveyed in Mr. Steventon's carriage. I chose to walk."

Steventon cleared his throat as if to speak when Lady Catherine de Bourgh swept into the room with a second, blabbering clerk following behind. The poor young fellow was mumbling apologies to his employer, who sighed wearily. "It is of no importance, Waverley. Bring another chair."

Lady Catherine eyed Elizabeth narrowly, believing her somehow to be the real cause of all the mischief. "Surely, you have no right to any expectation from my daughter, Miss Bennet. You knew her scarce a month." Lady Catherine did not sound disdainful; her tone was one of plainly stated and obvious truth.

Elizabeth met the comment without alteration in her countenance of benign equanimity. "And yet, Lady Catherine, hither I was bid, and here I am."

"Miss Elizabeth Bennet is named in the will, your ladyship, as you were previously informed," stated Mr. Steventon with a hint of impatience.

Moments later a carriage was heard, and Lady Catherine huffed and grumbled when Mrs. Collins and Mrs. Jenkinson entered the room.

"I would sit by the window, Miss Bennet, *please.*" Lady Catherine spoke with exaggerated civility, standing suddenly as Mrs. Jenkinson was seated next to her. Once all were settled to their liking, the little lawyer began his recitation of the Last Will and Testament of Miss Anne de Bourgh.

*"As the heiress of the de Bourgh fortune, it is incumbent upon me to act responsibly in the determination of the future of the fee simple Rosings Park estate and assets. I believe myself to be carrying the heir to Rosings, and should tragedy befall me, I must leave my financial affairs in good order for my child and the lasting betterment of the de Bourgh fortune. With these burdens foremost in mind, and being of sound mind and body* [Lady Catherine sighed noisily at this, to be met by the censorious eye of Mr. Steventon], *I make the following bequests:*

*"In the event of my passing, if I leave behind a child of my body of either sex, I request Miss Georgiana and Mr. Fitzwilliam Darcy stand as Godparents and Guardians, notwithstanding that at the time of this will, Miss Darcy is not of age. I request the child be raised at Pemberley and such London schools as are deemed appropriate to said child's interests and inclinations, and that visitation of the child by its maternal grandmother, Lady Catherine de Bourgh, be strictly limited in duration and always with the presence of one or both guardians."*

"This is not..." Lady Catherine began.

Steventon met her eye over his spectacles with a look that would not be gainsaid.

Lady Catherine's remarks died on her lips.

Steventon resumed. "There is a recent codicil to this portion, dated Friday, the third of April, 1812."

*"It has come to my attention through my acquaintance with Miss Elizabeth Bennet that she might be as fair a Guardian to any infant of mine as Miss Darcy. Because Miss Elizabeth Bennet will be of legal age before the birth of my unborn child, I name her the child's temporary female Guardian until Miss Georgiana Darcy is herself one and twenty. I believe Miss Elizabeth Bennet and Mr. Fitzwilliam Darcy will act for the benefit of the child."*

Not a head turned in the room. Even Lady Catherine met the request, which would never come to pass, with stunned silence. It may be assumed that Darcy and Elizabeth blushed in mortification. No one dared look at them.

*"I set aside in trust for my child the entire de Bourgh fortune and Rosings Park income with exceptions listed as follows:*

*"I leave to my cousin, Colonel Alexander Richard Fitzwilliam, the sum of 50,000£ so that, at such time as he retires from his military service, he will never know want and may be less beholden to his family. He is a man of merit who did far greater by his office than I have heard of most second sons, and he was a devoted friend to me as well as a relation."*

A surprised inhale of breath was heard throughout the room, contributed rather equally by all of its occupants. Elizabeth unconsciously glanced at the colonel; the sum, having been mentioned between them in jest, was astonishing.

The colonel remembered Elizabeth's words, a joke about the relative worth of a second son, and felt all eyes upon him. He dared not be distracted by the motion of Elizabeth's head. He found himself embarrassed in public for the first time since childhood.

Darcy saw Elizabeth's unguarded response to the colonel's enrichment, wondering whether it had anything to do with the man's blush. Was there already something—some familiar regard—between them? The very thought, although a notion that he would publicly support, caused him to frown.

*"Such a sum, I trust, will allow him a wider choice as to marriage and, I pray, will allow him a greater likelihood of marrying for affection should he be so blessed as to feel it.*

*"To my long-time companion, Mrs. Elspeth Jenkinson, I leave 5,000£. Please allow Mr. Steventon or some other sensible person to invest it for you in the four percents to secure a lifetime income surpassing what you were paid per annum by my mother, who will no doubt not think to see to your care if I am gone."*

It should come as no surprise that Mrs. Jenkinson began to quietly weep. Darcy noticed the movement as Elizabeth took one of the lady's hands.

*"A trust will be established on behalf of Mrs. Charlotte Collins in the amount of 10,000£. Andrew Steventon, Esquire, Mr. Fitzwilliam Darcy, and Colonel Alexander Fitzwilliam will stand as trustees. The funds and any interest accrued may only be paid out to Mrs. Collins at her request in the case of dire need (assuming agreement by the trustees), or immediately upon her widowhood. In the event of her death, the trust will be dissolved and divided for the provision*

*of her children. If there are none, the sum will be returned to the Rosings estate. Under no circumstances will Mr. William Collins hold any right to any monies from the trust, and he may make no claims against it."*

"Oh, Anne," Lady Catherine sighed in disparagement.

Mrs. Jenkinson was sufficiently recovered to titter nervously.

Elizabeth reached across the lap of Mrs. Jenkinson to clasp Charlotte's hand and bit her lip to keep from smiling.

"There is a last codicil, also dated from the third of April of this year," Mr. Steventon stated. His attention turned to Elizabeth.

*"Lastly, although our acquaintance is not one of long standing, I have come to know and admire Miss Elizabeth Bennet. The previous bequests will empty the readily accessible monetary assets of Sir Lewis de Bourgh as they were passed to me, but I am in possession of the de Bourgh jewels, and these I leave to you, Miss Elizabeth. I detect in you an intelligent and independent spirit, and knowing your family's situation, I would not like to think you might need to make a living at some demeaning occupation or marry beneath your value to secure your well-being. At the time of my coming of age a year ago, the gem collection was valued at 30,000£. I know you will wish to see to the settlements of your sisters, but I do hope you secure your future with a major part."*

Here Mr. Steventon handed a separate document to Elizabeth. "She has included an inventory of the jewels, Miss Bennet, and further says…

*"My mother is not to be trusted in this, and I include an inventory of the jewels, that you will know what the collection contains— "*

"This is ludicrous," Lady Catherine interrupted, leaping to her feet.

"Lady Catherine, sit down!" Darcy likewise stood and glowered at his aunt until she complied.

Elizabeth sat wide-eyed and nonplussed as Steventon continued.

*"Miss Elizabeth will also have the right to any clothing or personal effects of mine which might be of use to her or her sisters. There is much in my wardrobe that was never worn, as my mother insisted I have a new selection of gowns and folderol ordered with the coming of each Season."*

Steventon surveyed the room. "And we conclude with…

*"As regards my mother, Lady Catherine de Bourgh, my father's will stipulated that she continue as Mistress of Rosings Park for the term of her life until I marry. Were I to marry (which I never intend to do), she would be removed to the dower house. Should both my child and I be lost, I leave to Colonel Alexander Richard*

*Fitzwilliam the entire estate, fortune (as excepted by the above bequests), and its management. My dear cousin, I am told by the preparer of this document that the care of my mother is bound by the will of my poor father, and Lady Catherine de Bourgh will remain Mistress of Rosings until your marriage, but you may alter her allowance and household expenses as you see fit and prudent. I would advise a hasty marriage, and I wish you joy, Cousin Alex.*

*"And thus I end my Last Will and Testament and the disposition of my worldly goods. I name Andrew Steventon, Esquire, my executor in this, with payment of 50£ per annum from the Rosings estate for as long as his services in the execution of my wishes are required."*

Mr. Steventon looked up, smiling to have assisted in bringing such largess to them all. "This document and all of its parts have been registered in London with the Commons Court. Colonel, there is a sealed letter for you from Miss de Bourgh." He handed the missive to its recipient.

The letter was a single sheet, dated "3 April 1812" and read simply:

*My dear Cousin Alex,*

*If you do not secure the hand and affection of Miss Elizabeth Bennet, you are an utter damned fool, and I shall not have chosen my heir wisely. If Darcy will not have her, or as I expect, she will not have him, fill the void. Compromise her if there are no other means—seek atonement after. You will not succeed absent a wife of health and wit and capable of the sound management of my mother.*

*A de B*

Darcy had remained standing and was looking over his cousin's shoulder. Anne's hand was elegant and eminently legible. He strode slowly to the window, gazing absently through the glass.

The colonel folded the letter into his pocket as he watched Darcy stalk away, assuming correctly that Darcy had read it.

"Steventon, is this travesty to be published?" Lady Catherine demanded when it was clear that the contents of the letter would not be forthcoming.

"Indeed, your ladyship. As regards a fee tail estate, with bequests outside the family, and since all of the concerned parties have been apprised of its contents, the Last Will and Testament of Miss Anne de Bourgh now transfers into the public record."

"But my daughter behaved scandalously! I shall fight this. The will of a fallen woman cannot be legal. I shall have you know that I have my own will. You will hear from Messers. Phawcett and Drippe of London within the week." Lady Catherine glanced imperiously at everyone. "I take no leave of you, sir." She swept from the room.

Elizabeth and Charlotte stood as one. Having spent the early morning in the study of Anne de Bourgh's journals, each felt they should speak but knew not where to begin, particularly with the young Miss Darcy present.

It was this youngest lady who spoke first. "Am I to understand that my cousin was…" She glanced nervously at her brother and did not finish her thought.

Elizabeth moved to sit beside her and spoke gently. "Indeed, she was, Miss Darcy." Darcy turned to listen, and the colonel also leaned towards them. "Your cousin left journals, which are with Mrs. Collins and me. Miss de Bourgh had some uncommonly forward notions of the world, perhaps somewhat naïve, but she was strong willed as we have all heard. Much stronger in mind than in body…" Elizabeth took Georgiana's hand, watching the girl's eyes.

"But who…?" Georgiana whispered.

Elizabeth looked at Charlotte. After a moment, Charlotte nodded. Elizabeth leaned to whisper in Georgiana's ear.

"Oh!" Georgiana paled. "How horrid! How wretched of him! Did she *pay* him? He does nothing except for the love of money."

Elizabeth nodded with a lifted eyebrow. "That she did."

Georgiana began to tremble and twisted to embrace Elizabeth with dry sobs. Elizabeth glanced at Darcy, who watched unhappily. Elizabeth patted and rubbed his sister's shoulders, hoping to offer some comfort, and quickly Georgiana drew in a restoring breath and sat upright. She nodded her head as if coming to some conclusion and held Elizabeth's hand as it remained upon her shoulder. She spoke quietly, "Thank you, Miss Bennet. You were kind to be honest—to treat me as a fellow woman and not a child. I have always wanted a sister, and I have imagined she would treat me as you have with just your sort of gentle sympathy. How did you know I could bear it and be brave in the face of this?"

Elizabeth glanced at Georgiana's brother before saying with great purpose, "You are a Darcy."

Darcy was wholly engrossed in the scene before him. He thought he could guess the name whispered in his sister's ear, but he set that consideration aside once his sister was being consoled in Elizabeth's arms. He heard Georgiana say she had always wanted a sister, and Darcy's heart clambered against his ribs, feeling his failure with Elizabeth all the more painfully. And now, Anne wished Alexander to be Elizabeth Bennet's bridegroom; she would never be Elizabeth Darcy. *It is best for her.*

When Elizabeth had made her final response after meeting his eyes for a weighty moment, Darcy knew not what to think except to return to her velvet voice again and again. Elizabeth Bennet had said, "You are a Darcy," as if it were no small thing and nothing she despised.

*3 April 1812*

*This day is most interesting. Mr. S received my changes to the will with only the barest comment and must think me a weathercock, but as long as I do not make requests insupportable in the law—oh, that I could disinherit my mother completely, but that was my father's doing—he takes down my words and sees they are witnessed. The clerks draw the documents, and they are sent express to the Archdeacon's Court of Doctor's Common in London for registration. It is all most properly done.*

*After Darcy's abrupt departure from last night's little party, I had not seen him until this morning. I do not believe he has slept! His eyes at breakfast were hollow and dark. He said nothing other than yes or no to anyone. When Alex suggested they take their leave of the inhabitants of the Hunsford vicarage, I saw a distinct cast of distress about him, but he covered himself quickly, merely nodding. Alex looked quizzical, I thought. I made sure to be present when they returned, but Darcy returned alone and as melancholy as I have ever seen him. He would not sit with us. His excuse of seeing to his packing was patently specious. Alex returned a good deal later. Mama asked how the household did, and he admitted he had not seen Miss Bennet, that she was out walking.*

*What am I to make of this? Why would EB still be abroad during the morning calling hours? Assuredly, she knows my cousins intend to leave on the morrow. I heard Mama tell her so when we were about in the carriage the day before yesterday.*

*It is bedtime, and I feel as sluggish as I ever have, but I have pondered more on the day's events. There was no activity in the billiards room today. Darcy went to ground in the library and would not be moved. Throughout dinner, he said little, and if he swallowed so much as a mouthful, I did not see it. He is discomfited and wholly out of sorts. I looked a question at Alex, and he mouthed "Elizabeth Bennet" when Darcy was glowering at his plate. What can possibly have occurred, and when? Did he seek her out after she did not come here last evening? Mrs. Collins was eyeing him when she gave EB's excuses; surely, she would not attempt to encourage Darcy by her shrewd looks. Can it be? Has Darcy, of all men, suffered a rejection? Can Elizabeth Bennet have brought him to this? Not in the deaths of his parents, not after Georgiana's near scandal...no, never have I seen him so low. Perhaps I might get Alex apart for a moment before their departure. —A de B*

*4 April 1812*

*I had only a brief word with Alex. He knows not the particulars but believes Darcy and EB have quarrelled. He does not know whether Darcy made her an offer. I asked whether Alex had any interest in this, and he said Darcy had warned him off—chased him off is more like it. Alex said that, although he finds her good company, he has allowed himself nothing more. Given her considerable physical charms, I cannot say I believe him. They are both besotted in their way. Evidently, we are to see the Hunsford party for dinner after church tomorrow. I look forward to observing EB. —A de B*

# CHAPTER 7
## The Colonel's Marriage Prospects

*Tuesday, 14 April 1812, Hunsford village*

With funds came confidence, and Mrs. Jenkinson stayed with Mr. Steventon after the reading of the will to discuss her future, secure in the knowledge that she could afford to hire a carriage to return to The Bell in Bromley and thence to wherever her heart desired with her presumed income of 200£ per year. She was not at all sure of the propriety of becoming a lady of independent—if modest—means, but she meant to try.

The day had turned fair with a slight breeze, and the carriage that had brought the Darcys and Colonel Fitzwilliam to the reading was dismissed. When the colonel suggested escorting Elizabeth and Charlotte to the vicarage, an odd party was formed. The colonel fell in beside Mrs. Collins while Georgiana and Darcy walked on either side of Elizabeth.

Where Colonel Fitzwilliam had developed the habit of laughing at Darcy's arrogance when they were in the neighbourhood previously, Darcy now caught the idea and was just as likely to laugh at himself. His manner was dry and droll, to be sure, but he would now stop himself when in the midst of some conceited proclamation and shake his head, wondering at his presumption.

The first time Elizabeth beheld this spectacle, she was all astonishment. The topic was Anne de Bourgh's will.

"Will you assist your cousin in estate management, Mr. Darcy?" Elizabeth asked. She already knew the answer—of course, he would—she was merely casting about for a safe subject for friendly discourse.

"He had better return to university," came the reply. "I have not the least notion how to direct an estate in so mild a climate. I am accustomed to more challenging work in Derbyshire."

Elizabeth looked down and raised an unseen eyebrow.

There was an awkward pause before Darcy started, realising he might appear proud. "Listen to me! I only give orders. That cannot be called work." He laughed a little.

Georgiana looked at her brother. "No one works more tirelessly for Pemberley's success than you, Brother, even though you are not the one thrashing the grain or shearing the sheep."

He gave a mild snort that bobbed his head. "You are kind, Sister. Too kind."

Elizabeth hid her surprise and wondered whether the presence of his beloved sister inclined Darcy towards self-deprecation.

At reaching the garden gate of the vicarage, the group entered a general conversation, but Elizabeth noticed when Darcy turned ill at ease. He cleared his throat and asked, "Miss Bennet, when will you call to collect the de Bourgh jewels?"

Elizabeth blushed and stammered, "I-I had not thought of it. I can scarce believe they are mine and feel they ought not to be. Should they go to you, Miss Darcy?"

"I have my mother's jewels. How many broaches and bracelets have I need of? Precious few, I can tell you. It is years until I come out, or so I hope. You will not force me next year, will you Brother?"

Darcy looked fondly at his sister. "No, indeed, I shall not. If you care to wait, I leave it in your hands."

Again, Elizabeth looked at him with surprise. Although not directed at her, the warmth of his smile and tenderness in his voice seemed to strike a harmony within her chest. His devotion to his sister's comfort was most pleasing. No matter what he might think appropriate, this was evidence that he would allow Georgiana to choose the moment of her entrance into society. Elizabeth thought this wise, and unusually liberal, after the girl's ordeal of the previous summer. His forbearance was not what Elizabeth would have assumed a fortnight ago.

Colonel Fitzwilliam suggested Elizabeth accompany Mr. Collins in the morning for his daily visit to Rosings. "Georgiana and I shall present you with your jewels, madam!" He made a most cavalier bow, sweeping his hat over his toes. "Though you might wait until your birthday, which is soon, I understand?"

"It is, sir. I arrived in the world on May Day."

"Well, come along tomorrow and meet your booty anyway."

"You make me sound quite a pirate, sir!" Elizabeth laughed and noticed Darcy's eyes dancing with amusement.

The colonel glanced between them. "You *do* steal things," he said with a lowered voice, although all heard him.

It was Charlotte who quickly filled the uncomfortable silence by providing clarification. "Booty is taken on land, Lizzy, not at sea."

The colonel turned his gaze to the speaker. "Indeed, Mrs. Collins, you are correct. How do you know this?"

Charlotte raised her brows. "One hears things. One remembers."

He laughed. "A lady of mystery, Mrs. Collins! Well, to Miss Bennet's jewels, I daresay they are safer where they are for now. No thieves or pirates at Rosings, not on my watch! Perhaps I, or Darcy, might assist you in finding a reputable jeweller for the sale, and you will want to decide whether there is anything you might wish to keep."

"Thank you, sir, you are most kind." Elizabeth smiled in return.

"Miss Darcy," Charlotte said, turning to the girl. "Would you care to join Lizzy and me for tea? I could do with refreshments."

Georgiana turned to her guardians with a hopeful look.

"Of course." Darcy nodded, his eyes meeting Elizabeth's. "I shall send your maid to return with you. Or would you have a carriage?"

"I shall walk, Brother. I hope the exercise will improve me as it does Miss Bennet." Georgiana turned a smile to Elizabeth.

Darcy paused. "As you wish…" He faltered before adding, "Enjoy your time with your friends."

Elizabeth's stare after Darcy as he walked off with the colonel was so marked that Charlotte was required to call to her twice to proceed to the house.

Once inside and settled, Elizabeth ventured a suggestion. "Charlotte, would it be too much of a crush, or would my cousin disapprove, were I to invite Jane to stay? I very much wish her counsel about Miss de Bourgh's clothing, and then, perhaps, I shall not feel so much like a rag picker. The room you have spared for me would be ample for us both; we are accustomed to sharing, you know."

"Jane is your eldest sister?" Georgiana asked. A timorous look filled her expression.

"Indeed! Oh, Miss Darcy, if you can tolerate *my* company, you will adore Jane's. Everyone does. She is everything kind and benevolent, generous and sensible. She does not run about a place as I do, at a mad dash and venturing pert opinions. Am I not correct in this, Charlotte?"

"Oh, yes." Charlotte laughed. "Lizzy might teach you misdirected confidence with lively conversation, but to learn truly genteel behaviour, you have only to look to Miss Jane Bennet."

"A fine thing you are, by way of a friend!" Elizabeth exclaimed. The two women laughed.

Georgiana looked at them in astonishment. She longed to have sisters and such friends as these with whom to tease and jest. She sat up straight and decided that, to enjoy the company of these delightful ladies, she must unbend. Clearing her throat, she blushed as she requested, "Mrs. Collins, Miss Elizabeth, would it be too forward of me, do I ask too much, that I might have you call me Georgiana? In a small party such as this, amongst friends and family, those close to me call me Georgie…" Her voice trailed away as she feared she had put herself at risk. Would they surmise she truly had no confidants beyond her brother, her cousin, and a paid companion?

Charlotte nodded amiably.

Elizabeth's bright smile was all that could be wanted for a response. "I fully apprehend the honour, Georgiana! I hope you brother will approve."

"How could he not when…?" Georgiana started to assert that her brother felt much more than mere approval for Elizabeth but managed to silence the impulse.

Elizabeth pretended not to notice the girl might have said more and stood to curtsy to her new friend, making everyone laugh. "It is settled then! And do call me Lizzy. Charlotte only calls me Eliza when she means to scold!"

There followed a pleasant hour, passed in the discussion of all the benefits accruing to the friendship of like-minded women.

*Wednesday, 15 April 1812, Rosings Park*

THE COUSINS PAUSED IN THEIR MORNING RIDE TO WATCH ELIZABETH FROM afar, as she gracefully bent to pick wildflowers and grasses, making a loose bouquet. She seemed to wander idly, paying no particular attention to what she was creating in her hands and appearing lost in thought.

"Are you inclined to court her, Alex? Have you made up your mind?"

"Did I tell you of the conversation she and I shared Thursday last after Easter? You had informed me that she is a lady of little fortune with unfortunate connections. I let her know that any second son of an earl must be circumspect as to marriage. She instantly made a proper joke of it, saying I could not expect to fetch more than 50,000£, unless my brother is sickly."

"She said *50,000£*?" Darcy dropped his guard and stared.

"Yes. Oddly enough, that was the sum she pulled from the air."

Darcy mused a moment before saying, "It would not surprise me to find Miss Elizabeth employing any proceeds from the sale of her jewels to improve the likelihood of her sisters settling with men of consideration in the world at the expense of saving enough for herself, no matter our late cousin's wishes."

"Will she be able to accomplish so much?"

"Oh, yes. I have seen the de Bourgh jewels. You may well imagine our aunt dangling them before my eyes to increase my appraisal of Anne."

The colonel barked a shocked laugh. "No, Darcy! She did not!"

Darcy merely shrugged. He knew, in spite of his cousin's surprise, that he was believed. "In any case, you now find yourself well able to purchase your own happiness with a quite remarkable partner in life, who will have more dowry than we previously supposed. You could not wish for a more conversable companion, even though not a soldier. Let me be the second to wish you joy." Darcy stopped his speech abruptly. His throat tightened, and he found he could not carry the joke. He realised he had heard those words once spoken at himself—Caroline Bingley wishing him joy after his praise of Elizabeth's fine eyes.

"Except you do not." The colonel met Darcy's troubled gaze. "You do not sincerely wish me joy. So you see, I still do not have a clear plan of attack."

"What? The military man has no strategy? But she visits Rosings this afternoon!"

"No, she does not. I have heard that her call to see the jewels is set for tomorrow. But the material point is that I cannot attempt to win the affection of the lady who holds you in such sway, much as I might wish to.

Your eyes betray you, Darcy, each time you look at her or speak of her or hear her spoken of."

"But she will not have me. I love her enough to wish her settled with a man she can like, who will amuse her, as I, it is obvious, do not. And you said yourself she is the best marriage prospect we have seen in years."

"Glib talk when I thought I was furthering her suit with *you*."

"You need not have exerted yourself. She won my heart months ago."

"And she has it still," the colonel stated resolutely. The horses were restless, but the colonel had a sudden question for his cousin. "Darcy, if you were openly courting Elizabeth Bennet and I asked you to choose between myself and her, which of us would you choose?"

"Of all of the balmy suppositions I have ever heard, Alex, that is, without doubt, the most foolish." Darcy was staggered and confounded.

The colonel merely raised his eyebrows, waiting for an answer.

"*If* she had accepted me and *if* you were so momentarily unhinged as to ask such a sacrifice of me, I would choose Elizabeth." Darcy followed his words with a curt nod. "And so should any man choose when approaching matrimony. If you would not value the lady you are to spend your life with over every other consideration, well, then you should think on it again, sir.

"If you decide to court Elizabeth Bennet, you must learn to love her that much, for nothing less is her due." As the cousins conversed from their shrubbery cover, Darcy's gaze never left Elizabeth until she disappeared into the woodland. "It is to be hoped that I shall recover, Alex, but I have not yet. I would not for the world have you make the choice you just hazarded I make."

"Let me know when you are recovered, Darcy. It will make my decision easier."

Darcy evidenced a tight smile, but the colonel knew he had struck a frayed nerve.

"You will be the first to know." Darcy wheeled his horse around and trotted towards the Rosings stables.

Fitzwilliam watched his cousin's affronted back. *Yet you would have me make such a choice, Darcy…If I win her love, I drive you away, for I do not believe for a moment that you could bear it. You do not see that the question you denigrate is the very one you ask of me.*

He turned half around to watch as Elizabeth wandered back into the far grove. *Yes, a beautiful lady, lively, able in her pursuits, pleasing in conversa-*

*tion... It would be a splendid thing to bed her if she were in love. Plenty spirited with the right partner. But am I that man? Can I make myself love Elizabeth Bennet as Darcy loves her? Could one woman be the love of one's life for two men at the same time?*

He could not at present answer the questions. His own indecision frustrated him, and he chose to continue his ride.

As Darcy entered Rosings to seek the comfort of its library, his aunt beset him yet again.

"The search of the house is complete, Nephew."

"I am glad of it, madam. We have borne these absurdities long enough. Perhaps Georgiana and I may now make plans to return to London. My dealings with Mr. Steventon may be managed by the mails. It is an easy distance to return if Alexander—"

"Not so hasty, if you please. Your actions are not above suspicion."

Darcy rolled his eyes. "I have done naught but ride, play billiards, and attend you. How are these actions suspicious?"

"I have the pleasure of the fierce loyalty of my servants. Everything is reported to me." Lady Catherine drew herself up, causing the black ostrich feathers in her grey satin turban to flutter into her eyes. She blinked rapidly.

Darcy lowered his eyes and coughed into his hand to hide a smirk. *What has she to accuse me of now?* "Information for which you pay them handsomely if shillings be the measure of loyalty..." he muttered.

Lady Catherine would not be distracted. "After your departure a fortnight ago, the chambermaids reported a vast number of broken quills and nibs, paper ash in the grate even though you had not requested a fire be lit, and that you had the ink replenished twice in the night. What am I to make of this?"

Darcy was plunged by her description into the hours of his composition of the most fraught, difficult, and important letter he had ever written. Fearing he would blush, Darcy made to appear angry. "As I said at the time... a most pressing matter of business arose. It required some delicacy and finesse in the response. More than this does not concern you. Or do you require recompense for the ink?" After a curt bow, Darcy stepped around his aunt.

"No one leaves this house until Anne's diaries are found," came the dictate from his aunt as he strode away.

Darcy was best pleased, knowing the journals were safe with Charlotte Collins.

*25 March 1812*

*My male cousins are well, if not happily, settled here, and Mama dotes on them excessively. She chases them out of the billiard room if they tarry too long and generally makes them flee at her approach, for which she castigates me. If I were more amusing, she says—if I wore my gowns cut lower in the mode of fashion… I chuckle to myself. My bosom is increasing before the rest of me, and there would indeed be something for my cousins to notice had I any wish to attract either of them.*

*Speaking of bosomy attractions, Alex seems to be finding sanctuary from my mother in the drawing room at the Hunsford vicarage. I did ask him last night whether he found Miss Elizabeth a pleasant and lively girl, as I think they would take delight in each other. His reply was quick and affirmative: if only she had some little fortune. Both Darcy and I are aware that Alex is more frugal than is generally known, and more than once, I have heard him complain that Darcy, as heir of Pemberley, may marry at his whim. Not that Darcy is given to whims, far from it.*

*Still, I do not entirely comprehend the military mind of Cousin Alex. What I can learn lurking outside the door of the billiard room makes me think the man has never been in love and is certainly no romantic. He enjoys women in the usual male way, and he gets on well with them in society, but I do not detect any inclination to profound ardency. Alex's heart will not be easily touched.*

*Whereas I now think Darcy, if he allows himself, will be utterly devoted. Joyless and dour but utterly devoted. I do wonder why he does not get himself to Hunsford with Alex since I understand he was often in company with EB in the autumn. Perhaps he does not find her as pleasing a diversion as Alex does, but I cannot account for his behaviour.*

*The Hunsford party will join us for dinner on Easter, and I shall be able to observe everyone at close quarters. I would warn EB if I see she is forming an attachment to Alex. And perhaps Darcy will reveal why he is avoiding her, for I think her charming and bold. Oh! Perhaps she stands up to him in the same manner she behaves to Mama, and he does not like to be challenged. That must explain it.*

*I am of a mind to travel to the lawyer tomorrow. It is some folly of mind due to my delicate condition, I am sure, but I want to make certain all of my affairs are in order. But now Mrs. J arrives with my chamomile. —A de B*

# CHAPTER 8
## The Wrong Hands

*14 August 1811*

*It is not to be believed. Had I not heard the announcement myself, I would never ever have known my mother could sink so low. She has named William Collins as the vicar for Hunsford. I would have wagered the de Bourgh turquoise and diamond diadem that she would have chosen the more scholarly James Leigh. Mr. Leigh is two and thirty, from a fine old family, married with two children, and seemed well spoken when I was in his company for his interview with Mama. He is a Cambridge man, as I recall.*

*But, alas not.*

*A dinner was given today for the local dignitaries (such as they are) and the verger of the church, who will not be replaced (without regard to the flagrant embezzlement he seems to think part of the emolument of his office) since he has my mother's support, and Collins will not thwart her. They all came to stare at this repulsive and shabby fellow. Never ever, ever have I heard anyone lavish such praise and flattery upon her, yet I do believe the misbegotten creature to be utterly sincere. He is young, stupid, lacking all self-awareness, wholly without fashion, and sings his own praises behind a guise of humble servitude. He cannot reason, which renders him incapable of guile, at least any that cannot be seen through. His countless vain little niceties are, I presume, the product of much study, and if he tells me again that my ill health has robbed the court of its finest jewel, I shall run mad. No…I have not the energy for that, but I do think I could manage an oyster fork in his throat. His repellent Adam's apple makes a fine large target. Yes, that I would happily do.*

*He is unmarried. Mama will have him marry, and together these two jackdaws have mentioned something about Mr. Collins being cousin and heir to an entailed estate currently populated by a healthy incumbent, his wife, and five daughters, some or all of marriageable age. There is some plot afoot to send him off thither, to which I heartily subscribe. Let him visit his Hertfordshire cousins as often as may be. Tonight I am a disgruntled —A de B*

*Wednesday, 15 April 1812, Rosings*

After the unpleasant exchange with Darcy and a hurried meeting with her housekeeper, Lady Catherine sighed. The execrable Mr. Steventon had sent a note requesting Miss Elizabeth Bennet be allowed immediate access to the de Bourgh jewels, but she was not inclined to entertain the nefarious Miss Bennet so soon. *By what means did the creature lure Anne into such a paroxysm of generosity?* Lady Catherine was perplexed, and understanding the mind of her daughter was not possible without the recovery of Anne's diaries. She could only seek the righting of the situation. That the de Bourgh jewels should be sold to provide dowries for an upstart family of hoydens in Hertfordshire was truly repulsive.

There was nothing to be done about monies granted Charlotte Collins and the Jenkinson woman, and her nephew Alexander might prove difficult, but about Elizabeth Bennet…ah, now *in that* she might exert some control whilst there was still time. The young hussy could come on the morrow to see her ill-gotten gains. Lady Catherine narrowed her eyes. Yes, they could take tea together as the jewels were displayed for their new owner in Anne's chambers. It would be of no consequence whether the rugs were further soiled. The rooms must be done-up again in any case.

Lady Catherine was furious and rendered distracted by her daughter's will. She had already that morning sent several sheets of instruction to her attorney in London, the highly regarded Mr. Phawcett. Once matters were settled with Elizabeth Bennet to Lady Catherine's satisfaction, she would hither to London and press her points home in her own Last Will and Testament.

*The Hunsford vicarage*

Elizabeth closed the 1811 volume of Anne de Bourgh's journals and watched her friend Charlotte still musing over the next book. Although Elizabeth had read a few of the entries, and others had been read to her, she had not yet taken the time to give 1812 the study her curiosity demanded.

"Charlotte, do I dare take that volume to my bedchamber this evening, do you think? I fear I have nearly memorised the first book."

Charlotte looked at her evenly. There was nothing for it but to tell Elizabeth the truth or something near it. "I know Mrs. Jenkinson intended us both to read all of Anne's thoughts, but she cannot have known what is contained here."

Elizabeth shook her head. "My maidenly sensibilities have withstood the loss of her virtue, you know." She chuckled. "It was what my Aunt Phillips had warned us it would be, do you recall?"

Charlotte had to join in her friend's amusement.

"I cannot think there would be anything *more* alarming," Elizabeth coaxed.

"I am afraid there is, Lizzy." Charlotte could not help but blush as she remembered reading about the last couplings of Anne and her Mr. C, as she had called Wickham.

Elizabeth weighed Charlotte's embarrassed countenance. Given that Charlotte was a married woman of some months, what could possibly be contained in Anne's tales that was worse than had been already described? "Charlotte?"

"No, Lizzy. It would not be proper."

"Charlotte! I do not wish to be vexed, but I fear I might become so if you persist."

The two friends had decided in a previous conversation that the confined life of Anne de Bourgh—wholly occupied, thwarted, and subjugated by her mother—had adversely affected the thinking of what might have been, in other circumstances, a very fine mind. Elizabeth was wild to know what more could be said of the unpleasantness Anne had endured to get herself with child.

"I shall bear all your wrath, Lizzy, but you will not move me in this." Charlotte held the black leather binding to her breast. "I shall put it in my

Oakley. Mr. Collins would never dare venture into my dressing room."

Elizabeth stared after her friend as Charlotte quit the parlour and disappeared down the hall to the servants' stairway. She counted her thoughts off on her fingers, making an inventory of all she had already read in the second journal. *One: Anne mentions Darcy's change in demeanour with the passing years; two: her joy at learning she is with child; three: more ludicrous behaviour from her mother; four: the to-doings over Easter; five: Anne's view of the consequences of my ignoble refusal of Mr. Darcy's addresses—as much as she had surmised; and six: her surprising study of me… There is nothing in the whole of it that is more objectionable than any other part. What could Charlotte possibly oppose my reading?*

Charlotte returned with an air of self-satisfaction.

"What of her dreams at Christmas?" Elizabeth asked. "I suppose *that* was disturbing enough for anyone…"

"There is at least one more entry in January that I have read," Charlotte admitted. "More…more vividly wrought."

"And thus more distressing." Elizabeth reached for her friend's hand. "Dear Charlotte… you need not bear reading that alone."

"The dreams are not the only thing, Lizzy." Charlotte squeezed the gentle hand before releasing it. "You must trust me in this." She huffed and shook her shoulders to banish what was scandalous. "An express came from the Gardiners?"

Elizabeth was instantly wreathed in smiles. "Jane will be here tomorrow afternoon, perhaps as early as two o'clock. Shall we invite Miss Darcy to join us for tea? I know we are supposed to be in mourning, but perhaps Lady Catherine need not hear of it."

The change of subject brought much relief to Charlotte, and they were soon occupied writing an invitation. Their attention was thus claimed until it was nearly time to dress for dinner when the maid-of-all-work, Nell, brought a card addressed to Elizabeth.

"Ah…" mused its recipient with a raised brow. "I am to call in the morning upon Lady Catherine. She politely bids me arrive after breakfast to view the de Bourgh jewels. Odd we did not hear the bell."

"It is Wednesday when Albertine, Lady Catherine's maid, takes dinner here with her brother Donald, our footman."

Elizabeth's brows rose. "She is the sister of Donald, the proud Yorkshireman? You mean Lady Catherine's French maid is *faux française*?" The two women laughed.

Charlotte explained, "They compare gossip and line their pockets by telling the sinister secrets of the Hunsford vicarage to our *esteemed patroness*. Albertine will spend the night, for they chatter away quite late. I do not like that Nell must share her little bed, but I often entertain myself by planting some bit of mischief in the tidings carried back to Rosings."

"But Charlotte! It is revolting that you are spied upon..." Elizabeth lowered her voice to a hiss rather than be overheard. "And all this time I have been here?"

Charlotte laughed and shrugged. "We have behaved notoriously the entire time!"

*Thursday, 16 April 1812, Rosings*

Lady Catherine was all graciousness when Elizabeth arrived with Mr. Collins the next morning, even complimenting her for again wearing the grey shot silk that had been sent to the vicarage for her use at the funeral gathering. Her ladyship's new mourning gowns had finally arrived, and she looked less constrained than in the past week. Her air was decidedly not that of a woman who had lost her only child. It was as though she wished to be cheerful and obliging in all things, but Elizabeth could not imagine why. Lady Catherine's disapprobation had been plain enough at the reading of the will.

*Did she parade a grief she did not feel only when the situation required it?* Elizabeth wondered. The very idea of such unmotherly sentiments necessitated that she suppress a shiver.

"You will excuse us, Mr. Collins," said her ladyship. "I shall return to you shortly. I have some fixed ideas for your Sunday service regarding the generosity one owes to one's family. Think on this whilst Miss Bennet and I are upstairs."

"I serve at your beneficent and munificent pleasure, your ladyship. Indeed, for your counsel and inspiration, I would wait unto..."

With a rustle of black bombazine and pompadour taffeta, Lady Catherine rose to lead Elizabeth from the room without knowing to what ends Mr. Collins would await her return.

When the ladies were gone, Mr. Collins's favoured footman stepped into the room in much distress.

"'Tis a sad thing, Vicar, right sad. We lost the new stable boy last night. He took sick all of the sudden-like. His people are from Headcorn, so's we'll be buryin' him here."

"How very sad. Such a loss for her ladyship. And his age?" There was not much money to be made in holding services for the poor, and they insisted on having the women of the family present, which was always a trial. It was difficult to concentrate on the service when there was an abundance of whimpering and weeping.

"He were about fifteen years, 'tis said. Didn't have his full growth yet."

It occurred to Mr. Collins that, since the boy was under the employment of Rosings, the estate steward would see all fees were paid for a modest ceremony. He brightened. "When the lad's family arrives, send them to wait upon me. I shall do everything I can."

The footman was pleased, and he withdrew.

LADY CATHERINE CLIMBED THE MARBLE CENTRAL STAIRCASE IN GREAT state. It was her intention that Elizabeth Bennet have every opportunity to take in the many luxurious details of the house, details the young lady was not likely to see again.

"There you see my dear Sir Lewis. Such a loving husband and devoted father. Anne mourned him dearly. There is a smaller portrait in my room, of course, and one in Anne's." Lady Catherine waved a bejewelled hand at the oversized painting of a rather slender gentleman of undistinguished visage. "He took such great pains with the building of this house. Anything I requested was added. No cost was too great. We were married three years before we were blessed with Anne. It was *very* gratifying to her mother and father that she could enter the world in a perfect home."

Elizabeth merely raised her brows and minded her footing on the shining marble.

They turned to the right at the first landing. "You will apprehend the family wing is not intended for guests to see, and we are more humble in our appointments." Again, the hand waved to indicate the sumptuous tapestries lining the walls.

Elizabeth had never seen so much gold gilt in the whole of her life.

As they neared the end of the hall, Lady Catherine's maid stepped out of a doorway and curtsied. "Ah, you are returned at last, Albertine," Lady

Catherine scolded. "We have no need of you."

The maid curtsied again. "Excuse me, madame. I would speak to you, *s'il vous plaît.*"

This last was pronounced "sill vows plate," and Elizabeth turned away to hide a smile.

Lady Catherine followed her maid to just inside her chamber doors. Elizabeth proceeded to view the prospect from the windows at the end of the hall. Lady Catherine stepped out to her again in a matter of moments.

"I apologise, Miss Bennet. I had every intention of attending you, but a matter has arisen that requires my immediate attention. That door behind you leads to Anne's bedchamber where you will find the jewels laid out for your perusal and a pot of tea steeping. I do hope you will enjoy it. It is my own special blend. And there is almond cake to enhance the flavour of the tea. Please do not hesitate to partake even though I cannot be with you. Take all the time you need, and drink as much tea as you like. I insist."

Elizabeth curtsied. "You are very kind, ma'am. Shall I ask my cousin to return with me to Hunsford when I am finished? Or will you have time to confer with him later?"

Lady Catherine's eyes narrowed a moment before returning to their benign expression. "You are good to think of Mr. Collins. Yes, my dear, take him with you when you depart." Lady Catherine left Elizabeth with a nod and what appeared to be a tender smile and proceeded into her rooms.

It was only then that Elizabeth turned to Anne's door and halted with a stumble on seeing the full-length portrait hanging next to it of a handsome, smiling Fitzwilliam Darcy.

For a moment, her heart stopped beating.

*Christmas Morning 1811*

*Damn it all! I am so entirely vexed. I spent the night very ill, tossing with disturbing memories. It began with the remembrance of the hideous smell of almond cakes. I do not recall when I developed a horror of the flavour, but I do believe that is what set off my mind's disquiet. I should have arisen and called for a draught.*

*Such sights I saw! Men writhing in agony in the stables, and the horses crying and rearing in alarm…why would I imagine such a thing? And then Papa's last illness, coming after that ghastly argument with my mother. I remember her screaming at him.*

*I am certain the coming of my courses brought on the distressing night. Not with child yet! I thought that Wickham, whom I now think of as Mr. Charming for the way he seeks to captivate me, had visited enough to get the thing done. Now I must send a message to bring him hither again, and he will complain for he is pursuing his little heiress.*

*What if I am barren and have endured the attentions of Mr. C for nothing? This brings me no joy. I want most dearly to be done with this. I have no patience left. What if the fault is with him? I have heard of marriages bringing forth no issue, then the husband dies, and the widow becomes fertile after making a second marriage. The deficiency could be with him…*

*And it is Christmas. Another cheerless, stifling, witless day, worse than others by the necessity of attending church and sitting through a longer than usual homily by our ridiculous vicar, just returned with his new wife. What sort of woman can she possibly be? She must be sensible enough to know what a vacuous hot air balloon she has married, or is she wholly lacking? I must not allow speculation on their private relations, but I cannot think she has any more or less joy than I do with Mr. C. If anything, I pity her more than I can pity myself, for I may end my arrangement at any time. This unknown creature must endure and spend her days with him for the rest of her life. It is all unpleasant duty. Poor creatures, women! —A de B*

# CHAPTER 9
## Thunderbolts from Venus

*Evening, Christmas 1811*

*This day became worse than I could have possibly expected. Mama would not be put off by my complaint of a headache, which was not in the least a malade imaginaire. She insisted I wait upon her in the drawing room then made a great spectacle of presenting the de Bourgh jewels to me as if they were hers to give and not already mine since April 19 last. But just as I thought she was exhibiting an altogether base and ungenerous frugality, she revealed that she had indeed made an expenditure by way of a "splendid gift" for me. She has given me two paintings.*

*One is of Pemberley. Speaking objectively, it is a lovely rendering of the approach to the house as one first sees it through the woods from the carriage road. If only it were not meant to hang over the mantle in my sitting room. Am I to have no escape even in my private apartment? No, says Mama. I am to be prompted to act, but I doubt my inclination to defenestration is the action for which Mama wishes.*

*The second painting nearly inspires suicide. It is Darcy at his full height. I am told there is a match to it in the gallery at Pemberley, and Uncle Darcy had this second made for Mama. I do not know where it has been these past six years since it was painted, but now it is ostentatiously framed, and it hangs outside the door to my bedchamber. I shall be using the servants' passage to come and go for the foreseeable future.*

*What am I to do? —A de B*

*Thursday, 16 April 1812, Rosings*

The service of Lady Catherine's ire demanded and aroused all of her capacities. Her annoyance at Elizabeth Bennet's inheritance of the de Bourgh jewels was nothing to the scorn she would heap upon the man —when she found him—who had defiled her daughter. When Albertine showed her the final volume of Anne's journal rescued from the vicarage, Lady Catherine was certain she would learn the truth.

"Very good, Albertine," she whispered. "But just the one volume?"

"Yes, ma'am." Albertine's eyes grew large, and she glanced around her mistress, fearing Miss Bennet had heard her from the hallway. "Ah! *Oui, Madame*!" she said more loudly.

"One moment…" Lady Catherine returned to Elizabeth Bennet, but was back at Albertine's side behind a closed bedroom door in what seemed a heartbeat.

The black-bound volume was taken into Lady Catherine's sitting room, and her ladyship was made comfortable in front of a good blaze. Although it was early in the day, the requested wine was brought, and Lady Catherine was left to read in quiet and solitude.

*Outside Anne de Bourgh's bedchamber*

Elizabeth unconsciously matched Darcy's painted smile with one of equal affection, for who could observe the expression on that handsome countenance and not return it? This man had loved her as he loved the person who was the focus of his attention as he posed—Georgiana, she supposed. Here was a man whose life's betrayals and losses had closed him into himself, and he unfolded only when entirely certain of his surroundings and company. How had he instinctively chosen a woman of intelligence, and with what sure knack for self-preservation had he sought her lively manners to lighten his burdens when society would have him choose otherwise? The sting in her eyes presaged her tears. That he had not expressed himself well should have come as no surprise. He had already admitted he had not that talent of easy conversation. Indeed, at Netherfield, they did not converse at all, only debate. Why did she not realise? How had she been so unforgivably blind?

*Would he have smiled at me had I accepted him? Harridan that I was, how did he come to love me? It is unlikely I shall ever have the chance to ask. The moment for requesting that mystery be divulged is long past.* A single tear slid down the side of her nose and sat poised on her lip. She licked it away. *I deserve to taste nothing but the salt of my tears.*

She took a deep breath and silently admitted: *What a silly chit of a girl I am. I love him.*

Nodding to the painting as though it were the man himself, Elizabeth entered the bedchamber. Were there not a compelling, indeed captivating, portrait of her beloved hanging just beyond the door, the sight of so many glittering parures, plus aigrettes, broaches, earrings, tiaras, chokers, hat pins, bracelets, pendants, rings of every colour and size, and loose gemstones would have been confounding.

She touched a delicate bracelet, but she could not stay. She wandered into the hall again and gazed at the painting. Elizabeth admired Darcy unabashedly. Her fingers nearly touched his lips before she pulled away, embarrassed in the face of emotions too wild and vast to contain. She could not touch this face, for it would not be warm and responsive; it would only be rough canvas and oil paint. Her fingers touched her own lips. She closed her eyes and kissed her fingertips, allowing a moment of giving herself before him as if he would see her yearning to be forgiven.

Elizabeth would not sob aloud for her loss as she had done in the woods of Rosings Park over her letter from him…no, she must confine this.

She re-entered the bedroom. Anne de Bourgh had died here, yet in this moment, the only ideas in her mind were floating away and encircling the portrait. All of the jewels were worth nothing. She glanced over them without seeing until a modest, pink diamond ring caught her eye. It was such a ring as might have suited her as a betrothal token, if ladies were given a choice in such matters. She slipped it into her pocket, took another glance about the room, sighed over the waste of Lady Catherine's tea and cake, and decided the task at hand ought only be attempted once Jane was with her.

Elizabeth quietly closed the door and addressed the painting. Still acting as if Darcy might see, she held out her hands and placed the little ring on her finger. A last tear spilled on her cheek.

"Were you ever to ask me again, sir, I would know how to deal much better." She spoke with a wavering voice before again returning Darcy's smile. She turned away, but looked back a moment later. "Only you." She held up the ring upon her finger. "Only ever you."

Elizabeth was tolerably composed when she stepped into the small sitting room to inform her cousin that Lady Catherine was detained. As they walked to Hunsford, Mr. Collins rattled away in his usual manner, asking only once about the de Bourgh jewels. He did not notice the one simple ring perched upon her finger.

Receiving merely a slight sort of answer, Mr. Collins proved himself fully capable of providing imagined details of the glories his fair cousin had seen. He was proud of her for earning the admiration of Miss de Bourgh. "From a jewel, many jewels to another jewel." He looked into the distance, admiring his turn of phrase. He tripped over an exposed tree root, stumbling to keep his balance.

Elizabeth looked away, vowing to write of Mr. Collins's thick sentiment to her father.

Once in her chamber, Elizabeth slid the ring onto the ribbon she used to bind the pages of her letter from Darcy together. *Someday, when I am a rickety old spinster, this ring will be my comfort, my memory. I was once loved, and by such a good man.*

*But Jane is coming! Dear Jane!*

*In the afternoon, outside the Hunsford vicarage*

Darcy and Colonel Fitzwilliam slowed their horses as they made their way through the village after a brisk ride. It was well past the noon hour, and by unspoken agreement, they had followed the bend of the main road towards the vicarage rather than passing the palings into Rosings Park. Darcy meant to further his cousin's intercourse with Elizabeth Bennet. For the colonel's part, he hoped for a cup of the superior tea Charlotte Collins served to her guests.

The men did not know the ladies were expecting Jane Bennet's arrival or that Georgiana was already there. As they dismounted, a fashionably spruce landaulet with a driver and two horses pulled to a stop in front of them. Almost immediately, Elizabeth Bennet burst from the vicarage, followed more slowly by Georgiana, Charlotte, and Charlotte's sister, Maria.

The hood was down, and Darcy recognised with no little surprise the fair features of Miss Jane Bennet. He could not have said which astonished him more: that Jane Bennet should arrive in Hunsford, or that she would do so in such an obviously private and stylish vehicle. If this equipage was the property of the Bennet's uncle in town, then he was a tradesman of obvious substance and excellent taste. Indeed, Darcy could imagine Georgiana employing such a little carriage to make her morning calls when she attained the age where such activity would become a necessity.

Elizabeth handed down her sister before the driver could alight, and the women proceeded to embrace with laughing tears. Georgiana stood apart at first, but she was brought into the circle by Elizabeth's gentle beckoning. Jane was introduced to Miss Darcy with curtsies on both sides.

Darcy heard Elizabeth laughing. "You see, Georgiana? My Jane does not bite though the same might not be said for my youngest sisters!"

Darcy turned to the colonel to explain their relationship. "We are witness to the arrival of Miss Bennet. She and Miss Elizabeth are exceptionally devoted sisters. I had the privilege…" He stopped speaking upon noticing the colonel's unusual, perhaps unprecedented, expression of besotted delight.

Darcy followed his cousin's gaze to see the handsomely turned-out Jane Bennet warmly addressing the other women and handing a gift to Elizabeth, which Jane explained was from their aunt. Darcy's eyes travelled back to his cousin. The colonel's smile of pleasure was broadening, his eyes bright. *Is he…?* Fear for Elizabeth's feelings turned Darcy's eyes to her.

Elizabeth watched with detached amusement as, in the face of Jane's more *au courant* beauty, her own attractions sank to insignificance in Colonel Fitzwilliam's estimation. Elizabeth did not evidence surprise as she had seen the like on more than one occasion. Since she harboured no expectations of the colonel, she did no more than allow a lifting spasm to one corner of her mouth before stepping forward to her sister and, with an arm around her shoulder, manoeuvred Jane to view the two gentlemen.

Darcy did not notice Elizabeth's aplomb, instead forming a fury at his cousin's rudeness, or so he deemed it. He hardly knew how to suppress his displeasure other than to remove his cousin from the place. "Cousin, let us not disturb this joyful reunion. The Miss Bennets have not been together for some months. We ought not intrude."

Elizabeth introduced her sister to Colonel Fitzwilliam, avoiding so much as a glance at Darcy, and Jane curtsied to both gentlemen with a faint serene smile. The men bowed, but the colonel continued to gaze openly at Jane even as he bent at the waist until she blushed and looked down.

"We shall not detain you, ladies. I am pleased to see you looking so well, Miss Bennet." Darcy touched his cousin's arm to steer him to the horses.

The colonel would not be moved, but neither could he speak after making the initial proper remarks. The ladies all looked at him strangely, excepting Elizabeth, who laughed.

"Ah. Another conquest, Jane! And you have only just arrived!"

"Oh, Lizzy." Jane's reply was softly amused. She turned for the house, led by Charlotte, who looked back over her shoulder at the colonel with a brief, absent frown.

The colonel did not notice Darcy's disapproving huff.

*Late afternoon, Rosings Park*

IT WAS NEARLY DINNERTIME WHEN A HIGHLY UNSETTLED AND SLIGHTLY inebriated Lady Catherine emerged from her sitting room. She crossed the hallway to her daughter's apartment and looked into the bedchamber. All was as it had been when she laid out the jewellery and prepared the tea. Miss Elizabeth Bennet was not there. Neither cup had been dirtied, nor had a portion been taken from the almond cake.

Lady Catherine pursed her lips. She had more important concerns than Elizabeth Bennet. After pouring the contents of the teapot into a potted citrus, she wrapped the almond cake in its linen cloth. It was still needed. She carried the tea tray to a table in the hall for the servants to take away and then locked Anne's bedchamber. She could have returned the jewels to their coffer, but at that particular moment, she felt no loyalty to preserve the gems for the current and, in her view, unrightful owner. If thieves broke in and stole the lot, it was no longer the chief of her concerns.

Lady Catherine paused, full of conflicting impulses. Should she confront "Mr. C" now? Clearly Collins had a history of seductions, difficult as it was to believe, and did not mean to stop. But the journal had been hidden in Mrs. Collins's Oakley amongst the out-of-fashion (and too small for her ladyship) mourning gowns sent to the vicarage. What did his wife know of this? *Something, surely, since the journal was in her possession...* Lady Catherine smiled with flattened lips, proud of her generosity of spirit and the impulse of the previous day to send more gowns and then Albertine's pleasantly surprising resourcefulness in offering to carry them upstairs for

Nell. "Yes," Lady Catherine hissed aloud, further gratified to know from her observant maid that Mrs. Collins was at least folding her gowns properly, even if a foolish husband deceived her. No wonder Anne had left Mrs. Collins a bequest. *Guilt.*

If only the volume still missing would come to light, she would know the entirety of the affair. But who else had read Anne's entries, and who might be in possession of, and was reading, the six months prior? Did "Mr. C" know Anne was writing a journal? And did he know the truth of Sir Lewis's death? Would some attempt at blackmail be forthcoming?

So Anne had hated her, *ungrateful child.* However the clandestine couplings had started, Anne had seen being with child as a means of escape. And a dalliance with a married man meant Anne could not be made honourable. Lady Catherine was reminded of the many dull, insipid evenings with the Collinses in attendance while Anne sat quietly, appearing every inch the nescient spinster, doubtlessly wrestling with what to leave in her journal and what to omit like every other diarist who hopes to create something sensational. Such depth and bitterness! There were no easy answers in Anne's puzzles and curiously little religion given her chosen partner. Anne made her immoral decision not knowing what a foe her mother could be.

That Anne had played the part expected of her extremely well could be no great source of amazement. She thought only of herself. "Selfish girl," her mother muttered. Lady Catherine was quite put out.

*Later that day, after dinner, Rosings*

"You utter sod."

The door to the Rosings billiard room slammed after Darcy followed his cousin into it. "You scoundrel!" The volume of his voice grew with each new insult. "You cretinous pillock. Have you no shame, Cousin? When did you become a recreant lout? Where is your sense of honour? What can you be thinking?"

"I am thinking Miss Jane Bennet is the most beautiful lady I have ever beheld. Never have I seen a prettier blush."

Darcy's hands grasped his face as he inhaled and tried to manage a more fruitful comment. He pushed his eyebrows up into his forehead, and slid his hands over his head as if to hold his skull in place. He exhaled a long sigh. "You have no thought for Elizabeth Bennet? Not one spare explanation to the lady you are supposed to be courting? You simply jilt her for the sister?"

"There is nothing spoken between Miss Elizabeth and myself. She has not been encouraging. You may be pushing me, along with Anne from beyond the grave, but I have not written to her father." Colonel Fitzwilliam assumed a haughtiness usually employed by Darcy. "If you cannot speak kindly of Jane Bennet, Darcy, I would rather you not speak of her at all."

"It is not Jane Bennet with whom I find fault, you immense stinkard, it is YOU! I have said nothing against Jane Bennet." Darcy was glaring.

"Miss Elizabeth has laid into you with halberds, Darcy. For that, I am sorry. I have looked into myself and decided not to pursue her even before the arrival of her enchanting sister. The only thing to save you from constant torture is distance. Once Miss Bennet is Mrs. Fitzwilliam, I shall not allow Miss Elizabeth to visit Rosings, and at those few times when we venture into Hertfordshire, you will not be included in the party. Let Elizabeth Bennet be another man's destruction."

"Wait on! *Mrs.* Fitzwilliam?"

The colonel looked infatuated. "Indeed."

"This is too much. You do not know her. Jane Bennet is not a woman given to expressing passionate opinion. Such of her heart as she has revealed, that I have been told of, might belong to another. She is not well read. Miss Elizabeth possesses a most exquisite taste in every species of literature. Miss Bennet does not play or sing. You have heard Elizabeth; she is a charming performer. She is a much greater prize."

"Darcy! If you must continually cry up Miss Elizabeth as the most uniformly virtuous of the Bennets, then *you* marry her. Oh...sorry, Cousin" —Colonel Fitzwilliam sneered—"you burnt that bridge."

The colonel stalked out of the room, leaving Darcy too mortified to speak.

After a moment to gather himself, Darcy turned heal with a muttered, "Bloody ass..." and proceeded to the escritoire in what had been Sir Lewis de Bourgh's study. He drew a sheet of fine parchment and began to write.

*Rosings Park, Kent*

*Dear Charles,*

*Let me thank you for the kind letter you sent upon learning of the death of my cousin.*

*It is not the usual way between us for me to require your assistance, but a matter of some importance has arisen at Rosings to which you are uniquely situated to lend support. I hope it does not inconvenience you too keenly to join me with all possible haste. Plan to remain for several weeks if your time permits.*

*With apologies for remaining so vague,*
*F. Darcy*

The letter was addressed to Mr. Charles Bingley in care of Mr. Augustus Hurst, 16–19 Grosvenor Street, Mayfair, London, and sent express.

Darcy could only hope his cousin would not be so rash as to compromise Jane Bennet in the next two or three days and that her heart was indeed everything Elizabeth said of it: constant, honourable, and firmly affixed to Charles Bingley.

# CHAPTER 10
## The Reunion of Dear Sisters

*11 July 1811*

*How very interesting the little village of Hunsford has become. In addition to interviewing companions for Little G, Mama has already begun interviewing for a new vicar. An interesting candidate is a handsome figure just arrived in the last day, known only as George Wilkins. While I have not laid eyes on George Wickham since I was ten years old, I believe this man is he. He must be aware that Little G is here. I saw him whilst out in the phaeton with Mrs. J. He cuts a dashing figure, I must say. Not the sort of young man one would associate with a seminary. He doffed his hat to me in a manner most insinuating, and he assumes I do not remember him.*

*If he has come here to cast a line out for Little G, I shall cut it. But she is not the only heiress in the neighbourhood nor the richest, is she?*

*Perhaps I could make him the means of my escape. I must think on this. —A de B*

*15 July 1811*

*As I chanced to request my phaeton be drawn down a lane behind the High Street shops, for it is no secret I have an abhorrence of the filthy debris of commerce left piled on the main road, I was most gratified to find an applicant for the position of vicar tussling with the giggling daughter of the bookseller. His hand was up to his elbow in her bosom. The silly slattern dashed away, and Wickham, looking quite proud, smirked at me and tipped his hat after putting it back on his head. I sent my driver into the apothecary's shop before I beckoned Wickham, much to his surprise, to the phaeton and made him aware that I knew his identity. Seeing I was amused rather than alarmed, he attempted a rather paltry joke about educating Darcy's betrothed by what I had seen. When I responded that there was much more I cared to learn and might seek him out for instruction, he was a vast deal more surprised—astonished, I may say.*

*He looked me up and down brazenly, for he is such a man. Seeing he could not discompose me, he pronounced himself at my service in all things. I explained to him the location of an empty tenant's cottage at the far south end of the estate. He will meet me there tomorrow. —A de B*

*16 July 1811*

*It appears a deal has been struck. Although he believes himself charming, there is an obsequious quality to Wickham that reminds me vaguely of one of the other candidates for vicar, William Collins. What an odious, pompous, greasy dish of mincemeat he is. Collins I mean… Wickham is much more clever, which I would want the father of any child of mine to be, and handsome enough to improve the de Bourgh features. I avoided the Fitzwilliam Roman nose of my mother, and perhaps with the right sire, my child will too.*

*I am to give Wickham a sum of cash to settle some pressing debts in London. He will return hither in late August or early September, when I shall pay his commission in the militia currently stationed at the old Sissinghurst Castle, though wearing a red coat for his duties to me I shall prohibit! Joining will give him a plausible reason to be in the area, as long as his identity is unknown to Mama until it serves me to reveal him. Other than myself, he is wholly unknown here, and his deplorable dealings with the Darcy family will be of little matter. I have further told Wickham that he must not attempt contact with Georgiana. If I learn of it, our little bargain ends. He and I shall have no assignations until Little G is well and truly away from Rosings.*

*Therefore, in late August or early September, my grand scheme begins. I do not know when I have been so filled with hope. —A de B*

*Thursday evening, 16 April 1812, the Hunsford vicarage*

Elizabeth shut the door to the bedroom she would now share and looked fondly at her sister. They were at last alone.

"Jane! I have so much to tell you!"

Elizabeth sat next to her on the bed, and Jane turned to allow her agitated sister to draw the pins from her hair.

"And I have *no* news, Lizzy." Jane gave a weighty sigh, "I shall say, however, that I quite approve of the way Mr. Darcy looks at *you*. It is not like before."

"Then it is with him that I shall begin the tale."

By the time Jane's hair was down and the complicated plaits worked loose, Elizabeth had related Darcy's proposal and the substance of the letter regarding his dealings with Wickham without mentioning Mr. Bingley. Nor did she mention her tender viewing of Mr. Darcy's portrait that morning or her drastically altered sentiment. It was never easy for her to admit mistakes, even to Jane.

"Oh, Lizzy, how could we have been so deceived? Mr. Wickham had all the appearance of goodness."

"Wickham is much worse than even Mr. Darcy knows, Jane. But what did you think of Miss Darcy? Do you see that she never mentions the tenant of Netherfield? I would not say I told you so, but…" Lizzy raised her brows and chuckled.

"She is a pleasant girl. Not at all what I expected. I am surprised by Caroline thinking her enamoured of Mr. Bingley, but perhaps she never did say the affection was mutual."

Elizabeth huffed. "Caroline Bingley used you most ill, Jane—as if you were a toy, a doll to be played with and discarded. I am convinced her motives through our entire acquaintance were to secure Mr. Darcy for herself without respect to her brother's happiness, or Miss Darcy's, and certainly not yours."

Jane looked sly. "Or Mr. Darcy's wishes. And *you* had secured his heart without even knowing."

Elizabeth looked down. "I could not have been more blind."

Jane found the opportunity to tease her sister so rare that she could not resist. "*He* was not blind, what with all his staring at *you*. We must admire his taste."

Elizabeth shook her head. "You must think me so very foolish to not have accepted him."

Her sister sounded so pitiful that Jane hugged her impulsively. "Dear Lizzy…he insulted you when you met, disputed every word you said whilst we were at Netherfield, and you say he insulted our family when he paid you his addresses and in his letter. He did not make his goodness known to you, and you could not respect him. You did as I would have expected you to."

After some moments of comfort, Elizabeth brightened and turned away. "Now you must see to *my* hair whilst I tell you the scandalous tale of Wickham and Miss Anne de Bourgh."

"Yes, please! I wish to know how my beloved sister came to inherit a fortune in jewels!"

Once Jane's delicate sensibilities had been first agitated and then soothed, and both sisters were ready for bed, Jane asked, "What can you tell me of Colonel Fitzwilliam?"

"He is pleasant company, and being a military man with sharp wits, he is well informed although his reading tends to that one interest above poetry or novels. He reads music well enough to turn pages and is a great walker."

"I thought him rather too forward when we were introduced."

Elizabeth laughed. "I am certain he is smitten with you, Jane. You ought to do as Charlotte once advised: show him more regard than you feel, and you will likely secure the heir to Rosings Park."

Jane was quiet for a moment. "I must forget Mr. Bingley first," she said with more conviction than she felt. Forgetting Charles Bingley did not seem at all a likely occurrence. She sighed dramatically. "Charlotte had the right of it, I suppose. Had I been more…*obvious*, I should have been so very happy by now. But I could not conscience the gossip, Lizzy. It was all intolerable enough as it was."

"I know how you dislike being the centre of attention."

"But what of Mr. Darcy, Lizzy? Is it not mortifying to be in his company so soon after…?"

"I was distressed at first, but I reread his letter and found some comfort in it. Anne de Bourgh had a high regard for her cousin even if she did not wish to marry him. And his manners have decidedly improved. He has been most forbearing to *our* cousin since his return. I cannot think why."

It was Jane's turn to raise an eyebrow as Elizabeth and their father would do when of a dubious state of mind. "You cannot?"

"Oh, Jane, I know I have said somewhat of how brutally I refused him, but it was worse than I care to admit, even to you. He has every reason to think ill of me. It was most improper of him to give me his letter and for me to have read it, but it gives me the advantage of knowing him better. Sadly, it would be tantamount to indecency for me to respond in kind, and then he *would* know me to be as degenerate as the rest of our family, excepting you. In you, at least, he sees a proper lady." Elizabeth stroked her sister's hand.

"Little does he know me!" Jane laughed.

*True enough, for he could not judge your capacity to love*, Elizabeth thought ruefully. *And now I love* him*!*

Jane saw the turn of her sister's spirits. "What is it, Lizzy?"

Elizabeth raised woeful eyes to her sister. "Dear Jane, I am so relieved you are come. Every lingering struggle against him grows fainter and fainter. I find, as regards Mr. Darcy, I am ashamed of myself."

"He seems to look at you with kindness. Perhaps there is a friendship to be salvaged. He certainly appeared solicitous of you when the colonel paid me too much attention."

Elizabeth smiled at the way Jane always tried to see the best. "Well… I can say for a certainty that there is no one here to take any notice of *our* feelings, exaggerated or sincere. Every topic falls before the infamous death of Anne de Bourgh." Lizzy screwed up her face as if considering something important. "And as to Colonel Fitzwilliam, do not overlook his one great flaw…"

"What is that Lizzy?"

"It is the same as Mr. Darcy's: their aunt is Lady Catherine de Bourgh!" And so saying, the sisters laughed, and Elizabeth blew out their candle.

As they drifted off to sleep, Jane took Elizabeth's hand. It was a godsend to be returned within her sister's cheerful sphere. The heavy grey winter of London had taken its toll upon Jane's spirits. It was no easy thing to admit that the sisters of Charles Bingley were not the allies they had presented themselves to be in Meryton. She could not understand such behaviour, but at least with Elizabeth's help, she could accept what had been.

The journey to Hunsford had been lovely, and Jane had requested the hood be down once they had watered the horses in Bromley. Now it seemed that wherever her sister was, so was the joy and hope of spring.

Elizabeth smiled sleepily as she felt Jane take her hand. As children sharing a bed, they had often held hands at the end of a trying day. It was a comfort. Jane knew her so well, and Elizabeth knew Jane would soon discover her partiality for Mr. Darcy. It was to Jane she could look for an example of proper behaviour in the face of having made a glaring error in judgment.

Now she had compounded the problem by allowing herself to fall in love. This was no paltry, changeable affection. No…her body's response upon seeing him appear as Jane arrived had convinced her of that. What a thing to have no control of the rate of one's breathing, the beating of one's heart, or the blush on one's cheeks.

It was almost Shakespearean, but a drowsy Elizabeth could not decide whether it was a comedy or a tragedy. Would Mr. Darcy have an opinion on the subject? The hand in hers slowly ceased to be delicate and soft. It grew larger, warmer, and more enveloping. Elizabeth was flooded with a calm that did not quiet but rather stimulated her senses. She was in bed with Fitzwilliam Darcy, and he was gently stroking her hand. It was not frightening or awkward; it was strengthening and secure.

The dream would sadden Elizabeth upon remembrance of it when she awakened later in the night, but within its duration, she was safe and loved. That she might have many such dreams was all she could hope for.

*10 January 1812*

*I have awakened just now from the most awful dream.*

*Because of my mother's height and hawk-like nobility, looking down at her inferiors is a necessity as well as her pleasure. I believe Mr. C is frightened of her, which should not surprise anyone. I shall be too if I keep on with such nightmares. Mama was only a little shorter than Papa as I recall. Mama and I took almond sponge cakes once to the stable men when I was but a girl. It was just before my father took sick. He and Mama had been quarrelling. I did not like to listen, and for the most part, I was taken from them when there was discord.*

*I know I am making little sense. In my dream, I was a little girl again. There had been an argument, and afterwards, Papa came to me to apologise. He wanted me to know that his wish for more children was not meant to diminish me in any way. I was his first and eldest child and would always be foremost with him. He said Mama had told him that his insistence on more children worried and frightened me, causing an upset to my stomach. I assured him, with all of the vehemence of a serious child, that I did not feel so. I did not understand why Mama would say such a thing. I told him I longed for a sister to play with. Of all things, another sister was what I most wished for in the world. Even more, I would take greatest delight in having <u>two</u> sisters. I had said so to Mama. She was wrong to lie.*

*Papa laughed as only he could and wrapped me in his arms. He said that I must be prepared for a brother and must accept such a possibility, but he and Mama would be equally happy with a baby of any stripe! I laughed that a baby might have stripes and asked what my stripes had been.*

*But wait… No. That was not a dream but a memory, coming to me now as I write. I am remembering Papa and me talking about sisters. Later that night, yes, that same night, came their worst set-to. Although my nursery was not close to their rooms, I could hear Mama shouting. She was trying to defend herself for misleading my father about my feelings. I ran to the noise and peeked into Mama's sitting room. He called her a liar and said he must be mad to want more children with such a wife. She struck him. I wanted him to hit her back, but he did not. She hit him many times more. He only grunted, and when she bloodied his nose, she finally stopped. There was blood on her dressing gown, but it was his.*

*Papa saw me. "No!" he cried. He came towards me, but Mama tripped him and he fell across a chair.*

*"Look at what he has done to me!" Mama said.*

*"You hurt Papa's nose," I accused. At that moment, old Mrs. Moore arrived with all apologies to my parents, and I was hurried back to my rooms.*

*The next morning, I was called before my parents and told that Mama was going to be living in the dower house in a fortnight's time. But before that happened, Papa became sick.*

*Why is this coming back to me now? Why do I dream of the horses shrieking? Or is that also a memory? —A de B*

# CHAPTER 11
## Schemes & Observations

*Friday, 17 April 1812, Rosings,*
*the small summer breakfast parlour*

The niece and nephews of Lady Catherine de Bourgh noted in silence the aimless agitation of their aunt throughout the morning meal. All were mainly quiet, what with Georgiana's natural reticence and the newly hatched quarrel between the two gentlemen. Her ladyship often seemed about to speak but managed only nonsensical mutterings and false starts.

Colonel Fitzwilliam wolfed down his meal and stood to bow himself out of the room, saying he had some urgent letters to write. The brother and sister remained, deep in their own thoughts.

*I suppose the balmy bastard is off to write Mr. Bennet*, Darcy fussed privately. *Ought I to write? No…it would be improper, although the man should know about Wickham. My letter may not have convinced Elizabeth of his perfidy; however, now that she has met Georgiana, she must understand. Still, Mr. Bennet has other daughters requiring protection…and I might slip a word in about Alex and Elizabeth, preparing the way.*

*What charming ladies the Miss Bennets are.* Georgiana cautiously eyed her brother, but he was lost in his own musings. *What stops my brother from paying his addresses to Lizzy? She appears to hold him in high regard if her blushes of yesterday afternoon are any indication. Why does he push our cousin at her when he so plainly has his own feelings? And shall we not be seeing more of her as she sorts through Anne's clothes? Of course, he will not be a party to that, but still… Oh! I know!*

"Lady C-Catherine..." Georgiana began hesitantly.

Their aunt looked at Georgiana as though she had forgotten the girl and her brother were in the room.

"Would it be inconvenient... Um, uh..." Georgiana glanced at her brother, who appeared quizzical.

Darcy nodded his support for he knew not what, but if Georgiana felt courageous enough to ask a favour of their aunt, he was ready to play his part.

"May I invite the ladies from the vicarage in for tea this afternoon? Miss Jane Bennet, Miss Elizabeth's eldest sister has arrived. I met her yesterday and took tea with them. I should like to return their kind invitation... I believe you will find Miss Bennet quite agreeable."

Lady Catherine raised an eyebrow. "You were invited there?"

"Yes, ma'am."

Darcy spoke quickly. "She has formed a friendship with Miss Elizabeth Bennet. Alexander and I have encouraged it." He nearly winced, waiting for the burst of invective he felt sure would follow.

Lady Catherine's mind had wandered. She looked vaguely at Georgiana. "As you wish, my dear, as you wish. Though I may not attend you, and I shall certainly not be present if you include Mr. Collins."

"Oh, no, ma'am," Georgiana responded, wide-eyed. "Just the ladies."

While she could not like that Darcy and the colonel were allowing such a confederacy of women from mixed classes to develop, Lady Catherine was wholly distracted by other concerns. "Send a footman to me when your guests arrive, and I shall look in if my time allows."

She stood and left them without a notice for Georgiana's hurried curtsy and Darcy's bow. She had not been gone more than a moment, without enough time for brother and sister to comment on this new form of oddity, before a footman entered with an express for Darcy. It was from Bingley.

*The Hurst's, ~~Grover~~ Grosvenor Street*
*London*

*Daer Darcy,*

*How delightful fortitudinous!* [Darcy smiled, assuming his friend meant "fortuitous" and was taking the trouble of finding—or inventing—four syllable words.] *Had not your note arrived when it did, this morning would have seen me off to Bathe with my relations. The rare opportunity of doing ~~you~~ you a ~~favour~~ service is one I would lothe to miss.*

*I expect to be with you by noon twelve o'clock noon with my carriage to follow slowly, as carriages do.*

*Best regards and faithfully,*
*C. Bingley*

Darcy grinned at the letter, for once feeling nothing but affectionate forbearance with his friend's errors of penmanship and spelling.

"You seem pleased," Georgiana teased, sensing his lightened mood.

"Charles Bingley will be here in time to greet the ladies from Hunsford when they call this afternoon. He is acquainted with them, you know."

She made a slight frown. "I was perplexed by some of the conversation between the ladies yesterday. Was there something—a failed courtship, perhaps—between Mr. Bingley and Miss Bennet?"

Darcy gave her an arch look. "It is my intention to see it all mended."

*Later that day, Lady Catherine's private sitting room*

"Sit, Nephew." Lady Catherine ordered Colonel Fitzwilliam to take the chair she had positioned in front of hers. It had a low seat, and if she sat particularly straight, they would be at the same height.

"I am surprised by your summons. What have you to accuse me of? Oof!" The colonel sank into the cushion with his knees higher than his waist.

"Accuse you?"

"Darcy informs me that you have accused him of being the father of Anne's unborn child. I was with my regiment throughout the winter, I assure you."

Lady Catherine frowned and waved his impertinence off with an impatient hand. "I know who the father was, and I expect you to uphold the family honour."

"Do you?" The colonel's attention was engaged, and he sat forward in his seat. "Who? No wait…I want a chance to solve the puzzle. Might I have a clue?"

Lady Catherine's eyes narrowed. "This is not some parlour game, Nephew."

"Do not be coy then, ma'am!"

His aunt waited until he was no longer chuckling before hissing, "Mr. Collins."

The colonel looked about them as if the named man had entered the room. "What about him? Do we await his attendance before you will reveal all? I suppose this is the kind of information one would like to repeat as little as possible."

"Silence! Insolent puppy! Mr. Collins was the father." Lady Catherine raised her eyebrows to see how her larking nephew would like the truth.

There was silence. The colonel turned red with the effort not to laugh but finally exploded with loud guffaws.

Looking thoroughly annoyed, Lady Catherine paused until her nephew was merely giggling and wiping his eyes.

"Have you proof?" he finally gasped.

"I do. Your cousin kept a journal, going back to her twentieth year. She wrote daily, sometimes morning and night. The entries are of little consequence, as you may imagine, until the past year. Coming into her fortune changed her and *not* for the better. The second half of last year is missing, July through December complete. This year's beginning journal was just found and brought to me yesterday. It indicates Mr. Collins is the culprit." Lady Catherine chose her words carefully. "And apparently the local midwife knew. I have sent word to interview her. Likely she is telling tales even now..."

The colonel's eyes continued to water with suppressed amusement.

"Why are you not outraged, sir?" Lady Catherine asked with some heat. She reared back her fan to slap her nephew, but his quickness in thwarting the blow astonished her.

"Because I cannot take you seriously. What would you have me do, call out William *Collins*?"

"Precisely. That is *precisely* what I would have you do."

The levity of the situation diminished rather precipitously. "Are you suggesting I engage in an illegal activity?"

"Anne's honour must be defended. You are a respected officer, your father is a well-placed peer of the realm, and I am not without influence. Nothing would come of seeking retribution against a philandering country vicar. It could certainly be hushed up."

"If I may remind you, murder by duel is a capital offense, no matter who engages in it or the provocation. Anne has left Rosings Park to me. She would not have her heir jeopardise himself. What *she* wanted was for me to settle here immediately with *her* choice of wife."

Lady Catherine sat with balled fists. "And her choice?"

"Elizabeth Bennet."

"Gah!" Lady Catherine beat her fists upon her knees. "No! Promise me you are not engaged to her, nor that you will become so."

The colonel smirked insolently. "I promise, dear Aunt, that I have no intention of making an offer to *Elizabeth* Bennet. You have my word."

She heaved a relieved sigh, but then looked back at her nephew's face, sensing a prevarication. "Yet a letter was sent from you to her family's seat..."

He silently cursed her servants. "My promise stands. I shall never marry Elizabeth Bennet."

Lady Catherine raised an eyebrow and hummed between her lips. Setting her shoulders, she asked again, "Still, you will not defend Anne?"

"At the risk of my freedom and life? No, I shall not." Colonel Fitzwilliam stood.

Once more, he allowed himself to be diverted by the situation. "Are you certain, completely and irrevocably certain, that Anne was referring to Mr. Collins? I simply cannot accept..."

"Go, Nephew. I have no use for you."

Lady Catherine had only her fan in hand to throw at the laughing back of her stubborn nephew, and it flew with a flutter, wide of its mark. "Then what must be done, I shall do myself."

*Meanwhile, in the main drawing room of Rosings*

WHEN THE LADIES FROM THE HUNSFORD VICARAGE WERE SHOWN INTO the room, Georgiana and Darcy were standing together, happy to meet them. Mrs. Collins glanced around the room as though looking for someone then curtsied her greetings, followed by the Bennet sisters. Jane wore a pearlescent grey that Darcy thought quite flattering to her complexion. He mused on the kindness the women at the vicarage showed by joining in the general air of mourning with their choice of gowns.

Jane advanced, holding out a hand in greeting. "Mr. Darcy, I am sorry for your family's loss. I should have said as much yesterday." She curtsied as he nodded over her hand.

"You are very kind, Miss Bennet. My aunt may be joining us any moment, as well as another guest to Rosings only lately arrived. Please"—Darcy directed Jane to Georgiana—"make yourself comfortable."

Georgiana smiled timidly at Jane, and they sat together upon a settee facing the doors. Darcy bowed to Maria Lucas and nodded at Elizabeth, who would no more meet his gaze today than she had done the prior afternoon.

Charlotte spoke when she saw Elizabeth would not. "Another guest?" She had noticed that, although Darcy and her friend seemed to be striking up a better friendship since the funeral, in the last two days, Lizzy had withdrawn. "This may be the largest party I have seen at Rosings apart from the funeral gathering. I trust Lady Catherine enjoys the larger audience?"

Darcy smiled enough to show his dimples. "My aunt is closeted with Colonel Fitzwilliam for reasons I know not. But she has always encouraged Georgiana and me to treat Rosings as our home. Even though this is a time of mourning, I have taken the liberty to invite a friend."

Maria, with a young girl's guileless enthusiasm, had moved to the table between two windows upon which was artfully heaped every manner of cream cake and preserved sugared fruit. Georgiana rang for the tea service to be brought, and an awkward silence descended.

Elizabeth moved to a window beside the refreshment table, but turned suddenly when she heard a familiar voice preceded by the rapid advancing of a man's steps on the intricately inlaid floor.

"I say, Darcy, Georgiana, I must apologise for being late. Are the ladies…?"

The voice of Charles Bingley trailed off to nothing as he found himself face-to-face with Miss Jane Bennet.

Jane stood abruptly at the sound of his voice.

"Miss Bennet!"

"Mr. Bingley!"

Elizabeth looked at Darcy, who was watching her. He raised his brows, gave her a little nod of irrepressibly gay satisfaction, and moved to the other window flanking the refreshments.

Bingley bowed with unnaturally stiff formality as Jane made the most ungraceful curtsy of her life.

"Your family was well, Miss Bennet, when you left Longbourn?"

"Certainly, sir, but I have been in London these past few months since the turn of the New Year. I know they are well only by letter."

Bingley gaped a moment before recovering. "All this time! And you have not called?"

Jane looked down to hide a smile that everyone could still see. "Ladies do not call upon gentlemen, Mr. Bingley."

"But my sisters…"

"Were not true friends to me, sir. I shall not pretend otherwise."

Elizabeth wanted to cheer and glanced at Darcy's calm profile.

"B-but at Netherfield…" Bingley stuttered.

"I was but an amusement to them, a trifle."

The servants entered with the tea service, and all was quiet until the footmen receded. Georgiana acted as hostess in the absence of her aunt, adding leaves from an ornate Chinese chest to the teapot.

Bingley made another attempt. "I do not remember a happier time than those few short months we spent in Hertfordshire."

"Ah," replied Jane, "that must explain the unexampled rapidity with which you returned once you had gone."

Elizabeth's eyes flew wide, and she spun to face the window, fearing that, once unbridled, Jane would say too much. Again, Elizabeth glanced at an unmoved Darcy. *Enough, Jane…enough!*

The room was silent. Darcy continued to look out the window. Although he had never before been half so well entertained in that room, he knew he must accept the blame for his friend's discomfort.

Bingley sighed and grew serious. "Miss Bennet, may I call upon you tomorrow? Perhaps a walk after breakfast if the weather holds fair?"

Jane smiled serenely. "I would be most pleased, Mr. Bingley. A private apology for subjecting a lady to months of her neighbours' pity cannot come too soon or be more welcomed."

Bingley paused a moment. "Welcomed?"

"Yes. A lady will always welcome the apologies of a truly amiable gentleman."

"Amiable? I am…you think?"

Jane smiled at him.

Darcy turned in time to see genuine regard in the eyes of Jane Bennet. Hers was the smile of a woman making sport with a man for whom she felt a real affection. Jane could tease as readily as her sister, it appeared, if more gently. He glanced at Elizabeth's profile.

"Yes, I have always said you are the most amiable man of my acquaintance —that is, when we are *in* acquaintance. When *you* are in London and *I* am in London, and you do not know it, you are not nearly so amiable."

Bingley laughed. "If you like, I might apologise now. We need not waste the morning."

Jane continued to smile. "No, sir. I would prefer you have the night to perfect any little compliments with which you might wish to embellish your statement."

Elizabeth involuntarily choked on a laugh before covering her mouth though she did not turn into the room. *At last, Jane takes Charlotte's advice!*

Darcy had seen enough and turned back to the window. After hearing Elizabeth's laugh, he chanced a look at her.

Elizabeth sensed his eyes upon her and felt hot and cold together. Mr. Darcy's shameful boast of what misery he had been able to inflict upon his friend was, in an instant, put to rights. And in that instant, all wrongs of which Elizabeth had ever accused him—every blame so liberally bestowed—were dissolved away, leaving in her heart astonishment, confusion, and a pain she could only assume was a healthy measure of unrequited love.

Darcy was watching her still, so she plucked up her courage, met his eyes, and whispered with great care, "Thank you."

Darcy could not hear her. Charlotte was laughing with Jane and Bingley while Georgiana and Maria poured the refreshments and murmured instructions to each other about how the guests took their tea. But Darcy had dreamt of the lips of Elizabeth Bennet often enough to heed their meaning.

He smiled at her, opening his heart. He had never felt such love for another human being in the whole of his life. He had done this for her to protect her heart from his cousin's fickle turn—to make right what he had blundered over—and she had thanked him. There was nothing for it but to meet her enchanting eyes and smile as only a man in love might. She began to blink back tears, and he fought to keep from careering through the food to take her in his arms.

Elizabeth stood motionless. Her inclination was to glance behind her to see whether Georgiana was there, attracting Darcy's smile. But no, Georgiana was approaching from the tea table; Darcy's look was for her alone.

"Lizzy?" Georgiana held out a cup of tea to her.

The moment was broken, but Elizabeth had seen it, and she would never forget. Mr. Darcy had smiled at her as if still in love. It was the smile of a man eager to please. She had to place her cup and saucer on the table, for it was quite full, and her hands were shaking too severely to avoid dowsing her borrowed grey- and white-striped gown.

Darcy and Elizabeth watched through their respective windows as Lady Catherine drove by in a somewhat erratic fashion in a brightly coloured curricle, along a cart path towards the south of Rosings Park. Amidst such an amazing sight, they failed to notice the entrance of Colonel Fitzwilliam.

Upon entering the room, the colonel beheld Maria and Georgiana at the pianoforte discussing music, and he smiled a little. Seeing Darcy and Elizabeth at separate windows with their backs to him changed his expression to one slightly more sardonic in nature. Upon a settee, Charles Bingley and Jane Bennet, *his* Jane Bennet, engaged in a blushing, stuttering tête-à-tête. He cleared his throat with extreme disapproval, not noticing Charlotte Collins watching him with her spirited grey eyes.

"Would you care for tea, Colonel?" she asked, rising from her chair.

Bingley stood at once and happily held out a hand to the new arrival. "Colonel Fitzwilliam, spanking to see you again!"

As if performing mirrored dance steps, Darcy and Elizabeth turned into the room. Separated though they were, they seemed united.

The colonel held out his hand to Bingley for a somewhat limp handshake, and they exchanged bows. Was Mrs. Collins repressing a smirk as she handed him his tea? Behind Bingley, Jane Bennet was watching his back with something resembling appreciation in her eyes. The colonel knew that look. With nearly audible clanking, the blinkers fell from his eyes. *That is her idea of manly perfection, is it? That prancing jackanapes? That giggling prat? Then she is not the woman for me.* He looked towards Darcy, feeling less heartbroken than thwarted. His cousin wore a sunny smile of airy unconcern. *Damn the man!*

Elizabeth and Charlotte looked from cousin to cousin with perceptive expressions. For reasons each her own, the two ladies smiled equably at the transitory and foiled affections of Colonel Alexander Fitzwilliam.

*29 December 1811*

*What would you have me say of the vicar's wife? What a conundrum she is. Her name is Charlotte Collins, formerly Lucas, and her family are near neighbours of the estate Mr. Collins is to inherit.*

*She is not tall, neither fair nor dark, and of middling figure. But her grey eyes are intelligent, and she must occasionally hide a blush at some foolish pronouncement of her husband's. As to the nonsense of my mother, Mrs. Collins will learn to hide her astonishment better in time. I cannot think why she would marry into a situation such as this. Relations with the man must be most distasteful, and she cannot have had any accurate information about the disposition and manners of my mother. Given the exorbitant praise heaped upon his patroness by Mr. Collins, I am certain this is so.*

*Poor Mrs. Collins must have entered the neighbourhood assuming an independent control over her household that she will never have while Mama yet lives. Given that the lady appears to be on the wrong side of five and twenty—she may be older than me—Mr. Collins must have been seen as a welcome pis aller, and she must be happy to no longer be a burden to her family. But the fact remains, she has married one of the stupidest men in England. How can she make herself easy with such a man as her master and my mother as his exacting benefactress?*

*Soon and very often, Mrs. Collins is going to wish the current incumbent of Longbourn might die of a sudden fit, no matter how intimate and pleasurable her friendship with the family. Most assuredly, when the letter comes announcing Mr. Collins is to inherit, the lady will get herself to Hertfordshire before the dust has settled from the express rider's horse. —A de B*

# CHAPTER 12
## Death Comes for Breakfast

*2 February 1812*

*The horror of what I can now describe is beyond measure, but with my dreams and recent memories, I am suddenly able to illuminate the death of my father at my mother's hand.*

*Their squabble escalated into something nearer a brawl, but Papa would not defend himself. I was taken away but was called to them the next morning only to see the damning evidence of my mother's brutality upon my dear father's bruised face. He would not meet my mother's gaze, and the decision for her to move into the dower cottage appeared mutual in its achievement and equally pleasing to both. But subsequent events did not bear this out.*

*My mother began to spend hours on end in the library. The door was locked. After a week of visiting that room more than she ever had before, her research, if such it was, ended as quickly as it had begun.*

*One evening at twilight, she bid me walk with her to the stables, where I was a great favourite. She had made a treat for the stable hands and trainers, and she shared it in equal measure with all the men there.*

*As a child, and a sickly one, it meant nothing to me that it was soon reported some illness had swept through the stable servants, and the smallest of them, a boy not much older than I was then, had died. I did not connect her treat with their illness until these mad recollections beset me.*

*To keep me from fussing that mere servants had been given a sweet and I, the heiress, had not, a similar sponge cake was presented to me when we returned from the stables. It was not redolent of almonds, as the other had been, but was instead glazed with citrus, which suited me much better.*

*Some days later, we returned to the stables. There was much activity, for my father had just returned from London where he had gone for matters of business—likely his will. My mother insisted the men stop their work to partake of her treat, but they resisted. She labelled them all ungrateful wretches, and nearly stuffed the cake into the mouths of those not inclined to take it. Soon many of the men were writhing upon the ground and crying aloud. It frightened the horses, and most began kicking and snorting, stamping and squealing in an ear-splitting cacophony that terrorised me.*

*My parents took their breakfast without me the next morning. All the servants I encountered mentioned the illness that had beset the stablemen the previous evening, but they made no mention that my mother and I had been there. I later learned all the men had died!*

*That afternoon, my nursemaid reported Papa had taken ill. That evening, I was sent to him, and never had I seen anyone so changed. He was all over red and sweating. My mother was most solicitous, holding cool cloths to his face. He spoke little except to murmur he loved me. I was not allowed to stay long. It was the last I saw of him.*

*My mother murdered him, poisoned him with something reeking of almonds, to spare her the risk every woman faces. She did it for greed and control. She practiced her dark arts on the stablemen, killing nearly a dozen, to refine her methods.*

*Will anyone wonder why I have made the choices I have done and wish for nothing more than to be free of the daily sight of her? And mark me well, I shall be. —A de B*

*Saturday, 18 April 1812, the park at Rosings*

ELIZABETH ROSE EARLY, SLIPPING QUIETLY FROM THE BED TO DRESS FOR A walk. She placed Darcy's letter in her pocket, careful to note that Jane was still asleep and would not see its hiding place.

The morning was fair, but the air was heavy with dew, and every leaf she brushed by left a wet mark upon her pelisse. She found her favourite stump in the sun and sat to read. In what she knew was an act of the purest folly, she placed the pink diamond ring upon her betrothal finger and set to her task.

The reading was made more poignant by Mr. Bingley's appearance the previous day. It was all made right; everything Mr. Darcy could do to correct his errors had been done. As her fingers moved over the dear words, the ring glinted in the morning light.

Elizabeth could not help imagining her bejewelled hand held in the masculine firmness of Darcy's. She closed her eyes.

"Miss Elizabeth?"

Her eyes opened in a panic, and she saw Colonel Fitzwilliam standing at the edge of the glade. She crammed her letter into her reticule, hoping he had not seen it.

"Colonel Fitzwilliam! Good morning, sir!" she said brightly, trying to sound unperturbed. "What brings you into the wild places? Another tour of the park?"

He stepped forward. "I received a queer note this morning. The midwife wishes to meet me here."

"In this place?"

"Yes, I believe so. Are there many meadows hereabouts with single stumps at their centre?"

Elizabeth became pink-cheeked, embarrassed at the interruption in her reverie. "If the midwife wishes a private word, I should take my leave." She curtsied to go.

"Please wait, Miss Elizabeth. I have been foolish. You must have seen the forceful attraction I felt at meeting your sister. I was powerless to hide it, but it has passed. She has set her heart on another."

Elizabeth nodded with a faint smile. "Indeed, sir. You could not have known it, but when you spoke of Mr. Darcy separating Mr. Bingley from the threat of an imprudent marriage, you were speaking of my sister."

She imitated the colonel, "'I understand there were some strong objections to the lady,'...or so you were told. I had some notion that he was involved in separating them, and you were my confirmation."

Elizabeth had a singularly gratifying moment of beholding the colonel utterly staggered. She held up a staying hand and continued. "You owe an apology to your cousin more so than to me. In a most mean-spirited and unkind manner, I have held Mr. Darcy's actions against him. In truth, he only wished to protect his friend, and Jane was ever reluctant to reveal her feelings." She looked down. "Do you know of...of the proposal?"

"Ahem...yes. I do know something of it."

"Yes, well, this episode was one I threw in his face. I was impolitic." She paused before murmuring in wonder, "And now Mr. Darcy has made it right." *Did he do this for me?* "Oh, I only mean that now Jane and Mr. Bingley are in proximity and may find their way forward as foolishly as two people in love may be supposed to do without interference."

"Darcy tried to warn me that Miss Bennet's regard might centre on someone other than me." The colonel shook his head as though confused. "It is as if I had a brief, startling illness and have now recovered. Please forgive me for any distress I may have caused you."

"Me?" Elizabeth's voice sounded slightly alarmed.

The colonel laughed ruefully. "I understand you."

"Explain me to myself then if you would be so kind." She attempted to sound nonchalant.

"It would seem it is not the fate of Alexander Fitzwilliam to win the heart of either of the eldest Miss Bennets." He motioned towards her reticule, held by the hand wearing the ring. "But am I to wish you joy?"

"Oh! Oh, no!" She took off the ring and placed it in her pocket. "No, that is nothing. Girlish silliness. Please, say nothing of it. Forget you saw it."

The colonel looked at her curiously. "As you wish."

"Ah! Colonel Fitzwilliam! My apologies, sir, for being late." Mrs. Spiggotson hurried into the glade.

"Mrs. Spiggotson, I am Colonel Fitzwilliam, and this is Miss Elizabeth Bennet."

Introductions were civilly exchanged.

"I should leave you," Elizabeth said. "You have matters to discuss that do not involve me."

Mrs. Spiggotson responded, "Not directly, no, ma'am. But I must advise you, if you please, do not accept any invitation to take tea or any refreshment *alone* with Lady Catherine. She is not to be trusted, and"—she looked more particularly at the colonel—"sir, I fear your aunt is not in her right mind."

The colonel laughed abruptly, trying to pass off the warning. "Within the family, this is not exceptional information."

"I am not in jest, sir. You see, I know all of Miss Anne's… um… situation. As I believe this lady does…" The sturdy little midwife glanced at Elizabeth. "But Lady Catherine has it all wrong and will not be corrected."

"LIZZY! Lizzy! Oh, Lizzy, I am so glad I found you!"

Maria Lucas came sprinting to a stop amidst the threesome.

"Maria!" Elizabeth took the girl by the shoulders to still her, and met her gaze. "Steady yourself. You are all in a lather! What can be so dire?"

"It is Charlotte! She is in a panic. I have never seen her so hysterical. She says you are to return at once—that she requires your help."

"Of course, Maria."

After hasty civilities, the two young ladies were away as fast as propriety would allow with a man watching their retreat. As soon as they were beyond the meadow, Elizabeth began to run with Maria following behind.

Charlotte was indeed quite frantic when they found her in her sitting room. Every drawer was opened, every cushion was on the floor or cast about; the entire room was upset. "Lizzy! Oh, Lizzy, please tell me you found the last volume of the journal and have taken it away to read."

Her eyes were beseeching, but Elizabeth had no good news to impart. "I do not know where you kept it, except that you said it was in your Oakley where Mr. Collins would not venture."

"Damn it…" Charlotte muttered, much to the shock of her sister.

Elizabeth was known to speak ill under her breath when provoked and ignored Charlotte's slip of the tongue. Her older friend had taught her most of the infamous words she knew, which Charlotte in turn had learnt from her several brothers. "Where *did* you hide it?" Elizabeth asked. She removed her pelisse, slipping her ring from its pocket to the pocket of her gown, and handed the pelisse to Nell, who had appeared to take her outerwear.

"Amongst the mourning gowns from Rosings." Charlotte made a dash up the stairs with Elizabeth hard upon her heels.

"And Albertine brought more on Wednesday?" Elizabeth asked.

Charlotte started. "Oh, bloody bollocks…" The dressing room was a madhouse of gowns and camisoles, stockings and petticoats, spread hither and yon as if a modiste's warehouse had exploded.

Maria stepped back with her hand to her mouth.

Elizabeth put her arm around Maria's shoulders and steered her from the room. "Perhaps you should stay in your room, my dear? Shall I come for you when your sister is in a better humour?"

Maria nodded, her eyes seeming permanently widened by her elder sister, a vicar's wife, cursing with such ease and facility.

When Elizabeth entered Charlotte's dressing room, her friend had sunk to the floor, now in a pelter of ungovernable tears. It was an unprecedented sight.

Elizabeth shook Charlotte's shoulders. "What is in the journal, Charlotte? What can be so very bad? I read nothing more or less untoward than any other part."

After several deep breaths, Charlotte was able to speak. "The—the material point is that Lady Catherine will know we have read it. You and I know the truth."

"On my walk, I came upon Colonel Fitzwilliam. He was to meet the midwife at her behest, and I talked with her myself. She says Lady Catherine is undone by this and is not to be trusted. Her ladyship has drawn incorrect conclusions from what she has read, and we are not to accept any invitation where we may be alone with her."

Charlotte pulled herself up on her knees and frowned. "What could be misconstrued?"

"You would know better than I, Charlotte. Perhaps Lady Catherine does not remember Wickham, or—"

Charlotte jumped to her feet. "Wickham is not named in the second volume. He is only ever 'Mr. C.' Lizzy…this morning Mr. Collins received a note to arrive early—to take breakfast with her ladyship."

"Where is Jane?"

"Out with Mr. Bingley.

"That is a blessing. Charlotte, we must go!"

Mrs. Collins nodded, and the women scrambled to their feet, stumbled down the stairs, and made their way as fast as they could for Rosings.

*The same morning, Rosings, the small summer breakfast parlour*

Mr. Collins was in awe. Never had such an honour been bestowed upon him, to take an entire meal alone with her ladyship. The food was arrayed on warming trays along the sideboard. Upon the table, tea and coffee were already steeping and a perfectly luscious-looking sponge cake with a thick glaze was awaiting them. The room was redolent with the aroma of almonds, which was one of his favourite flavours. He breathed in the scent. The knowledge that Lady Catherine had remembered his preferences swelled his chest with pride. He and his beloved patroness were of one mind.

"Ah! Mr. Collins, prompt as ever! I do so appreciate that you take my requirement for punctuality to heart." Lady Catherine swept into the room with a rustle of black skirts and passed Mr. Collins who was making a deep bow of deferential submission. He owed her nothing less.

Lady Catherine stood by her chair, and as no footmen were present, waited for Mr. Collins to rise from his awkward position to draw out her seat. He was all obsequious concern as the great lady settled herself.

"I have arranged this *assignation* with you to demonstrate my approval for the *penetration* of…your *understanding* during this most difficult time."

Mr. Collins sat, feeling immensely pleased, and opened his mouth to respond, but Lady Catherine continued to speak. He flattened his lips over his teeth to silence himself and nodded.

"Anne was most *appreciative*, it seems, of your many, *repeated attentions* to her. Pray, fetch me that black volume upon that chair."

Mr. Collins stood. "Of course, your ladyship." He had not noticed the finely bound book before and handed it to Lady Catherine with another bow.

"I shall read to you from this journal she kept, for she mentions you often, most especially in January, but first, let us take a little to drink and some of this digestive cake." Lady Catherine fixed her hawk-like visage upon Mr. Collins, expecting him to give away some guilty emotion in learning that Anne had written of him, but instead, he appeared not only surprised but pleased. She gave him a creamy smile as she poured out his tea and then coffee for herself.

"Your ladyship does me a great honour."

"Yes, well, you must be repaid for the many *little honours* you did my Anne," Lady Catherine said as she filled their cups.

Next, she cut the cake and placed a large portion on Mr. Collins's bread and butter plate. There was a tap at the closed doors.

"I am not to be disturbed!" Lady Catherine reminded whoever was on the other side.

The rapping came more loudly.

Exhaling a sigh that revealed great agitation, she called, "Come then, and be quick about it."

Her butler entered. "Please, I do apologise, your ladyship, but if I might have a word. There is a grave problem in the stables."

Mr. Collins stood as his splendid but visibly irked patroness quit the room, closing the doors behind her. He sat back down and felt he might drool for the delightful smells. Perhaps a sip or two of tea and the merest few crumbs of cake would not be noticed by her ladyship, for he longed to partake.

After taking a swallow of tea, it occurred to him that Lady Catherine was fond of dipping cake and biscuits in her coffee. He noticed she would create a layer of residue in the bottom of her cup, which she would finally eat with a spoon after drinking off the liquid. Although not appetising to him, would she not appreciate his courtesy if he ministered to her coffee as she would do for herself whilst it was still hot?

After another swallow of tea, Mr. Collins noticed specks of glaze and crumbs on his plate, which he tucked into his mouth with relish. They were delicious. His stomach growled. Deciding he would seek Lady Catherine's forbearance after the fact, for he was quite hungry, he ate a bite of cake, followed quickly by a larger one, filling his mouth and leaving him unable to speak as, without warning, she returned.

"You have started? I should have known."

"Murf…snerk," Mr. Collins managed, as the cake had gone rather gummy before he could swallow.

Lady Catherine observed that his tea was half gone as well as the cake. She took up the book, turned to a page at a bookmark, and read, *"Seventh of January. I dwell upon the mouth of Mr. C this morning with only the fondest of remembrance."* She watched as Mr. Collins began sweating and started to colour. *"When I recall him suckling as his fingers pressed inside me, I can conjure his touch again and revisit every pleasure."*

From within his gathering physical distress, Mr. Collins did just manage to make some sense of what her ladyship was reading. Its salacious nature, written by the virginal Miss Anne de Bourgh, was confusing. She had written "Mr. C"? Was she given to flights of fancy about him? His guts twisted. "Gck…" he sputtered.

Lady Catherine stood, backing away from him, for she knew what was likely to occur. She continued reading. "'*That such delight could come from a man's mouth, from beyond a kiss on the lips. And his whispers! The words Mr. C placed in my ears as he had at me, his heated description of his own sensations, will warm me to my very bones for all my lonely nights to come...*'

"How did you agree you would not meet again?" Lady Catherine asked just as Mr. Collins forced his chair back from the table and vomited all over his knees.

His eyes were wild. Lady Catherine could not know whether this was caused by what she was reading or was a symptom of the poison. Then his body gave a great jerk, sending him over backwards in his chair, banging against the sideboard and causing the contents of a tray of kippers to land on his shoulders and slide down his coat. He continued shallow convulsions as she heard his bowels give way. He made inarticulate sounds that seemed to have some purpose, so Lady Catherine drew out her chair and picked up her coffee, preparing to watch the death throes in case anything of sense should be uttered. She would not sound an alarm until he was quite dead.

She absently took a large swallow of coffee, followed by another. Lady Catherine preferred her coffee strong and dark and did not notice the infusion of almond in her drink until she had a third mouthful. It was spit out unceremoniously. She looked aghast at her cup, and poured out its contents. As she felt herself becoming breathless, she beheld the sludge of sodden cake drip and pool onto the plate.

She stood at the table, staring as her hands reddened. She would not be sick. She would not fall into the squalor of Mr. Collins's death. Her body began to tremble with her effort and the effect of the poison. She would *not* be killed by the likes of the ninny William Collins. And such were her last thoughts.

Darcy had desired a morning ride, only to find the bodies of three large stable hands being seen to by Dr. Roberts. The physician instantly pronounced that the men had been poisoned. Suspecting his aunt had some knowledge, Darcy proceeded into the house.

As he reached the doors to the small summer breakfast parlour, he could see Colonel Fitzwilliam approaching at a furious pace from the opposite direction. Darcy flung open the doors, and they watched in horror together as their aunt, with skin now turned quite red, quaked and quivered, at last expelling a volume of bloody bile and collapsing dead upon the floor.

The room smelt dreadful, a wretched stench of bodily effluvia, kippers, and most heavily of almond. Darcy covered his lower face with a handkerchief and crossed the room to throw wide the windows. The midwife appeared behind the colonel.

"Oh my!" She crossed herself.

"The physician is at the stables. I shall bring him hither," Darcy said and disappeared down the hallway from whence he had come.

He had not been gone a moment when the sound of loudly panting ladies and billowing skirts announced the arrival of Elizabeth and Charlotte. They stood gasping at the door.

"We are too late!" Elizabeth exclaimed.

"Damnation! I would not have had you see this," the colonel shouted and just managed to slide a chair behind the knees of a stunned and sinking Mrs. Collins.

Charlotte could only stare at her dead husband.

Elizabeth stepped into the room and leaned against an open door, slowly taking in the whole appalling tableau: her cousin and Longbourn's heir supine in a chair tilted against the sideboard, covered in kippers and goodness knows what; Lady Catherine collapsed upon the floor, reduced to a bundle of black-clad and bloody joints with a black ostrich plume bobbing in the draft from the window; the table with the remnants of tea and cake; the missing journal lying open with the spring breeze idly fluttering a page to and fro, breaking the silence.

The cake looked the same sort as the one set out for her a few days before in the bedchamber of Anne de Bourgh with the same scent of almond dominant in the air. Elizabeth felt her thoughts labouring until she forcibly realised she had narrowly escaped the same fate as her cousin.

Darcy and Dr. Roberts rushed into the room. Elizabeth stared at Darcy, certain in the knowledge that the moments of falling in love with him—enthralled to distraction by his smiling portrait—had saved her life. Then, emitting a quiet sigh, she fainted into the arms of the doctor.

# CHAPTER 13
## Into Mourning

*Saturday, 18 April 1812, Rosings,*
*the small summer breakfast parlour*

Dr. Roberts was not a large man and of a wiry configuration. Thus, he was chagrined to find himself draped with the limp body of a goodly young woman not much smaller than he. *Now this one will be a fit breeder,* he mused absently in the manner in which a learned physician assesses a patient. *Far more robust than Miss de Bourgh.* Elizabeth's fichu had gone astray, giving him an intimate view of just how robust parts of her were.

"Er, uh…gentlemen?" The doctor squirmed to hold Elizabeth upright. "Would either of you…" He looked from Darcy to Colonel Fitzwilliam. It seemed as if they had momentarily turned to stone.

Darcy's startled gaze landed upon his cousin. *Damn it, Alex… Carry her upstairs. Exert yourself for her. You are a military hero, for God's sake!*

The colonel returned his cousin's expression. The family resemblance of the two men was briefly apparent when they scowled together. *You are in love with her. Make the grand gesture for once in your life. Send a-begging any thoughts she may have for whoever sent her that ring.*

"Oh, bother," muttered Mrs. Spiggotson. She moved to Elizabeth's slumped body and called, "Mrs. Collins!" in rather a sharp voice.

Charlotte had returned to something resembling awareness when her friend fainted, and she stood.

"I am adept at moving unconscious women. We will make a basket of our arms." Mrs. Spiggotson showed Charlotte what was required, and the doctor managed to slide Elizabeth into their grasp. He then adjusted her fichu.

Darcy and the colonel were shamed into action, making way for the women and their burden with Darcy calling ahead of them to have the housekeeper open a bedchamber. She chose Anne de Bourgh's, knowing it to be cleaned and recently aired for the viewing of the jewellery.

As they neared the room, Darcy saw his portrait. "Dear God! Poor, poor Anne."

Colonel Fitzwilliam snorted. "I shall have it removed."

Upon entering the room and catching a faint whiff of almonds, the colonel glanced around suspiciously. "Smell it?" he asked Darcy so the others would not hear.

"*I* smell it," whispered the doctor. "Cyanide."

The colonel and Darcy each took two corners of the velvet cloth upon which the de Bourgh jewels were displayed on the bed's counterpane and bundled them as if the treasure was so much kindling. It was set atop the remainder of the jewels on the tea table in an indecorous heap.

The ladies set Elizabeth upon the bed rear-end first, and Charlotte swung the yielding legs upwards as Mrs. Spiggotson settled Elizabeth's shoulders upon the pillows. The physician followed with salts, and Elizabeth was soon sputtering and awake.

She threw a hand over her eyes and pulled Charlotte close. "Oh, please, Charlotte, reassure me I am nothing like my mother."

Something in the plaintive tone of her voice brought laughter, or at least a smile, to everyone in the room.

But Elizabeth was not amused. "I am *not* squeamish."

"Dear girl," Charlotte cooed, placing the cold cloth that had been handed to her on Elizabeth's forehead. "I know. You are strong as an ox."

"And you...you have lost a husband, yet you did not swoon." Elizabeth squeezed Charlotte's hand.

"I plan to run mad later—at the next full moon, perhaps. I think it would suit me better than fainting."

"Dear Charlotte..." Elizabeth smiled crookedly.

Mrs. Spiggotson approached. "If I may say, miss, in all my years as a midwife, 'twas the prettiest swoon I ever saw. So gentle and graceful-like."

Elizabeth looked solemn. "Thank you, Mrs. Spiggotson. I may add another accomplishment to my credit: swoons prettily." At hearing Darcy chuckle, Elizabeth looked carefully around Charlotte, spying the colonel and Darcy. "Who carried me?"

"Dr. Roberts caught you, and the midwife and I carried you."

"Thank God for small mercies," Elizabeth said, lying back upon the pillows.

Darcy approached with a weighty question but was too overwrought at being in a room with Elizabeth Bennet on a bed to look directly at her. "Miss Bennet, did our aunt serve you tea when you came to see the jewels?"

"Yes, sir, but she was called away before we entered the room. I…" Elizabeth paused, unsure how to state what had occurred. "I, uh, was distracted by…everything. I did not partake of the tea and cake."

Unable to resist, Darcy looked into her widened and luminous eyes. "Whatever it was that distracted you, saved you." His throat grew tight and he croaked, "Do you understand me?" That those beautiful eyes might have been forever dimmed was nearly more than he could bear. He stepped closer.

Elizabeth spoke in a low voice only Darcy and Charlotte could hear. "I understand you, Mr. Darcy, and I understand myself a little better." She looked down, embarrassed to be so bold.

Charlotte was caught between them and felt rather certain that, without her presence, Darcy might have taken Elizabeth's hand or sat by her side on the bed. Charlotte chanced a glance over her shoulder at the colonel. He caught her eye with slightly upturned lips and shrugged.

"Lizzy!" Georgiana sped into the room and leaned over Charlotte to look at Elizabeth.

Darcy stood back, unable to take his eyes from his beloved. The proximity of her death brought the return of his usual stony countenance. He dared not risk any other expression.

"I am well, Georgiana," Elizabeth said with a smile. "Abominably silly, but otherwise well."

"What has happened?" Georgiana looked to her brother for answers.

Darcy held out his hand to his sister and led her into the hallway.

Charlotte stood away from Elizabeth and turned to the colonel. "It would seem, sir, that you are now the owner of Rosings Park, free and clear. May I be so forward as to act as your hostess and call for tea?"

"NO!" came the loud chorus from everyone in the room.

Colonel Fitzwilliam laughed. "Perhaps the better idea would be for you to bring some of the excellent tea you serve in your home. I am certain no one could wish to drink the Rosings tea until assurances are made that I have laid in a new store."

Elizabeth heartily seconded the suggestion. "Oh, do, Charlotte. Jane must be returned by now and worrying. And poor Maria! Please bring some of my aunt and uncle's Indian tea, and bring Jane to me. And I shall get myself upright."

As Charlotte departed, the colonel called for a fire to be laid in the hearth of Anne de Bourgh's sitting room. The midwife helped Elizabeth to stand, and after settling her charge into the soft chair by the fireplace, departed to make her morning calls. The colonel kept Elizabeth amused for a few moments before being beckoned into the hall by Darcy. The doctor returned to the small summer breakfast parlour to see to the bodies and try to verify what he believed had occurred by interviewing the servants. The magistrate was sent for. The private sitting room of Anne de Bourgh had never seen such activity as it became the heart of comings and goings. From its mantelpiece, the benevolent portrait of Pemberley and its landscape waited patiently to be noticed.

Georgiana spoke in a low voice once she and her brother had gained the relative privacy of the hallway. "Brother, I want you to tell me honestly: Has our aunt attempted to kill someone?"

Darcy took in a deep breath and regarded his sister. She stood still and solemn in a grey gown, looking more mature than her sixteen years. Georgiana was clever, and there must be some good reason she had reached this conclusion. He would not lie.

"Indeed, she has made attempts and at times succeeded. I believe the tables were turned on her today, and now she has died by the same poison she used upon others. Our aunt was thwarted by her own despicable cunning."

Georgiana nodded as though this answer was not unexpected.

"May I ask how you know of this?" Darcy asked.

"I found something in the library—an altar of sorts. It must be where she concocted her poisons."

Instantly alarmed, Darcy sought reassurance that Georgiana had not endangered herself by handling anything.

"You will think me quite silly when I tell you how I came upon it. I have been reading *A Midsummer Night's Dream* and thought to play Puck. I had an idea that if I could devise the proper herbal potion, I could compel Miss Bennet…Elizabeth, that is, Lizzy…to fall in love with you."

Darcy felt his cheeks warm. He pursed his lips and attempted a frown. "Say on…"

"Or I might make a truth serum so that you could not deny your affection and would speak of it to her."

Darcy rolled his eyes. "Oh, Georgie…"

She shrugged defensively. "Well, I like her. She is kind and joyful, at least she is when in the company of other women. She is more subdued in your company. You love her, do you not? And I already owned I was silly. Thus I went looking for an herbal or perhaps an old book of spells or—"

"No more Shakespeare," Darcy grumbled.

Georgiana huffed in reply. "Let me tell it."

"By all means…"

Charlotte Collins passed them. "I am to bring Jane and some proper tea from the vicarage. Lizzy has been moved to the sitting room."

"Thank you, Mrs. Collins," Darcy said with a brief bow.

Darcy and Georgiana were once again alone. "Please continue, Georgie."

"Where the herbals and old books of alchemy are kept, there is a false shelf. I found it accidentally when I moved a large book of old remedies, and three shallow shelves lifted to show a little cache behind them. There are beakers and a mortar and pestle with a little scale and jars of powders. There are notes in our aunt's hand. Her intentions are made clear by them."

"You must show me."

Darcy went to the door of Anne's sitting room and motioned for the colonel. He said nothing that might disturb Elizabeth until they were in the hallway. "Georgiana has found something. Please bring Dr. Roberts and join us in the library."

When Colonel Fitzwilliam met the physician in the small summer breakfast parlour, he noticed the black bound book.

"It is the journal of Miss de Bourgh," Dr. Roberts informed him.

"I shall keep it safe," the colonel promised, tucking it under his arm. "It may be of assistance to the magistrate."

Thus it was, between the evidence in the library and Anne's memories in her journal, that the murderous business of Lady Catherine de Bourgh was fully understood.

Charlotte squeezed her eyes shut for a few steps after walking away from the Darcys to avoid them hearing her irrepressible giddiness. It was not so annoying to be called "Mrs. Collins" when there was no longer a *Mr.* Collins. Once outside in the spring morning air, she began to skip and found herself laughing. Upon reaching the palings out of Rosings Park, she stopped to gather her breath. *Do not let freedom render you deranged, Charlotte.* She tittered again. *Lady Catherine has proved herself even more useful in death than she was in life!* Fearing to give the appearance of losing her wits in front of Jane, Charlotte took a deep breath and proceeded to the vicarage.

After telling Jane everything except of Elizabeth's narrow and unwitting escape—leaving that onerous task to the lady herself—the two women sorted through the mourning gowns and donned deepest black. Jane selected a gown of charcoal grey barège for Elizabeth.

"I look rather well in black, I think." Charlotte turned her figure at profile in the mirror while Jane laced the back of the gown. She was grateful that Jane, although full of incredulous alarm for the safety of the living, was not excessively sentimental for the dead.

Jane reflected, "You did not come to love my cousin, did you, Charlotte?"

"No. I did manage to convince myself for a time that I was content, but I do not know how much longer I could have pretended. No, it must be said, I shall enjoy wearing black for a year, for it means I am free. And with so little expense! There are ever so many gowns here."

"Where will you settle? Surely Colonel Fitzwilliam will not wait long to name a new vicar."

Charlotte shrugged carelessly. "Yes…where shall I settle? I shall have some independence, thanks to Anne de Bourgh. Not much for frivolity, but certainly enough for security. But I have come to love these woods and hills. With an affable gentleman like the colonel as the neighbourhood's preeminent fixture, who may well marry an amiable wife, Hunsford will be a pleasanter village. Perhaps I might carry on here."

Jane nodded. "I suppose a woman of independent means might not want to settle too near her family."

Charlotte met her eyes as they gathered the tea things. "It is but three miles from Longbourn to Netherfield."

"Yes, so it is." Jane gave an imitation of her sister's arch look. "Perhaps that is Mr. Bingley's one imperfection." She broke into a laugh. "It is fortunate he has only leased the place."

ELIZABETH STOOD AS JANE ENTERED THE SITTING ROOM, AND THE SISTERS embraced. "What a thing to have seen, Lizzy—the two bodies. I should have fainted myself."

Elizabeth looked at Charlotte.

Charlotte shook her head to indicate she had not told Jane everything.

"That is not why I fainted, Jane. I must tell you, Lady Catherine would have poisoned me too. She made her evil tea and cake the morning I came to see the de Bourgh jewels, but she was called away." Elizabeth's eyes darted down. "I became distracted by my emotions. I cannot explain more exactly than that, but I could not concentrate on looking at the jewellery, nor was I hungry or in need of tea. I was more in need of you! When I stood looking at our dead cousin, and saw the same kind of cake on the table, I realised my escape and what had saved me. It was then that I swooned."

Jane took her sister's hand. "That explains it. I was sure you could not be so delicate." She smiled a little.

Elizabeth sat more upright. "I should say not!"

"But how terrible for the Darcys and the colonel to have a murderess in the family!" Jane shook her head.

"Yes," said Charlotte, watching Elizabeth, "and Mr. Darcy always so particular about his family's reputation."

Elizabeth did not respond but rather stared into the fire. Such crimes as these would see the light of truth and the subsequent inaccuracy of modern journalism—or what passed for it. There was no hiding what had happened this day even if he would wish to. What must he be feeling?

Jane did not like to see her sister so dispirited. "Lizzy, the world will know of this, but it does not reflect upon Mr. Darcy or his sister. Mr. Bingley says he is quite highly thought of. And by the time Miss Darcy is brought out, there will be other scandals for the *ton* to devour. This will be long settled."

At the mention of Mr. Bingley, Elizabeth brightened. "And what of Mr. Bingley, Jane? Were his apologies handsomely worded?"

Jane laughed. "Oh, yes, and profuse in number. He is quite vexed with Mr. Darcy for knowing I was in London, and I fear there may be some cross words, but I cannot fault Mr. Darcy; I was too withdrawn. I was so fearful of appearing complaisant about Mr. Bingley's affections that I would not reveal a hint of mine."

"Have you declared yourself, then?" Charlotte asked.

Jane tilted her head and attempted to appear mischievous. "No, but Mr. Bingley has made his regard plain to *me*, and so, at the proper moment, I shall do the same for him. As for today, I enjoyed his apologies far too much to interrupt them. It was very wrong of me!"

Elizabeth embraced her sister. "Oh Jane, I have always loved you, but you are even more lovable when *you* are in love! Do you not wish to shout it?"

Jane laughed quietly. "Indeed. To speak of my feelings aloud to Mr. Bingley will be a great relief."

Darcy was just about to enter the room to tell the ladies of the magistrate's arrival and that Elizabeth and Charlotte would be questioned. He wished to determine to his own satisfaction that Elizabeth could withstand the rigours of an interview. He stopped when he overheard Elizabeth's teasing enquiry after Bingley's apologies and Jane's reply. Mr. Bennet had raised *two* clever daughters, but the elder was more likely to cover her keen observations with a thick veneer of benign goodwill. Elizabeth, to the contrary, withheld nothing and seemed to relish a challenge. She was his severest critic. *And she was nearly taken from me—can I ever forgive my aunt?* His thoughts reminded him that he must write to the Archbishop. He turned away without speaking.

Georgiana, Colonel Fitzwilliam, and Mr. Bingley joined the ladies in Anne de Bourgh's sitting room. Charlotte made an exaggerated pantomime of presenting the tea and how she was making it, to everyone's amusement.

"Lizzy, might we open the curtains now? I believe they were drawn for fear the bright sun would give you a headache." Georgiana moved to the windows.

"Please do! I had wondered why the room was being kept so dark. Pray, do not keep it so for me." Elizabeth moved to Georgiana's side to view the prospect. When she turned, the light illuminated the painting over the fireplace, catching Elizabeth's attention. She had never seen a mansion so simple and so happily situated, and she moved to the picture as if under a spell. "What is this place?" she asked, before drawing close enough to read the nameplate on the frame.

"Ah!" The colonel moved next to her. "That is Pemberley, Darcy's estate."

Elizabeth's eyes moved over the painting as Georgiana came to stand by them, and the colonel put his arm absently around his cousin's shoulders.

"Is it *truly* so lovely, or is there some artistic license?" Elizabeth's voice was low with wonder.

"That is exactly as it looks as one approaches on the coach road from a village called Lambton. You approve?" Georgiana asked.

"I think there are few who would not approve," Elizabeth murmured. *He loved me enough to envision me as the lady of his manor? Or was it simply some manly desire he could not fight but did not think through? He has surely thought better of his inclinations now… No, Lizzy, that is unfair. He has made improvements based on my cruel complaints. He has restored Mr. Bingley to Jane. Did he do it because it was right or because it would please me or perhaps both? How much of this can I bear—to know I have thrown such a love aside?*

Jane smiled fondly at Bingley, who had begun extolling the particular virtues of Pemberley. He explained his favourite features, wholly unaware of Elizabeth's mounting distress.

Feeling tears sting her eyes, Elizabeth turned away. "I have stayed too long indoors. I shall take a walk."

Jane saw the colonel and Georgiana exchange a significant look. *Will they think my sister mercenary for taking such an interest? But she has never cared for Mr. Darcy's good opinion. Or she never did before…* Jane was surprised at herself; she *wanted* Lizzy to soften towards Mr. Darcy. Perhaps opinions were already altering in Mr. Darcy's favour, but Lizzy was ever too vain of her own powers of observation to easily admit a mistake. Jane became determined to speak with her, for what a grand thing for dearest Lizzy to be in love with Charles Bingley's best friend.

"Lizzy," she said. "Charlotte and I brought you a dark grey gown. We should observe the mourning of our cousin when we go out. And we must write to our father when you return."

By mid-afternoon, it was clear the magistrate would require two days to conclude the necessary business, and he would return on Monday. Darcy and the colonel invited the ladies from Hunsford to a light repast, and Maria was brought to join them. It was all anyone wanted for dinner after such a day.

After the meal, a carriage was called immediately, and the colonel rode back to the vicarage with the ladies. Charlotte had agreed to give him the 1811 volume of Anne's journal.

Meanwhile, Darcy and Bingley awaited his return in the billiards room. Darcy admitted everything to Bingley: his mistaken notions of Jane Bennet and, more painfully, his affection for and benighted proposal to Elizabeth.

Bingley felt far too sorry for his friend's failed offer to attempt any remonstrance of his own. Elizabeth's near brush with death at the hands of Lady Catherine de Bourgh made him even less inclined to speak harshly to Darcy. Bingley knew Jane would have been devastated to suffer such a loss. This thought lead to others, both more pleasurable and confusing. He lost his concentration for the game.

Bingley aligned a shot, taking enough time about it as to annoy Darcy. For all his effort, Bingley missed. "It seems, due to my ineptitude at Hertfordshire and my being so easily persuaded to feelings not my own, that Miss Bennet no longer assumes that the quality of likeability testifies to goodness."

Darcy studied the table. "You think she no longer believes you to be a good man?"

"Why would she?"

"That I cannot say. Who knows why anyone loves anyone else? No, I shall not speak of why, only that I overheard the sisters speaking after Jane arrived here today. You need have no fear for her affections, Bingley."

Bingley's smile lit the room. "What did she…?"

Darcy held up a hand. "Do not ask. I shall not disclose particulars. Women cannot love proud men—trust me in this—and I shall not make your head swell by supplying details I was not meant to know. I have influenced you more than I should. Whether you love Jane Bennet enough to make her an offer, you must be above my paltry persuasion."

*21 September 1811*

*What in heaven's name have I gotten myself into, and how low can be the character of the man I have chosen to father my child? I pray daily for a quick conception, and twice a day when I have been with him, which now totals four times.*

*He thinks to play me the fool. I gave him the funds for his purchase of a commission in the regiment stationed at Sissinghurst. Today he has revealed that they are to be moved to a place called Meryton, in Hertfordshire, for the winter.*

*Firstly, he will be nearly fifty miles away instead of less than ten. Damned annoying not to have him easily at my beckoning. But now comes his perfidy: he has explained, using insultingly simple terms—have I not proved my wits and that I have the measure of him?—that he has been advised by some vague acquaintance already within the regiment that 'tis better he waits to join after they have moved to Meryton. This was of little consequence to me, excepting he requests a duplicate of the sum I have already given him that he might buy his commission later. He thinks… Well, I am sure I do not know what he thinks except that I am a foolish woman and part easily with my money. His new frock coat, the ghastly scent he wears (doubtless thinking it alluring), and perhaps gaming debts have wasted the original sum.*

*Such knavery is to be expected, I suppose. Is this not why I selected him? He is the worst sort of fellow, and no one would ever suggest we marry.*

*Damn the man. —A de B*

# CHAPTER 14
## A Knight Sardonic Arrives

*Saturday evening, 18 April 1812,*
*the Hunsford vicarage*

After sending Maria safely to bed, Jane, Elizabeth, and Charlotte gathered in Charlotte's sitting room. They talked of desultory topics, and none could find any comfort—not in reading, as Charlotte attempted, in handwork in Jane's case, or in writing letters. Elizabeth felt a letter to Mrs. Gardiner was owed but could not string two words of sense together nor properly mend her pen.

At last, Jane spoke of something substantial. "Lizzy, had you some understanding with Colonel Fitzwilliam?"

Charlotte looked up sharply.

"Colonel Fitzwilliam is no longer an object, Jane. I cannot say truthfully he ever was." The corner of Elizabeth's mouth curved; she was amused at herself. She had only ever wanted the colonel to be a window into the soul of Fitzwilliam Darcy—at first to confirm she should dislike him and now to offer her some hope that Mr. Darcy did not dislike her.

"I am relieved to hear it. It was my instant fear, when I arrived and the colonel behaved so oddly, that I had been the means of your heart being broken. I own I thought badly of him, Lizzy." The relief was plain on Jane's face.

Charlotte continued to look at Elizabeth, and Elizabeth was provoked by her expression to respond, "Charlotte, I have found the colonel to be pleasant on every occasion, and he will, without doubt, make the right lady an amiable husband. But to make a felicitous match, he will need his equal in sly, discerning humour and guarded candour. She will need to be quick and observant and have a compassion for the trials he has suffered in service to his country."

Elizabeth observed her friend as she spoke. Never had she felt herself to be more the centre of Charlotte's attention. "Now tell me, Charlotte, when did you first know you were in love with Colonel Fitzwilliam?"

"Lizzy!" Jane exclaimed. She appeared mortified at what her sister was suggesting about Charlotte's character.

Charlotte blushed swiftly, confirming Elizabeth's suppositions. To ease her friend's agitation, Elizabeth suppressed her smile. She and Charlotte were captivated by men who could not return their affections. It was both comforting and sad.

"You will not believe this of me, Lizzy, but it was love at first sight."

The two friends reached across the table and held hands. "How truly maddening, dear Charlotte, to discover your true love whilst married to a man you had just learnt to tolerate."

Jane's surprised stare swept from one of her companions to the other.

Charlotte nodded ruefully. "You saw when you arrived that I had convinced myself to be happy, Lizzy. I could have lived contentedly had I never met Colonel Alexander Fitzwilliam. Love is humbling…is it not?" She met Elizabeth's gaze as if waiting for a glimmer of recognition.

"Whatever do you mean, Charlotte? You imply I am in love."

Jane smiled softly at her sister. She took one of Elizabeth's hands as Charlotte clasped the other. Both women spoke at once: "But you are."

Elizabeth looked at their hands as Jane and Charlotte completed the circle. "I know," she said. "It is too dreadful."

*1 April 1812*

*I must write again today, for I am all astonishment. It would seem my cousin Darcy is God's own fool—an April Fool. He is in love with Miss Elizabeth Bennet! I could not be more delighted by this latest of life's absurdities. She is certain of his disdain.*

*I stopped outside the vicarage during my afternoon excursion, and Mrs. Collins paid me her attentions. As I often contrive, I asked Mr. Collins to bring me some trifle from the house. I knew Darcy had called in the morning, and Mrs. Collins informed me he had found Miss Bennet alone, its being a market day. She revealed, with some amusement, that he had appeared puzzled and seemed thrown by his time with Elizabeth. I believe Mrs. Collins suspects him.*

*I had the advantage of her in watching him frown, fidget, and fuss through last night's dinner and the quiet family evening afterwards. He displayed every mannerism a discomfited Fitzwilliam Darcy ever did: twisting his signet ring, rubbing his hands over his lips, appearing to muse on ponderous matters as he paced, running his hands through his hair distractedly, all of it. But to this, he added something new: the occasional fleeting smile.*

*Oh, yes! But now, how is the lady to be worked on? This is a Sisyphean task, because I suspect Darcy of some deceit as he will never speak to EB of her elder sister. What has he done? —A de B*

*Sunday, 19 April 1812,*
*the Hunsford vicarage and church*

Charlotte Collins stood at the doors of the Hunsford church. There was no vicar to lead the Sunday service, and early in the morning, the black hangings of deep mourning were spread around the doors and various architectural impedimenta of the building's exterior. The Cold Cook had prepared Mr. Collins to be seen by those of his parishioners as cared to view the remains of a man known to be murdered by the high-born harridan who had managed him and the entire town with an iron fist. Needless to say, the numbers of people so moved were legion.

His widow gave every appearance of strength and grace, keeping her astonishment private. The grandeur of her widow's weeds was much admired, for the town ladies knew they were hand-me-downs from the murderess and thus did not begrudge Mrs. Collins her elegant, if slightly outdated, bereavement. Few of the villagers travelled in such lofty circles as to judge silk bombazine *de classé* and that sateen under sarcenet was now preferred.

Elizabeth and Jane assisted Charlotte as villagers came and went during the hour when services would have been observed. Sorting the de Bourgh jewels was a brief topic, and again the task was put off for another day.

*Meanwhile, at Rosings*

Lady Catherine de Bourgh was laid out as her daughter had been in the grandest receiving room, but no one was inclined to venture forth, and Albertine was made to sit with the body.

The family, small though it was, even including Bingley, kept to Anne de Bourgh's sitting room, the most cheerful setting in the manor. They were quietly relieved when an invitation came from the ladies at Hunsford for an early dinner. It appeared there was an abundance of food, more than four ladies could possibly consume unaided.

It was not thought that a letter would arrive from the Archbishop of Canterbury until Monday morning, and only then if by a church messenger, so the party at Rosings knew they must wait to arrange the funeral. At noontime, Darcy jumped up purposefully and left the room. Unbeknownst to the others, he had remembered the horrifying raven-feather wreaths unnecessarily adorning the hatchments on the front doors. He removed them with no little vigour.

This burst of energy did not expend Darcy's disquiet. There was much to consider, some of it entirely not his concern, but worry he would. He paced the broad top step of the Rosings entrance, pondering the disposition of Longbourn now that its heir was no more. Were there other absurd cousins to inherit? What became of estates for which there was no heir? Could he buy the estate and turn it over to the Bennets by deed of gift? And if he could, what was the possibility of doing so secretly?

His thoughts turned to heirs and the improbability of ever marrying. It would fall to Georgiana's eventual marriage to produce Pemberley's heir, perhaps the child taking the Darcy name, or some adoption could be arranged. There was little romance in the legalities of inheritance.

He further considered the necessity of teaching his cousin a great deal about estate management in a very short time. It was nearly May with its need to interrupt the Season for the annual trip to Pemberley and remain a fortnight to oversee the spring planting. Perhaps Alex should join him; they must speak of it and also of when Alex would resign his commission. What a transition, to cease thinking of him as a colonel and begin to think of him as landed gentry.

His thoughts returned to Georgiana, and he worried over the absence of Mrs. Annesley. She had stayed in London to collect the remainder of the orders placed for Georgiana's mourning clothes and would join them as soon as everything was assembled. Surely, the various modistes and milliners knew time was of the essence. If he did not have a message from Darcy House in the morning stating his sister's companion was on her way, he would be writing to *her*.

He began to think of his new position as trustee of the money left to Charlotte Collins by Anne. It would be a short-lived task, but how was he to advise her? She had been seven and twenty when they met in the autumn, and now she was a widow. There was no reason to withhold anything from the entire sum, but she should buy a little cottage in Meryton and invest the remainder in the four percents.

*"I do not mean to say that a woman may not be settled too near her family,"* came a fondly remembered voice. As did every word exchanged with Elizabeth, these haunted him. That simple sentence innocently led him to believe he would be accepted should he decide to pay his addresses. Considering all that followed, he had been mistaken to cling to this speech and had not properly attended the rest of what she had said. Elizabeth had meant to explain that his pride kept him woefully above such menial considerations as to how a woman, or anyone not of his class, might travel about the country. She meant him to know that she thought him shallow and unfeeling for those beneath him. Of course, she was right.

The colonel stepped outside, and watched for a moment as his distracted cousin stood gazing with apparent absence of mind, holding a raven-feather wreath of substantial proportions in either hand. "Toss them onto the lawn, Cousin, if you are of a mind to..."

Darcy startled. He then laughed at himself. "You see me considering my failings, Alex."

"Cease torturing yourself. None of this is of your making. It is time we departed for our dinner with the ladies. I have heard enough of Bingley asking about the propriety of carrying on a courtship during a lady's time of mourning for a cousin she thought little of." Colonel Fitzwilliam shook his head ruefully, and Darcy laughed.

"I find it difficult to imagine Miss Bennet thinking little of anyone."

"She has told Bingley that Mrs. Collins has advised her to be more forthcoming with her feelings." The colonel snorted. "Bingley may be in for it now! Perhaps there is a shrew under the placid exterior of Miss Bennet."

"Oh, I doubt that. Perhaps simply a more garden-variety woman who has seen the error of holding herself to a higher standard of comportment than is sensible." *I know this error, for I have seen it in myself.* "Are we to walk?"

"Yes, all of us. Bingley and Georgie will be down directly."

Darcy took the wreaths to the butler and urged him to dispose of them in a manner that would assure their never being seen again.

DARCY STRODE OUT AHEAD, REACHING THE GARDEN GATE AT THE VICARAGE a few moments before the rest of the party, and saw Elizabeth, Jane, and Charlotte on benches in the side garden. Like blackbirds in a flower garden bursting with daffodils, their black skirts and lace were jarring against the bright gold and yellow. After a moment's alarm, he reminded himself that one had lost a husband, however bumptious, and two had lost a cousin, the heir to their father's estate, howsoever ill esteemed. He looked down to hide a smile; he preferred them in their simple country muslins.

He watched Jane Bennet blush prettily as Bingley greeted her. Charlotte Collins maintained perfect aplomb, but her eyes followed the colonel. Elizabeth engaged Georgiana directly, and Darcy felt very much an afterthought in her greeting.

The dinner was a subdued meal as anyone would have expected. Colonel Fitzwilliam and Charlotte managed small talk that included everyone. Elizabeth was uncharacteristically silent, and Darcy could not believe she would be so affected by the death of Mr. Collins. Perhaps the near loss of her own life was the more sobering influence. It was an oddity, to be sure, for Georgiana to be the one attempting to draw Elizabeth out. Bingley and Jane existed in a world of their own, and Darcy tried to hide his envy.

The sexes did not separate after the meal. Given the mixture of dishes offered from the best of those brought by the villagers, it was little wonder that Charlotte suggested they delay the dessert course until the coffee and tea were prepared. Darcy could scarce imagine what ostentatious and insipid sweets the local ladies might have fashioned, but he knew it was all, every bite, most kindly meant.

In the best parlour of the vicarage, Charlotte had just begun an unnecessary apology for the erratic quality of the previous courses when the Sunday quiet was disturbed by the approach and halt of a carriage upon the road. Maria ran to the window.

"Lizzy! Jane! It is your father!"

Elizabeth followed her, and indeed, Mr. Bennet had emerged from their family's elderly chaise and four and was veritably dashing along the path to the front door.

Much to the surprise of the rest of the party, Mr. Thomas Bennet entered the house in a rush. Although Elizabeth was moved to seek a fatherly embrace, for she had missed his company these eight weeks away, something in his bearing stopped her progress. "Papa! You have come all this way on a Sunday?" she cried.

"What would you have me do, child? First, I receive a letter telling me you are an heiress to a fortune in jewels, but my curiosity might have survived that. Next, I receive a *demand* from a man I have never met in the whole of my life insisting, in a highly unsuitable manner, to bless his marriage to my eldest daughter, asking me to take the word of Mr. Darcy as to his character! I might have invited the fellow to Longbourn after giving the matter due consideration, but last night an express arrived announcing so many deaths that I have lost count, and my dearest daughters in the midst of it. Your mother is in a state of panic, and this once, she is more than justified. I set off at first light, hoping to prevent further slaughter. Charlotte, *your* father is not so impolitic as to travel on a Sunday, having merely lost a son-in-law, but Sir William will arrive tomorrow to see Maria home."

Bingley and Jane stared suspiciously at the colonel.

The room was silent but for Mr. Bennet's laboured breathing, and his eyes searched each face.

After an indecently long pause, which neither Darcy nor Elizabeth was inclined to end, the colonel stepped forward with a sheepish expression.

"Mr. Bennet, please accept my apologies. I am Colonel Alexander Fitzwilliam." He bowed formally.

"Yes, young man, you *should* apologise for being Colonel Alexander Fitzwilliam. You must be a great burden to your family; the insane generally are. I believe the Fitzwilliam family is sadly marked." Mr. Bennet turned to look again at Bingley, who bowed. "Mr. Bingley…" He glanced at Jane. "My dear, how many suitors have you?" Mr. Bennet made a show of looking under the straight chairs. "Are there more?"

Jane's blush darkened, and she looked down. "The colonel has realised his error. To me, he never was an object." She glanced at Bingley then down again.

Mr. Bennet saw Bingley smile broadly, and he rolled his eyes. He gave the colonel a disparaging glance. "Fickle are you, sir?"

Colonel Fitzwilliam had not felt so diminished in confidence and authority since his first days in the army. "So it might seem, Mr. Bennet."

Darcy was Mr. Bennet's next victim. "Mr. Darcy, we meet again. You have taken some pleasure, I understand, in insulting my Lizzy. At this moment, I am happy—no, *relieved*—that she is not handsome enough to tempt you."

Elizabeth closed her eyes, thinking her mortification complete.

Darcy had also closed his eyes and did not know Elizabeth was his competition in exhibiting humiliation.

"Mr. Bennet…" Darcy began after another momentary silence.

He was ignored as Mr. Bennet fired another volley. "Charlotte, I am sorry for your loss, perhaps sorrier than you are for yourself. You have lost a pompous, insensible husband, but I have lost my heir unless you are…?" He waved his hand vaguely around his own middle.

Charlotte coloured and shook her head. No, she was not with child.

"Ah, well, I should have known Mr. Collins would fail me in this. Now I must exert a great deal of effort, and likely expense, to save Longbourn from reverting to the Crown when I am gone."

"Father…" Elizabeth hissed, trying to effect some amendment to the flow of his indignation.

She too was ignored. "But that is of little matter compared to the placement of my dearest daughters into a viper's nest. I would not have thought it of your *esteemed* family, Mr. Darcy. A mad and murderous aunt and a witless cousin, however decorated in the wars."

"Papa…" Elizabeth made another attempt.

Mr. Bennet's eyes landed on Georgiana. Her obvious fear of his wrath slightly quieted his savage breast, and he enquired in a gentler tone, "And who might you be, my dear?"

Darcy spoke. "Mr. Bennet, please allow me to present my sister, Miss Georgiana Darcy."

She curtsied. Mr. Bennet bowed properly and then turned to Bingley. "She is a charming child, Mr. Bingley. Are we to wish you joy?"

Elizabeth's fingers pressed against her brow as she bowed her head. She recalled everything Darcy had written about the impropriety shown by her father. She wondered how she was not fainting at this when she had swooned easily the day before. Oblivion would be most welcomed and sooner rather than later. She thought briefly of all the times she had wished her father would exert himself in the family's defence. Now was not one of those times if an endless philippic was his method of protection.

"I do not have the pleasure of understanding you, sir," Bingley said, bristling.

"Perhaps I was misinformed, but I heard in a letter from your sister Miss Bingley, which was read to the family by Mrs. Bennet, that my beautiful Jane was jilted for this young lady. She is pretty enough, I grant you, but she appears very young.

"However, I am not here to sort out squandered romances. Who here has enough information to apprise me of all I should know?"

"I believe I do, Mr. Bennet," Charlotte said.

"And I, sir." The colonel stepped forward. He caught Darcy's eye and the men exchanged nods of agreement.

"Let me show you to the book room, Mr. Bennet," said Charlotte. "It will be at your disposal for as long as you are with us." She led him out of the room.

The colonel started to follow but whispered loud enough in Darcy's ear for everyone to hear, "I thought you said the old boy was an indolent and indifferent father, Darcy. I have never in all my life been more insulted without hope of defending myself." With a joyless smile, he made a general bow to the others and left the room.

Georgiana looked from her brother to Bingley and back again. "I believe Mr. Bennet is not the only one owed an explanation."

"Would anyone care for a glass of wine first?" asked Elizabeth.

Everyone did.

When Georgiana's questions had been answered as truthfully as possible by whosoever in the room could best accomplish the consideration of each query, Mr. Bennet was still cloistered with Charlotte and Colonel Fitzwilliam. What might be done about feeding him and settling where he should sleep occupied Jane and Elizabeth while conversation continued in a less fraught manner between Georgiana and her brother. Maria was set the task of moving some of Charlotte's personal items into her room. The sisters would share to allow Mr. Bennet the best bed.

When Elizabeth returned to the drawing room, she raised her eyebrows to Darcy, nodding at him to follow her to the window. Her concerns were evident as she said, "You must allow me to apologise, Mr. Darcy. I know my father's faults, but I have never known him to be so injudicious. You must believe me, I am mortified."

In truth, Darcy found her earnest expression beguiling, and although he longed to tease her, he chose to respond seriously. "This is no reflection upon you. Mr. Bennet has been abundantly provoked. I do not blame him." He paused. "He seeks to protect you." *Would that the task were mine, not his.*

"You are kind. He has had little practice in coming to our defence, and he is clumsy, even indelicate."

Darcy's dimples nearly emerged. "We have been well instructed as to the value of practice, you and I. I know of no one as skilled as you at sketching character or better attuned to the atmosphere in a room." Darcy crossed his arms over his chest to resist the urge to calm her in his arms.

Elizabeth's eyes widened. "How can you say such a thing? You know what my failings have been."

Darcy lowered his voice to avoid his sister's hearing. "You were subjected to the arts of an accomplished dissembler. You could not have guessed—"

Elizabeth impulsively placed her hand upon Darcy's forearm. "It was not to *that* man I was referring, sir." She met his eyes pointedly before moving away, blushing to have touched the sleeve of his frock coat.

Darcy turned to the corner chair he usually occupied when in this room. The floor had suddenly tilted under his feet, and he was uncertain whether it was the effect of the odd meal or the fine eyes and soft voice of Elizabeth Bennet. He sat without grace, nearly missing the seat.

Only Georgiana noticed her brother's disquiet and the high colour of her new friend.

When the colonel and Charlotte had at last answered Mr. Bennet's many questions, they were released from attending him, and like comrades in arms who have been tortured together, their exchanged expressions spoke eloquently of a bond others would never comprehend.

They joined the party in the best parlour, and Charlotte approved the arrangements made by Jane and Elizabeth to organise the household around its new addition.

"Your father has asked us to send you to him, Lizzy," Charlotte informed her.

"I shall take him a tray." Elizabeth curtsied from the doorway. "I must say good evening. Once my father and I are alone and conversing after a long separation, it may be near morning before we emerge."

Immediately after she left them, Darcy and Colonel Fitzwilliam took their leave, returning to Rosings on foot, where they would send a carriage for Bingley and Georgiana.

The cousins walked silently at first, and then the colonel said, "I believe Mr. Bennet was not as taken in by the charms of Wickham as Elizabeth was, and even Charlotte could not imagine the extent of his profligacy until she read Anne's journals."

Darcy merely nodded.

"But I am not certain that Mr. Bennet is as convinced as he should be that the man is a thorough bleeder. The militia is on the point of removing from Meryton to Brighton, and there is talk of Miss Lydia venturing there in the household of Colonel Forster. I have always found Forster far too lenient."

Darcy became livelier at this news. "Bennet must not allow it! Surely you warned him."

"Mrs. Collins spoke of Lydia's wildness. I said what I could of Wickham, but Mr. Bennet was not inclined to think his youngest an object for a mercenary predator. I could hardly speak of Wickham's preference for spoiling fresh young things before Mrs. Collins now, could I?"

Darcy stopped walking. "Miss Lydia Bennet must not go to Brighton. It is courting disaster. I shall speak to the man first thing tomorrow."

The colonel said, "Good," and they continued walking.

*Later that evening*

A footman brought a note from Mr. Darcy directly to Mr. Bennet, in which he requested some moments of Mr. Bennet's time at an early hour. As Elizabeth had predicted, she was still with her father when it arrived. Mr. Bennet handed it to her after he had read it.

"I believe he comes to explain his dealings with Wickham, Papa." She dared not hope Darcy would call for any other reason. "Then you will hear. He has asked me to be silent on the subject, but I cannot say enough against sending Lydia to Brighton. Our family's reputation is at stake. Wickham is vindictive."

It was the same heated topic father and daughter had been debating before the brief message from Darcy was presented.

"Very well, Lizzy. Since he says you might join us, I insist you do so. But how is it you know some secret of Mr. Darcy's? Has your opinion of him changed so much, or his of you, that he has taken you into his confidence?"

Elizabeth sighed, wondering how much to reveal. She would not speak of Darcy's proposal. She was not sufficiently inured to recent circumstances to tolerate her father's barbs on the subject or stomach his amusement at Darcy's expense. "He had occasion to hear me speak in defence of Wickham—rather too warmly—and sought to explain the truth of the matter. Wickham is an accomplished liar, and I was well and truly taken in. I am yet ashamed to have spoken as I did in Mr. Darcy's presence once I understood the whole of it."

Mr. Bennet seemed intrigued. "Then I shall await the morning with bated breath, my child." He could sense his daughter's unease. "For now, let us speak of other things. Will Bingley offer for Jane soon, do you think?"

# CHAPTER 15
## Not in Sacred Ground

*4 April 1812*

*I have had it from the servants that Darcy did not sleep at all the night before last. Paulette has related that, yesterday morning when the maids entered his chamber, there was a riot of ash and spilt ink and pen nibs all over the desk, chair, and floor. The bed had not been disturbed.*

*Last night, Darcy went into the library very late, and his man had to employ one of the footmen to assist getting him to bed. The footman says he was blind drunk and dead to the world.*

*Now Darcy is on the point of leaving. Mama is at the end of her tether. Alex does not know what has happened other than Darcy is angry with him for spreading tales out of turn about something, and I have withdrawn to my room after a careful and quiet farewell to my cousins.*

*I am achy from the baby and plan to spend the remainder of the day in my room. Mrs. Jenkinson will put it around, if necessary, that my courses have come and I feel weak. Indeed, I do feel weak. —A de B*

*Oh! I have more news. EB has a letter, a thick one. The footman at Hunsford has seen her with it and told my mother's maid, who is his sister. He says EB mutters over it and is cross, but she hides it away when any but the servants are in the room. Darcy has written her, I am certain! Wherever would I be without the gossip of servants? Blessings on them, every one! As soon as I am improved, I must speak to her, and if she returns home before I have the chance to offer her a position as my companion in my new circumstances, I shall write to her. Not so long and vexing a letter as my cousin's, I'm sure, but perhaps as surprising, in its way. —A de B*

*Monday, 20 April 1812*

Before the early call upon Mr. Bennet, Darcy instructed the butler at Rosings to bring any message received from the Archbishop of Canterbury to him directly should one arrive. The spring morning was crisp and fair, and he was sorry his request to make an early call might cause Elizabeth to forego her morning ramble. Seeing the parkland through her eyes, he knew she would take delight at the first blooming of each new species of flower. He was sorry he had not been more observant when he walked with her before—before so rudely forcing his offer upon her. He wished he knew her preferences for flowers and colours.

Darcy did not know for certain whether Mr. Bennet would include Elizabeth in their conference, but he believed he had not misapprehended the man's esteem for his daughter's opinions. He began to gather a handful of flowers as he went, hoping he might be including a type she had not yet seen.

Elizabeth stood at the window of the stairway landing, which faced the road and afforded a view of the palings and gate into Rosings Park. She pursed her lips. *What a child I am, waiting for a glimpse of his hat!* The sill was deep and she leant against it on her elbows, her self-disapproval not drawing her away from the prospect. She longed to be out walking and wondered whether the handsomest man of her acquaintance would ever tread the paths with her again. *Doubtful, Lizzy, highly doubtful.*

Her heart attempted to escape her chest when, at last, the dark beaver approached in stark contrast against the tapestry of spring green. It then disappeared, only to reappear some distance nearer. Elizabeth wondered at this strange progress, and smiled with delight when Darcy appeared at the palings with an extempore nosegay in his hand. She did not stop to ponder the forwardness of opening the door for him as he came along the garden walk towards the house. Nor did she note with any disapprobation the strong tendency to vanity that assured the flowers were to be hers.

Mr. Bennet also watched Darcy's approach from the book room and heard his daughter's light steps descend the stairs. The front door opened, and Mr. Bennet watched the remarkable change in Darcy's countenance as he was welcomed. The gentleman was beaming as he made his bow. Elizabeth stepped into the view and curtsied. The open window made public their greetings.

"Good morning, Miss Bennet."

"Good morning, Mr. Darcy. My father has informed me that I am to join your discussion. We hope you will take breakfast with us afterwards if you are not too long about your business, in which case, you may have luncheon."

Darcy held out the flowers. "I offer these by way of apology for keeping you inside when I know my friend would as soon be afield on such a fine morning."

Darcy had removed his gloves to gather the flowers, and being at home, Elizabeth wore none. Their cheeks burned as their hands touched when the flowers passed from one to the other.

"I hope there might be something here you have not seen blooming before, or at least not here…this spring…in the park…since…since your arrival…" Darcy's spoken wishes dwindled to a stammered silence.

Elizabeth required a moment to catch her breath. Had he called her his friend? She hoped she had heard him correctly and unconsciously pressed the point. "This is indeed a kind and friendly gesture, Mr. Darcy. And most gentlemanly, too, to seek to redress for any inconveniencing of a friend—although you have not bothered me, for it is no trouble, you know, to sit with you…and my father…together."

Realising she was babbling, she looked up at him brightly. "There are cowslips, chequered lilies, and early purple orchids. I thank you!" She wiped pollen from her nose as Darcy chuckled.

Mr. Bennet watched and overheard their conversation with no little astonishment. This was not the daughter who loathed Mr. Darcy above all men. This was not the haughty and judgmental Mr. Darcy who would not be tempted by Elizabeth Bennet. There was much here to consider.

The couple entered the house, and Nell approached to take the gentleman's hat and linen duster. Darcy listened carefully as Elizabeth pulled the servant aside, and he was pleased to hear the words "water," "vase," and lastly, but by no means of least importance, "to my bedchamber."

He closed his eyes to gather his equilibrium as the floor became unsteady. Why did he never feel confident of his balance in this house? Something he had touched would now—and for as fleeting a time as the flowers would live —lodge in the bedroom occupied by Elizabeth Bennet. They would mutely observe her in ways *he* never would. He vowed silently to bring her flowers continually for the remainder of her stay in the neighbourhood.

Furthermore, he had hazarded the word "friend" and Elizabeth repeated it. She called his gift "gentlemanly." No matter how the conversation with Mr. Bennet progressed, he could do naught but count his visit to the vicarage a hearty success. They would be friends.

Elizabeth guided him into the book room where Mr. Bennet turned from the window to receive and return Darcy's bow. He then looked at the two young people in bemused appraisal, allowing the moment to stretch into their discomfort by not leaving the window. When he saw in their eyes that they understood he had seen the giving of the nosegay, Mr. Bennet gave a slight nod before saying, "What is our topic, Mr. Darcy? Are we to speak of flowers that bloom in the spring with a 'hey nonny nonny'?"

Elizabeth blushed profoundly and wondered whether the magistrate had taken *all* of the cyanide from Rosings.

Although becoming pink-cheeked, Darcy went straight to his point. "I fear it is nothing so pleasant. I wish to acquaint you with the true character of George Wickham."

Once all were seated, Mr. Darcy gave a candid and complete rendering of all his dealings with the man. Mr. Bennet cast the occasional glance at Elizabeth, who heard it all as though Darcy were not saying anything she did not already know. Even the explanation of the near elopement of Mr. Darcy's sister did not produce a blush to match her countenance when the subject of wildflowers had been broached.

"This all seems a rather sordid family business, Mr. Darcy. May I ask how Lizzy came to be aware of it?" Mr. Bennet raised his brows. He wanted to hear Darcy's mind in the matter. Mr. Bennet continued to find it difficult to understand the changed relations between Darcy and his most valued daughter.

"When I danced with Miss Elizabeth at Netherfield, she implied your family had formed a friendship with Wickham," Darcy explained. "One cannot speak against someone too strongly in a ballroom, however deserving."

Mr. Bennet did not smile too much. "No, certainly not. Harsh words are *never* heard in a ballroom."

Darcy suppressed his impatience. "When I had the chance of it upon meeting her again, I *did* explain everything."

Mr. Bennet studied Darcy's eyes. *Jealousy!* He was vastly diverted. Most assuredly, Mr. Darcy held Elizabeth in high regard. Perhaps there was even a tenderness of feeling? Such a proud man would never offer for her given the difference in their circumstances, but neither could he resist her, that much was obvious. That she had taken Wickham's word over his in Meryton must have been a burr under his saddle.

Darcy did not like the presentiment of being seen through, but such were his feelings. His annoyance was a challenge to contain. The warning to Mr. Bennet about Wickham's depraved nature seemed to be going unnoticed in the man's efforts to find amusement in the unease of his daughter. *I hope I shall never be such a father as this, where teasing my children is of greater concern than protecting them.* Darcy stood abruptly, "I have said all there is to say in this. It is for you to protect your family."

He turned with a sincere smile to Elizabeth. "Miss Elizabeth, you did offer me breakfast, did you not?" Darcy nearly forgot to bow to Mr. Bennet as he left the room after insisting, with rather more emphasis than was necessary, that the man's daughter take his arm.

Once the young people were out of sight, Mr. Bennet drew a sheet of writing paper from the desk and began a letter.

*Hunsford Vicarage*
*Kent*

*My Dear Wife,*
*It has come to my attention…*

Mr. Darcy had finished his breakfast with the ladies of the vicarage, and Elizabeth had seen him out the door, by the time her father emerged from the book room bearing a sealed letter. He held it in such a way as to be certain her curious eyes would see the direction. He called for the footman, and in Elizabeth's hearing, demanded the letter be sent by express to Longbourn, leaving no doubt of his intentions. He turned to his surprised daughter.

"I care nothing for Mr. Darcy's approbation, but I *do* care that he respects you, and there is much improvement in him. Did I not always say you and Jane would be valued wherever you go? For myself, I value only *your* good opinion, Lizzy, and thus I have written your mother, forbidding Lydia to travel anywhere outside the boundaries of Meryton.

"It will be some time before I am home to hear the lamentations, and that recollection made the letter much less burdensome to compose. It is to be hoped that when we return to Longbourn, there will be talk of wedding lace." He raised his brows at her. "I find I can tolerate lace more equably than Lydia's protests of ill treatment and the constant unfairness of life's trials."

Elizabeth rolled her eyes but was so relieved that she was required to retreat to her bedroom to cry for five minutes complete. However, when her eyes beheld the flowers from Mr. Darcy, the flow of tears magically ceased.

*Later that day, Rosings*

THE SEVENOAKS MAGISTRATE—MR. HUMPHREY KNOCKER—ALONG WITH Darcy, Bingley, Colonel Fitzwilliam, and Georgiana was taking some light refreshment in the music room when The Most Reverend and Right Honourable Lord Archbishop of Canterbury, Charles Manners-Sutton, was announced without forewarning. Darcy introduced his distant cousin (his paternal grandmother had been a Manners) to the magistrate, who was the only person in the room wholly unknown to the Archbishop.

"This is capital, Cousin Darcy," his kindly and reverend relative announced. "I had hoped to consult the magistrate before making any recommendations as to Lady Catherine's funeral. I shall speak to him and return to you directly."

The Archbishop was closeted with Mr. Knocker in the small parlour where Lady Catherine had often met Mr. Collins, since no one had died in it.

An hour later, Mr. Knocker departed and the Archbishop returned to the music room, taking Darcy and the colonel aside to speak privately out of deference to the delicate sensibilities of Miss Darcy. Bingley sat with Georgiana, turning pages for her at the pianoforte. She chose Bach and played ponderously as she thought befitted the occasion.

The Archbishop was sombre. "No one is more aware than I of appearances, Darcy, and it will not look well for your family, but I cannot perform a funeral service for a murderess. Indeed, I shall neither speak by her grave nor see where she is laid out. Nor shall I allow her to be entombed in the de Bourgh crypt in the churchyard. She cannot suffer her earth bath in hallowed ground. Our Lord may forgive her, and we ought to do so in our hearts, but that is all. There cannot be one rule for the high-born and another for murderers from the lower classes."

The colonel nodded in agreement.

Darcy sighed, looking as stone-faced as the Archbishop. It was the first time he had given a thought for the reputation of his family since being refused by Elizabeth Bennet.

"This is God's will, Darcy. It cannot be otherwise. Lofty as I am, I cannot flout the law, neither the King's nor God's, and in this instance, they are the same. The noble Fitzwilliam family is better rid of this canker upon its family tree. Am I to understand the current local physician was not yet in the neighbourhood at the time of Sir Lewis's death?"

"That is true, Your Grace," Darcy replied.

"And we have the evidence that the local magistrate had then received a bribe from her ladyship?"

"So Mr. Knocker says, as well as the unscrupulous verger of the church, who had caught wind of it and avoided taking tea with Lady Catherine all these many years," the colonel explained. "It will all come out now."

The Archbishop nodded. "We have only the diary of her late daughter informing us that Lady Catherine was at this vile trade for some time and unrepentantly using the stable grooms as test cases." The Archbishop made a sound of disapprobation. "'Tis a sorry business, and I am certain we are all well rid of her, as are all good Christians."

Darcy nodded and knew there was nothing to argue.

"Now, gentlemen, there is one funeral service I *do* intend to conduct. I would be honoured to lead the service for Mr. William Collins. Might we manage it tomorrow? I understand that the incumbent to the estate for which Mr. Collins was heir is currently in residence at the vicarage along with two female cousins of Mr. Collins and his widow. Is Mrs. Collins…?" He motioned his hand over his belly.

Darcy and Colonel Fitzwilliam coughed into their hands. "She says not," the colonel muttered.

"I wonder whether the marriage was consummated," the Archbishop mused aloud, causing even the colonel to blush. "Mr. Collins was a simple soul, a most tedious toady, it cannot be denied. But he acted as God's cat's-paw in effecting a justice of perfect symmetry."

The colonel had ceased listening, having read, as he knew Charlotte had, the explicit descriptions of Anne's final assignations. He devoutly hoped Charlotte had not read such things as a maiden, but could only wonder with grim interest about her marital relations. From her wish to protect her friend's innocence, Charlotte had unintentionally set the death of her husband in motion. The colonel surmised that, in this, Mrs. Collins was struggling with no little guilt.

Darcy looked at his cousin's blush with open curiosity but said nothing. It took a great deal to make the colonel turn any colour but tan from long hours upon his horse. Darcy addressed the Archbishop instead. "One of Mr. Collins's cousins is the lady who escaped our aunt's tainted tea and cake. It was only by some miracle, which she does not explain but says that it saved her."

"So I understand from the magistrate. The crime of attempted murder is counted amongst Lady Catherine's sins. I would like to be introduced to this young lady. Miss Elizabeth Bennet, is it?"

The colonel's spirits lightened, and he knocked Darcy in the shoulder. 'That falls to you, Cousin. You are well practiced in making her known to the quality."

The Archbishop was relieved to see the cousins smiling again. He much preferred performing weddings and christenings, and even the odd coronation now and again, to funerals. "Darcy, Colonel Fitzwilliam," he said, "I absolve you from mourning your aunt, or even Miss Anne de Bourgh. And Cousin," his lively eyes lit upon Darcy's impassive countenance, "I should be honoured to celebrate your wedding, should I live so long."

*Later that evening*

THE SERVANTS WERE SET INTO TURMOIL AS A PRESENTABLE MEAL WAS COBbled together for the Archbishop and his retinue, though served rather later than typical for dinner in the country. Guest rooms were aired and bedding freshened. The crowd from the Hunsford vicarage was invited, including Sir William Lucas, who was prevailed upon to stay for the service of his son-in-law since the highest man of God on earth—absent the King—would perform it.

It had been Sir William's first inclination to flee the county with his youngest daughter, as if worried that something in all of the recent deaths was of a catching nature. The auspicious character of the officiate for the next day's funeral was such that Sir William's stories of his investiture at St. James's might be eclipsed by new tales, at least for a time.

Because the best drawing room could not be used—given that it housed the corpse of a murderess—the ladies withdrew to the music room and were eventually joined by the men. Mr. Bennet made a considerable study of Elizabeth and judged her withdrawn. When Darcy was not speaking to others, he was as absorbed by staring at Elizabeth as he had ever been, while she appeared to study the pattern on her teacup or the painting over the mantle. Mr. Bennet noticed Elizabeth slowly and somewhat stealthily (to anyone's eyes but her father's) following Darcy's progress around the room, staying near enough to hear his conversations but hanging back from being drawn into them. Mr. Bennet could not like what he saw. Given the friendly terms the two had evidenced that morning, he could only resolve to puzzle out his daughter's uncharacteristic behaviour later in quiet and solitude. A cot had been erected for him in the book room at the vicarage since the father of the mistress of the house deserved the best bed. Mr. Bennet was well pleased with the arrangements.

Darcy requested a bath before bed, and as he and his valet awaited the footmen with the water, the keeper of the Darcy wardrobe cleared his throat. When his master made no acknowledgment, Stafford repeated the noise at greater volume.

Darcy looked up from idly running a manicure stick under his already immaculate fingernails. "Stafford, are you unwell?"

"No, indeed, sir. I am fit as ever."

"I fear for your tonsils all the same."

"If I may, sir?"

Darcy knew his man must have gossip to impart. "I am yours to command, Stafford."

"It has come from the servants at Hunsford to the servants of Rosings, and thus to me, that a certain gentleman only lately arrived sent an express to Longbourn directly upon your departure from the vicarage this morning."

Darcy smiled slowly and, he had to own, rather victoriously.

"The maid, Nell, also let it be known that stems of wildflowers were seen tucked into the bodice of one of the Bennet sisters in the afternoon before she changed for dinner. It was the younger, dark-haired one, Miss Elizabeth. The purple orchids were quite noticeable against the lady's black silk, I am told. She was thought irreverent. Not setting the proper example, it was said."

Darcy was still laughing when his bath was poured. He settled into the soothing water with Anne's journal, which Colonel Fitzwilliam, with a leer, had turned over to Darcy for his perusal.

"Mind you," the colonel had said with a convincing expression of vulgarity, "it will keep you awake. Or perhaps alert. No, a better word is 'aroused.' Yes."

After several pages, Darcy began to feel genuinely discomfited. Anne's revelations were far more disturbing than appealing. Darcy shivered with distaste for what he was reading. To be naked and discovering the arts and allurements that a man he assumed was Wickham used to coax eagerness from Anne left Darcy disgusted with them both and with his own shameless male member.

When he flung himself into bed, his thoughts turned wanton without his leave. His imagination was too energetic: leaping from purple orchids against smooth skin to suckling at the bosom of a gently moaning bride. Thus, the actions Wickham visited upon his cousin, Darcy imagined performing upon Elizabeth Bennet. If mere musings roused such a mania of passion, Darcy must fear sleeping.

*Just before midnight, the Hunsford vicarage*

The night air was cool, too cool for the light nightgown Elizabeth wore as she leaned indolently against the window of the room she shared with Jane. She had been overheated the entire evening at Rosings. The sensation grew worse after her brief but sobering introduction and private word with the Archbishop of Canterbury. He knew she would have been a victim of Lady Catherine's but for some happily timed distraction, and he enquired what her thoughts might have been.

"My dear, were you bewitched by the jewels you have inherited?" His eyes were kindly but not disinterested.

Elizabeth could not lie, for this was a man to whom one should deny nothing, but she was loath to expose herself, even to one bound by God to keep any secret to himself. "The distraction was not in the bedchamber of

Miss de Bourgh, Your Grace, but rather, it was something I saw in the hall."

After looking quizzically at her, the Archbishop's right eye appeared to twitch as the corners of his mouth rose. "I have toured Rosings, Miss Elizabeth, and can recall nothing remarkable in that part of the house"—his voice dropped—"excepting the portrait of my cousin Fitzwilliam Darcy." His eye twitched again.

Elizabeth wondered whether it was voluntary; was the Archbishop of Canterbury *winking*?

Upon remembering their exchange in the dead of night, she was certain her response had been as flimsy as the garment she was wearing. She raised the cowslip she had been playing with to her nose, breathing in the sweet, clean scent. If she pressed some of the flowers, she could keep them in a small box with her letter from Darcy and the pink diamond ring. It would not be enough, but it was all she could expect.

She sighed and breathed in the scent again. No, there could never be enough to sustain her through the long years of spinsterhood ahead, but she had managed to make a friend of him. She was certain Mr. Bingley would offer for Jane, and the newly forged friendship with Mr. Darcy would make the married life of her dear sister easier.

Elizabeth returned to bed and fell asleep with the cowslip held over her heart.

# CHAPTER 16
## Two Funerals

*Tuesday, 21 April 1812*

Darcy and the congregation stood in the Hunsford chapel as the Archbishop progressed up the aisle. Because of the girth of the deceased, Mr. Collins's eternity box was built around him. The pallbearers, Darcy included in their number, would only be burdened for the brief distance to his grave in the churchyard.

Darcy glared at his cousin, who was at last prevailed upon to behave seriously. He next looked to Bingley, who was, in his turn, watching him with a countenance full of concern. Mr. Bennet was watching the ceremony with a mien of gravity Darcy would not have expected. Darcy could not know his friend and cousin were thinking only of him, and Mr. Bennet's thoughts were also absent from the proceedings, dwelling instead upon his daughter Elizabeth.

In the rear of the church, townsfolk of both sexes gathered to watch no less a personage than the Archbishop of Canterbury speak honestly, and therefore briefly, of the merits of William Collins. He had been a faithful husband, had mended a breach with his family, and had shown uncommon devotion to his patroness (the lady was not mentioned by name). Beyond this, not much more could be said without either speaking disparagingly of the dead or breaking the limits of truth.

The Archbishop offered a little homily about justice that amused Mr. Bennet, for there were precious few other lessons to be drawn from the life of William Collins. Many of the townsfolk did not understand the connection between the Archbishop's commentary and the death of their vicar excepting that they knew justice could be swift. This they had learned from years of being subjected to the inexhaustible righteousness of Lady Catherine de Bourgh.

The villagers from Hunsford and the tenants of Rosings Park were also keen to observe the man who was now widely known to be Anne de Bourgh's heir. Much good was generally known of Colonel Fitzwilliam, but speculation circulated swiftly as to whether or how soon he would resign his commission and take up residence in his inherited estate. Or would he spend much of his time in the de Bourgh London establishment hunting for a wife? There was chatter about his connection to one, perhaps even two, of the ladies visiting at the vicarage, but nothing substantial was confirmed.

Therefore, it was an interesting addition to the spectacle when the two Bennet sisters and Mrs. Collins's young sister arrived in the churchyard to witness the burial. These young ladies wore dark grey gowns and stood with their respective fathers, maintaining demure downcast expressions throughout the traditional burial verses.

It would not have been genteel for the grieving widow to make an appearance. The assemblage could not know Charlotte Collins was humming absently with a light heart as she oversaw the final preparations for the shoulder feast to honour the pallbearers, though half a dozen might suspect her true sentiments.

Mr. Bennet and Sir William Lucas turned away with their daughters and were the first to leave the cemetery. Bingley and the colonel fell in on either side of Darcy for the brief walk to the vicarage after seeing the Archbishop on his way.

Bingley rubbed his shoulder and moved his arm as though discomfited.

"Not made for such work?" the colonel enquired.

"No, nor do I wish to become so. I prefer fencing and riding to lifting weights for exercise. I say, Darcy…" Bingley hesitated. "Might I have a word with you later this afternoon or this evening…soon?"

The colonel leaned around Darcy to add, "Bingley, if you are going to speak of what you mentioned to me earlier, I would join you."

Darcy stopped. "I must complete the arrangements for our aunt's burial tomorrow. But it is a simple affair, so perhaps over port this evening?"

"That will suit," Bingley affirmed. He strode ahead to reach the Bennets.

Darcy glanced at his cousin. "And Bingley's subject?"

The colonel shook his head. "I shall not speak of it now and will only say that our first thought is to spare you any further dismay, Cousin." He patted Darcy on the back.

"You make an ominous start for one who will not speak of 'it,' whatever 'it' might be."

The colonel only shook his shoulders in an apologetic shrug. "Then I shall distract you with this: George Wickham was the father of Anne's baby. I have the earlier volume from Mrs. Collins."

Darcy stopped dead still. He closed his eyes, opened them, and schooled his countenance into its usual sanguinity. "I suspected as much. It all makes perfect sense except for calling him Mr. C."

"Mr. Charming..."

"Ah. Of course."

The cousins continued their journey.

"But what you and Bingley have to say is worse than this?" Darcy asked as they neared the fence of the vicarage garden.

"I have said all I shall say for the present."

THE GATHERING IN THE HUNSFORD VICARAGE WAS AT FIRST A CRUSH. MR. Collins had been so enamoured of his patroness that he had overlooked the social obligations most vicars and their wives view as part and parcel of their charge as leaders of their Christian flock. Charlotte understood her husband's failing but had not sought to redress it, assuming instead that the deficiency would sort itself with time. Hence, the great curiosity to see the improvements to the house boasted of by Lady Catherine was no surprise to Charlotte.

Maria and Jane served coffee and tea. Elizabeth assisted Charlotte with greeting guests and seeing to everyone's comfort, for she had now been in the country some weeks and was generally known as a particular friend of the vicarage household and a pleasant if temporary addition to the neighbourhood.

Most of the townsfolk did not stay above half an hour, enough time to partake of the food, bow to Colonel Fitzwilliam, peer at the lofty Mr. Darcy and his pretty but shy sister, and wonder at the absurd enchantment Mr. Collins had expressed for the rather unexceptional features of the dwelling's interior. The stairway in the main hall was no more perfectly situated than any stairway in any other home of middling means. The arrangement of the book room at the front of the house merely revealed Mr. Collins had been the busybody they all suspected him to be. Surely, anyone wishing to close themselves up with books would have preferred the lady of the house's charming sitting room at the rear of the building. Their inquisitiveness slaked, they departed believing that William Collins had been, in truth, as thoroughly pretentious as he had seemed whilst alive.

The Rosings and Hunsford parties were soon left to themselves in the best sitting room. Bingley conversed with Jane as she placed the tea service upon a tray held by Nell. Charlotte and Sir William sat with the colonel and Georgiana. Mr. Bennet was near to them but contributed only the occasional sage nod or sardonic smile. His attention was more involved with the faltering attempts at conversation between Mr. Darcy and Elizabeth.

Darcy cleared his throat. "Miss Elizabeth, are you surprised at the curiosity of the villagers?"

"Not at all, sir. I am perhaps most astonished that more of the Rosings tenants did not attend. Surely, they might wonder at how the dowager mistress of Rosings spent the funds they laboured to produce for her. Charlotte said no more than half of them were present."

"I hope they do not think my cousin will be so unappreciative a taskmaster as was my aunt."

"That may be, but I believe they did not care for Mr. Collins and wished to avoid the appearance of falsely honouring him in death. More than once, he was heard to admonish them to acquiesce to every demand of her ladyship."

"I know my aunt was unnecessarily officious in asserting herself into the lives of her tenants. I hope they will see she was an aberration in the family. The trust between master and tenants is a highly valued commodity. Much depends upon it. The Fitzwilliam name will have much to answer for, but the sense and amiability of my cousin will bring it all to rights, especially if he marries well..." Darcy looked at Elizabeth closely, hoping against his own wishes for some indication of her feelings for the colonel.

Elizabeth met Darcy's questioning gaze without expression then lowered her eyes. "Indeed, to be attached to such a family is not the feather in a lady's cap it once was, at least for the present. One can say of *my* family, Mr. Darcy, that whatever our other follies and weaknesses may be, at least there are no murderers in it. No one remarked on Mr. Collins's buffoonery more than I—excepting perhaps my father—but my cousin did not deserve to die. He was unjustly accused; his judge and jury were *not* impartial, and they were wholly misinformed.

"And I am not insensible to the great detriment to one's understanding when one is misinformed and then acts upon falsehoods without first learning the truth." Elizabeth cleared her throat, which had tightened as she spoke, glanced at her father before venturing to meet Darcy's sad eyes, and stood to make her excuses.

Neither Darcy nor Mr. Bennet knew what to make of her hasty retreat, but Darcy's dejected confusion was noticed by Mr. Bennet.

*The same day, after dinner, Rosings*

SINCE THERE WERE NO OTHER LADIES IN THE ROSINGS PARTY AND NONE included at dinner, Georgiana took the liberty of taking a tray in her rooms, leaving the men to themselves. Thus, Darcy, Bingley, and Colonel Fitzwilliam were still at the table in the family dining room, blessedly far removed from the small summer breakfast parlour, when the butler, knowing the men to be idle, brought the evening post.

Both Bingley and the colonel were quietly relieved to put off their discussion with Darcy for a few moments longer and welcomed the distraction. As the new master of the manor, the colonel was handed the salver, and he sorted the letters to their recipients. Bingley had a letter from Caroline, forwarded from the Hursts' London residence. She was not yet aware of his location, only that he was somewhere with Darcy. He read her scolding with amusement, recalling the great sensation of liberation that had accompanied Darcy's original offering of an alternative to Bath.

Darcy had a letter from his steward urging his master northward for the spring planting, hiding his concern under a carefully worded veneer of politeness. The second letter he read was from Mrs. Annesley and elicited a more energetic response.

"Bloody hell! Damn the woman!" Darcy was on his feet.

Bingley and the colonel waited in shock for an explanation.

"From Mrs. Annesley. It is her resignation." Darcy began to read as he paced. "*It has come to my attention that some evil tendencies dwell in the Fitzwilliam family, and a lady in my position cannot be too careful of her reputation. The news of the crimes of Lady Catherine de Bourgh to murder a man of the cloth and the questionable death of her daughter, with whom I had understood Mr. Darcy to be betrothed, lead me to sever my connection with Miss Georgiana. I apologise for the necessarily precipitous nature of my actions, but I have found another situation and shall be removed from Miss Darcy's establishment in London well before her return."*

The colonel huffed in anger. "I suppose this is what we are to expect now with the gossip spreading faster than our steeds can gallop. My father writes he will not join us for the burial and will not wear an armband. How will that look?" He waved the fine paper held in his hand.

"I suppose it will be impossible to find a new companion for Georgiana. If only..." Darcy stopped himself. *If only Elizabeth had accepted me, Georgie would have an estimable sister and no need for a companion.*

The colonel muttered something unintelligible and glanced under his lashes at Bingley, who did not return his look. Bingley coughed into his hand.

"Darcy..." the colonel began with no little trepidation. "As regards Elizabeth Bennet..."

Darcy flung himself back into his chair. "I was not aware we *were* regarding Elizabeth Bennet."

"Admit it, man," Bingley was moved to comment, "you cannot manage to spend a quarter hour without regarding her."

"What of it?" Darcy glared. "We cannot all be as lucky in love as you, Bingley."

"Well *someone* has been lucky with Miss Elizabeth, Darcy." The colonel spoke in a quiet, serious tone.

"What? Has she accepted you? When did you make an offer?" Darcy was incredulous.

"I have not offered for her, but she has accepted someone. Bingley and I have both seen evidence. On separate occasions we have found her in the groves of the park, reading letters and wearing a little ring."

"I am sorry to say it, Darcy, but it did appear to be a betrothal ring," Bingley explained quietly. "I surprised her this morning. When I greeted her, she blushed and tucked a letter in her reticule, and I could see her struggle to remove the ring to her pocket as if I would not see."

The colonel added, "When I saw her with it, she described wearing it as some 'girlish silliness.' But now Bingley has seen the same thing. The man in question must not have yet solicited the blessing of Mr. Bennet, else she would wear it in company, but she clearly has expectations." He paused before lowering his voice to utter a sincere, "I am sorry, Darcy."

Darcy looked at his companions, from one countenance to the other. It was rare to be the object of pity, and he did not like it. "You are quite certain? But you have no idea who?" He attempted to maintain a firm voice.

"No notion at all," Bingley said. "And she is keeping her own counsel. Jane was as thrown as I when I asked her. Their father brought no letters..."

"And in any case, I saw her wearing the ring and reading a letter before Mr. Bennet arrived," the colonel concluded.

The room was quiet for some minutes. At last, the elderly butler entered, asking whether the gentlemen would take port or brandy in the library, study, or billiard room.

"Bring at least a gallon of brandy here, if you would be so kind, Abernathy," the colonel sighed.

There was a last letter upon the salver that carried the post. It was from Messers. Phawcett and Drippe, attorneys in London. The colonel read it through and announced, "We are summoned to the reading of our aunt's Last Will and Testament on Thursday at eleven o'clock at Mr. Steventon's office. One of her solicitors will be present."

Darcy shook his head with exasperation.

When Bingley took his leave, the two cousins were left alone. There was an uncomfortable silence before Darcy also stood to say goodnight. With a pained expression, he turned back to his cousin before closing the dining room door. "You have no clue, Alex?"

Looking equally pained, the colonel asked, "Wickham?"

Darcy reddened. "No. No, I am certain he is not, and never was, a temptation on her side. Miss Elizabeth and I have struck a tenuous friendship. Together we convinced her father to cut any Bennet family relations with the man. No, not Wickham."

The colonel shrugged. "I am at a loss. It did seem that one of us should have her..."

Darcy trudged to his rooms and sent Stafford away immediately, eschewing a bath or any other service. He sat before the fire until it was reduced to embers, and only when the room was nearly dark did he undress and slip naked into his bed. Although he had not imagined he would sleep, as his eyes grew heavy, he reached a hand across the bed to the woman who was not, and never would be, there to take it. As Morpheus embraced him, the arms could have been Elizabeth Bennet's.

*15 December 1811*

*My charming consort insists upon regaling me with tales from the wilds of Hertfordshire. Much as I hate to admit it, he is occasionally amusing. The militia has settled in and ingratiated itself with the local populace. They are invited everywhere. It seems my mother's vicar has selected a bride, described by Wickham as a plain but intelligent woman, nearly a spinster. I had to ask, "How intelligent could she be?" and for once we shared a laugh. It is no small coincidence that Wickham finds himself in the same neighbourhood where Mr. Collins will inherit a modest estate, and we have remarked upon it more than once.*

*Wickham further reports there are now two ladies in the place who tempt him. One he describes as exceedingly comely and spirited, though not so wild as the two youngest daughters of some family who are allowed to chase officers morning, noon, and, one presumes, night. The lady he calls "Bouncing Bess"—he says, "Her titties jounce in a most appealing manner when she dances. I'd like to stuff my face between them."—is generally well regarded throughout Meryton but is of little fortune. Learning this was a great disappointment to him. He does not pursue her but has settled for a chaste friendship, much as he desires to bed her. But is that not his response to any woman who is fair of face or who boasts of a fortune?*

*The newer lady is a recently minted heiress, Miss Mary King, and Wickham intends to pursue her. She has been away with relations in Liverpool, but she was brought home when her mother's father died and left her in possession of a small fortune. She stays with an uncle as her mother is unwell and likely to die soon.*

*As an amusement, I informed Wickham he might call me Mary at his moments of urgency. This also made him laugh. We then got ourselves to our usual business...at least I have grown accustomed to it although I still wish the necessity to be acquainted with such a man, let alone allow him these liberties, would come to an end. —A de B*

*Wednesday, 22 April 1812*

Colonel Fitzwilliam set out early to tour what he now endeavoured to think of as *his* park. If he could again catch Elizabeth Bennet with a letter and her ring, she would not find him so willing to pass off the issue. For Darcy to have any peace, the truth must be known. It did not surprise him that his cousin was not out riding that morning. A great quantity of brandy had been consumed, and the colonel would stake his soon-to-be-abandoned commission that Darcy had brooded away some further portion of the night.

He wandered the glades and groves for some time before deciding to call upon the vicarage. It had been his intention that, upon his return to Rosings, he would send an invitation for any that were willing to attend the burial of Lady Catherine de Bourgh. Now that too many of the early hours had been spent prowling for Elizabeth Bennet, he determined it was better to present the invitation in person.

The colonel passed out of the park and approached from the side road, walking through the grassy verge to release its spring scent and, he hoped, soothe his spirits. He could see no activity around the side garden save the shapely rump of one of the ladies clad in a gown of black bombazine, bent over and plucking herbs. The ties of an apron accentuated a slender waist, showing the derriere to best advantage, excepting that it was clothed. He wondered idly whether it was Miss Bennet or Miss Elizabeth. The air was redolent of an herbal perfume from the bruised stems collected in the harvester's hand.

When he neared the low rock wall that formed the boundary with the road, his view of the backside improved. He stood for a moment in appreciation before he coughed quietly to gain her attention. The garden nymph stood. It was Charlotte Collins.

Her face was flushed from her exertions, and it became more so upon seeing the colonel. She nervously wiped stray locks from her face, for she had only stuffed her hair under a simple straw work bonnet with no lace cap. She curtsied as Colonel Fitzwilliam made a quick bow.

"Good morning, Mrs. Collins."

"Good morning, sir," she exhaled, having not completely caught her breath.

"The household is well?" The colonel was surprised at himself at the sudden call for propriety. All he could think was that Mr. Collins had been a most fortunate husband and likely did not appreciate it.

The colonel's decorum was amusing, and Charlotte's grey eyes lit with merriment. She would play along with his excessively civil behaviour. But after asking, "And those at Rosings are well?" she could not suppress a smile.

Her smile pierced him, and the colonel laughed. "Well enough in health but not in spirit."

Charlotte lifted her eyebrows and nodded, pleased to return to their usual banter and understanding.

"Today we bury our aunt, you see. That is why I have come. If you would care to attend us at two o'clock, we have a grave dug under the cedar of Lebanon beyond the conservatory. She did always hate the heat of a full west exposure."

Charlotte's smile grew wider. "I shall most certainly attend. It is the least I can do for her many kindnesses."

The colonel eyed Charlotte closely. If there was some irony in her speech, who could blame her? "You will tell the others? And there will be a meal afterwards. Perhaps the others will attend that if not the burial?"

Charlotte nodded. "My father and Maria leave us this morning." She waved the herbs in her hand. "These are for the carriage. But I shall give your message to everyone else."

"I thank you, Mrs. Collins," he said as he bowed.

"You are most welcome, Colonel Fitzwilliam."

Jane Bennet and Charles Bingley attended the burial because they believed it was the proper way to offer solace to their friends through a difficult day. Charlotte Collins would offer her heartfelt if silent thanks for being delivered in one stroke from her absurd husband and his overbearing benefactress. Darcy, Colonel Fitzwilliam, and Georgiana attended because they were obliged to do what was right. Elizabeth Bennet attended to offer forgiveness and to be in Darcy's company. She did not pretend otherwise. Mr. Bennet would join them for dinner.

Georgiana stood apart, and as the simple pine box was lowered into the deep hole, she stepped forward and threw a great handful of herbs onto the coffin. Her brother looked a question at her.

"Borage for bluntness," she explained.

There came a titter from everyone except Darcy and Elizabeth.

"What does it matter?" Georgiana asked churlishly. "She has driven away my companion, and it is put abroad that we are all touched by her madness. I shall never get a husband when I am ready." Georgiana had worked herself into a state of nerves. "Nor will you get a wife, Brother!" She glared at Darcy before turning to her cousin. "Nor you!" She burst into tears and threw herself at Elizabeth.

Elizabeth embraced the girl and allowed her to cry. Darcy could not make out what Elizabeth said to soothe her, but did hear something to the effect of the *ton* having a notoriously short memory.

Georgiana wept the only tears that day. Her brother started to speak something perilously close to a sermon, but after his first sentence, "Let us hope our aunt finds the peace in the hereafter that she never found on this earth," the colonel interjected rather loudly, "Amen!"

Colonel Fitzwilliam turned to catch the eye of Charlotte Collins, a glance that was noticed by Elizabeth and Darcy. Charlotte met the colonel's look, blushed, and turned away.

Darcy's quizzical expression caught Elizabeth's suppressed smile. She captured his eye and, looking from the colonel to her friend and back again to Darcy, said softly, "Will you be my ally in this?"

His dimples deepened, and he nodded. Charlotte Collins and his cousin would be an ideal pairing, and he was surprised not to have apprehended it sooner.

Georgiana, who was still quietly weeping in Elizabeth's arms, assumed Elizabeth's question was to her. "Yes, I am your ally." The girl stood straighter, wiping her eyes and returning her handkerchief to her pocket.

Elizabeth rolled her eyes, and could only imagine what Georgiana might have thought she meant.

# CHAPTER 17
## A Clash of Wills

*Thursday, 23 April 1812, Hunsford,*
*the office of Mr. Steventon*

Those who gathered not a fortnight before to hear the reading of Anne de Bourgh's will met once again in the establishment of Mr. Steventon. Sitting at his desk was the lately elevated, austere, and proper-looking Sir Chauncey Phawcett. He did not meet anyone's eye and fussed nervously with a thick stack of papers in front of him. The magistrate from Sevenoaks was also in attendance.

Mr. Bennet sat against the back wall. His second eldest daughter was still a week from coming of age, thus he chose to exert his fatherly authority. The various questionable events and her dangerous proximity to a murderess gave him a distinct sense of unease.

Lady Catherine's abigail, Albertine, joined the august company. She smiled timidly at the garishly dressed Mrs. Jenkinson, who alone of the party was not in mourning. Her bilious green gown stood out amidst the black, dark brown, and grey.

Once the hopeful Albertine was settled in a chair near the window, Sir Chauncey cleared his throat to announce the beginning of the proceedings.

"Good morning." He did not look at anyone. "We gather for the reading of the Last Will and Testament of Lady Catherine de Bourgh. The good lady's will, as originally written, was a simple document, leaving all her worldly possessions to her daughter, Anne. However, since Miss de Bourgh's death and the subsequent reading of *her* will, her ladyship sent a voluminous series of codicils to our London office." The attorney at last glanced up to his silent audience, a growing blush upon his cheeks.

Colonel Fitzwilliam wondered idly whether the man had taken strong drink to produce such a flush to his countenance.

"As may be seen," Sir Chauncey patted the documents in front of him, "Lady Catherine made many amendments to her wishes, I shall read only the most immediate and inclusive of these, as one codicil seemed to supersede the rest. *'I, Lady Catherine Martha Fitzwilliam de Bourgh, being of sound mind and body, leave all of my worldly goods, the de Bourgh jewels, and the estate of Rosings Park to my faithful and devoted lady's maid, Miss Bertha Donald.'*"

There was a massed audible inhale of breath throughout the room, and Albertine gave a little shriek of glee. "I knew it! She were a lady of her word, was her ladyship!" Albertine stood triumphantly. "She said I would be wondrously rewarded, she did, for finding Miss Anne's journal."

Mr. Steventon spoke up, as though to a child, "Yes, well, my dear Miss Donald, not all is as it seems. Please resume your seat. We are not finished here."

Looking contrite, Albertine sat.

"Unless I am much mistaken, Lady Catherine gives what is not hers to bestow," the colonel grumbled under his breath.

"Quite," Mr. Steventon nodded.

"If I might continue..." Sir Chauncey said. *"It is apparent from my daughter's spurious and faulty will that she was not in her right mind at any time during the period when her will was drawn and amended. Therefore, all of her estate remains in my charge, and I do hereby nullify all her bequests. And, because her named heir to the de Bourgh jewels has passed away due to a sudden illness, their ownership would revert to me in any case."*

Elizabeth coloured. "I do not understand; I have escaped her. What will be the disposition of the jewels?" Elizabeth cared not a jot for any but her pink diamond ring. She feared she must return it to its rightful owner if whoever that was could be determined.

"Right you should ask, miss," said Albertine. She stood again with new haughtiness. "He just *said* they are to be mine!"

Mr. Steventon again affixed the maid with a disapproving eye. "Please, Miss Donald, be seated." He did not raise his voice, but spoke with a pointedness that would brook no argument. Then more gently, "Miss Bennet, I believe all will be made clear to you shortly."

"Certainly, sir," Elizabeth said.

Sir Chauncey resumed reading: *"My late nephew, Colonel Alexander Richard Fitzwilliam..."*

"Late?" The colonel coughed in shock. "Great God! Did she mean to kill us all?"

"Ahem." Sir Chauncey had gone crimson to the tips of his ears. "If I may... *'My late nephew was, in life, of no fit inclination, by nature or ability, to see to an estate of the magnitude of Rosings Park...'"*

"What cheek..." muttered the colonel.

"Quite," rejoined Mr. Steventon.

*"... And the heir of my other lately deceased nephew, Mr. Fitzwilliam George Darcy, is my niece and not yet of age."*

"Ah," Darcy murmured, "I am pleased to have such excellent company in my fate. Purgatory will not want for entertaining conversation or an excellent dance partner." Darcy's dimples emerged. Although he did not look up, he peeked at Elizabeth from the corner of his eye then at the colonel.

Elizabeth was at first alarmed that Lady Catherine had plotted an ill fate for Darcy, but at his equable response, she settled back in her chair, and the corners of her mouth quirked.

"I seem to have avoided her tea and cake," Georgiana responded in a whisper to her brother.

"There is more," Sir Chauncey said. *"Because I am the obvious heir of both nephews, and they shared the guardianship of said niece, Miss Georgiana Darcy, I leave her guardianship to my brother, the Right Honourable Earl of Matlock, to whom it should have been left in the first place, as events have proven."*

"Of all the abominable..." Darcy reached for his sister's hand.

*"As to the living of the parish of Hunsford, which has fallen open with the passing of the reprobate William Collins, in whom I was most scandalously misled, if I have not elevated a candidate to that position already, I bestow the responsibility for the souls under my charge to Mr. George Wilkins, who had been considered for Vicar of Hunsford in July of 1811."*

"Wickham!" Charlotte and Elizabeth hissed as one.

Sir Chauncey stared at the two ladies a long moment before adding, "Every effort was made to find this Mr. George Wilkins, but to no avail."

"It was the assumed name of a vengeful, despicable man," Elizabeth explained with some heat. "You will find him parading amongst the officers in a militia quartered in Hertfordshire. I would be pleased to provide you with the imposter's direction."

Darcy's lowered head cast a sidelong glance at his cousin. He received a subtle nod of acknowledgement in return.

"Ah, this explains why our investigators could find no trace of the man at the direction provided by her ladyship. We have his last known address at the boarding house of a Mrs. Felicity Younge in London, where no such person has ever been registered."

"Oh!" Georgiana raised a hand to her mouth.

*"It may be seen by this, my Last Will and Testament, that I seek to nullify and redress the errors of my daughter, Anne. It is well known that she suffered uncommonly ill health in both body and mind, which was due, I remain convinced, to the perfidy and want of family feeling by my late nephew Darcy, whose selfishness led directly to her wasting death of a broken heart."*

Sir Chauncey looked up, clearly mortified to be reading what his office would not allow him to avoid. "And so she concludes her final codicil. A fair and witnessed copy of this document is provided to the magistrate of Sevenoaks to assist in his investigation of her ladyship's…um… exploits before and at the time of her death." The papers were passed to the magistrate.

The room was silent for but a moment before the sound of soft laughter was heard. Its source was Charlotte Collins. The colonel joined in her amusement, and soon all were chuckling, even Mr. Steventon.

Only Sir Chauncey Phawcett, the magistrate, and Albertine remained sober. For his part, Sir Chauncey was embarrassed beyond expression to have been a party to the machinations of such a woman as Lady Catherine de Bourgh.

"Here…what's all this then?" Albertine demanded.

Sir Chauncey acknowledged his colleague. "Neither Mr. Steventon, nor anyone else, has any reason to question the Last Will and Testament of Miss Anne de Bourgh. Although I have been given to understand her morals in the last months of her life did not strictly reflect Christian values, she broke no laws but God's. Given the will of her father and that she was above the age set forth in that document to inherit his estate with no prejudice or entailment, her will is perfectly legal."

"So I am to get nothing? Not a farthing?" Albertine's voice rose in outrage.

Charlotte turned to her. "Miss Donald, are you married to Malcolm Donald, the footman in my home, or is he truly your brother and your relationship of a more unnatural and unchristian nature? You stayed under my roof once a week for the whole of my brief marriage, and Nell has confessed that you rarely shared her bed for an entire night."

Albertine sat with a thump, looking about the room for an ally. After appearing to consider her course, she drew herself up, affecting high dudgeon. "I'll have you know I am *Mrs.* Donald. Her ladyship would not countenance a married abigail. I know of what I am being accused, and I know when I'm being cheated." She stood again and pointed at the magistrate. "You must arrest them all! They have no right to anything belonging to her ladyship!

The magistrate smiled and attempted the kindly benevolence of one speaking to the simpleminded. "You must understand, *Mrs.* Donald, the largesse Lady Catherine bestowed upon you was not hers to give. Her husband did not leave to her the family jewels, the estate, or any of its capital. He allowed her to continue the running of the estate only until her daughter married. At that time, her ladyship would have been allowed the use of the dower cottage but never the ownership of it or any other thing."

"But Miss Anne never did marry!" Albertine rejoined.

"That is of no matter, madam, for Miss de Bourgh left a will of ironclad legality." Mr. Steventon defended his deceased client and puffed out his chest a bit, taking pride in his work on her behalf. "She was the legal heiress and of age. The fortunes of Rosings Park were hers to distribute as she saw fit within the law, and however unconventional it may be, her will stipulates nothing untoward."

"Well, I never!" Muttering and protesting, Albertine flounced from the room.

"So, sir..." The timid voice of Mrs. Jenkinson addressed Mr. Steventon. "Miss Anne's will stands as you read it to us?"

"Yes, madam. My unfortunate colleague was required to read aloud her ladyship's will even though it is wholly without merit and entirely unenforceable. Her ladyship had no legal ownership of anything she sought to bestow or withhold."

Mrs. Jenkinson fairly skipped from the room with a giggle of relief.

Those remaining stood and, turning to leave the place, beheld Mr. Bennet, the tears on his cheeks giving evidence to the bottled mirth he had struggled mightily to contain throughout the proceedings. Once meeting his daughter's eyes, he emitted gales of laughter until he could not breathe and had to be helped outside to take the air.

"Oh, Lizzy! My Lizzy!" he cried when he regained his reason. "That was the most delightful hour I have ever spent in the whole of my life. Oh, indeed, it was. That far surpassed our first dinner with Mr. Collins. You must tell me everything about Lady Catherine de Bourgh. Oh…that I never met her!"

"Those of us that survived doing so will gladly answer your questions," Mr. Darcy said.

Elizabeth turned to look at him, all astonishment to see the droll cast to his features before receiving another of his portrait-like smiles.

*Later that afternoon, the Hunsford vicarage*

AFTER A BRIEF CONSULTATION WITH CHARLOTTE, MR. BENNET EXTENDED an invitation for the party from Rosings to take dinner at the vicarage. He believed they would make an altogether merry party, notwithstanding everyone being in some degree of mourning.

The meal was simple with no footman to serve it—Donald seemed to have disappeared—but the company was so convivial that the sexes did not separate for long after the meal. Bingley's courtship of Miss Bennet was openly conducted, the colonel laughed with Georgiana and Charlotte, and Darcy conversed with Mr. Bennet for an extended period. Elizabeth sat near them but contributed little, much as Darcy and her father tried to draw her out.

Mr. Bennet could not be happy with Elizabeth's withdrawn manners, for such was not her usual wont. He observed her most particularly and noted he was not alone in making jests and comments in her direction. Mr. Darcy also vied for her attention.

When the evening post arrived, it contained a letter from Mrs. Bennet to her husband. Mr. Bennet sat apart to read it, thinking some parts might be diverting for Elizabeth and that he would read aloud anything of a silly nature. But he was not prepared for what he found. His agitation increased as he progressed through her misspellings and exclamations. With heavy finality he muttered, "Damn the woman!" He thrust the letter into Elizabeth's hands and fled the room. The door of the book room was heard to slam moments later.

All stared overtly at Elizabeth as she read silently.

*Longbourn*
*Hertfordshire*

*Dear Mr. Bennet,*

*I do not know what you can be thinking! You may find yourself in That Man's company, but we know from our true friend—whom you now see fit to chastise, that his attention is fickle—of Mr. Darcy's foul nature, and the whole neighbourhood here adores Mr. Wickham. Can we all be mistaken? I cannot think so! I also cannot account for Lizzy taking against our dear Mr. Wickham when he was always such a favourite with her. Perhaps it is her envy of Miss King, but you must tell her that Miss King was lately returned to Liverpools, and Mr. Wickham's engagement was found to be only on his part, for her uncle never did holy endorse it. Poor Wickham's heart is quite broken. Indeed, he had me weeping as he spoke of it to me, for he sees me as a replacement for his own dear mother. Do tell Lizzy she may return with a litened heart!*

Elizabeth exhaled with vexation and glanced out the window for a moment, huffing her cheeks to cool them before she continued reading. All watched her with great interest.

*In any case, you need not worry about his "unhappy influence" over our girls, or at least not for much longer, and not about Kitty (Mary, I am sure, does not care). The militia is to remove to Brighton for the summer, so when you return with Jane and Lizzy, only Lydia will remain in any "danger", as you say, for it is now certain she is to go to Brighton as the particulur friend of Mrs. Colonel Forster. Lydia says she much prefers Captain Carter to Mr. Wickham, so there is nothing to your worry.*

*The militia departs in a se'nnight, and Lydia is to join them a week later, once Mrs. Forster has set up housekeeping. I cannot think a week of slighting a man who has been nothing but a friend to our family a good plan, and I shall not speak against him. Indeed, I shall not!!!*

*It would be wiser, to my way of thinking, for ALL of us to remove to Brighton for the summer. In that way Lydia could remain with her family, and all the girls could partake of the enjoyments of the seeside. What think you? Is it not a good plan? I think a little see bathing would set me up for life!*

*I bid you conclude your business there and return home. We must get to Brighton and hope Jane can catch an officer, now that the entail is broken, since her hopes of Bingley are blighted. Perhaps Lizzy can make something of Mr. Wickham, for I do not mean to slight such an agreeable young man, and we cannot expect Lizzy to do any better!*

*Your wife,*
*F. Bennet*

Lizzy blew out her lips and felt her eyes swell with tears. "Oh, Mama!" she cried with more irritation for her mother than she had ever felt before. In an instant, Jane was by her side.

"What is it, Lizzy?"

Elizabeth's eyes darted around the room, lighting upon Mr. Darcy. She was humiliated and could not respond to his quizzical expression except to look away. Would her parents always fail her? She handed Jane the letter. "You read it. I defy you to find any good in it. How can she think to go against our father in this? Mama may be foolish, but she has never been wilful before!"

Jane finished the letter, shaking her head. "Our father has indulged her more than is wise. She thinks he is not serious, because he has never been before, and she does not apprehend our reputation is at stake. She means to get us all married with no thought to our future happiness."

A tear escaped, sliding down the side of Elizabeth's nose. A gentleman's handkerchief was thrust into her hand, and she unthinkingly dabbed at her cheeks. Jane put an arm around her sister's shoulder. The warmth of the embrace removed all defences, and Elizabeth wept bitterly into her sister's neck.

Jane looked up and whispered to Darcy, who had tendered the handkerchief, "Our mother will not listen to our father and will not cease inviting Mr. Wickham to Longbourn. And Lydia is to follow the militia to Brighton for the summer."

Taking in several deep breaths, Elizabeth pulled away from Jane, and saw the initials on the black-edged cloth soaked through with her tears, "FD." Her fingers tightened around the wet fabric. She looked up, blinking. "I am sorry." She pushed the handkerchief back into his hand.

"You have no reason to apologise. As you have said, no *Bennet* has killed anyone." Darcy made a brief bow, met her eyes with a serious countenance, and turned to leave the room.

Darcy stalked back to Rosings, almost, but not quite, as disheartened as he had been the evening when Elizabeth refused him. He was once again determined to write a letter, one he knew he should have written months previously when he first saw a uniformed Wickham speaking with the Bennet sisters in the streets of Meryton. He would send an express to Colonel Forster, laying bare all his dealings with Wickham. Doing so might not win the hearts of the Meryton populace, but he would make it known that Wickham was neither a man of honour nor someone to be trusted with a spare tuppence or a young daughter.

He had never seen Elizabeth so defeated. Even in this dire moment, she had been beautiful. Her sobs in her sister's arms rent asunder his very soul. There was nothing left within him save his love for her and a will do to the right thing above all else, especially if it would protect her family.

The front doors to Rosings opened and closed forcibly when the colonel entered some few moments later. "Are you writing to Forster?" he asked when he found Darcy in the study.

"I am." Darcy spoke without looking up.

"You will send it express?"

"I shall."

"Let me include a letter of corroboration. It will carry more weight."

"By all means, but make haste."

The cousins were just finishing their work a half an hour later when they heard frantic knocking at the Rosings entrance.

"Where is Mr. Darcy? He must see this!" It was Mr. Bennet, sounding winded and rather hysterical.

Upon being shown into the study, Mr. Bennet stopped to gather his breath. His chest was heaving. He had run all the way from Hunsford. "He is dead. Whatever letters you may be writing to make the case against Wickham are not needed. He is dead." He sat heavily into a chair, leaning forward with his head in his hands. An express fluttered from his fingers to the floor. He retrieved it and read it to the staring colonel and Darcy.

*Longbourn*
*Hertfordshire*

*Oh Mr. Bennet!*

*You will not believe it! It has all ended just as I said it would! The man was not to be trusted, but no one would listen to me! He has come to a very bad end, and to think I foresaw it all!*

*That nice young man, Mr. Chamberlayne, the lutenant Kitty so admired, had formed an attachment to the youngest of the Gouldings' daughters, little Alyse, only just turned fifteen. No one knew! It was all on his side though, and late last night Chamberlayne caught Wickham sneaking like a thief from her window! She had been vilely seduced by no one other than Wickham. This morning there was a duel! Although Mr. Chamberlayne was wounded, he shot Wickham clean through his heart! He is dead! And it is all he deserved!*

*I am so very glad our girls are better bred than any child of the Gouldings. Poor little Alyse is to be sent away to relatives to the north, somewhere around Newcastle, it seems.*

*It has all just now been revealed, and I hope you will not begrudge the expense of an express to tell you. I know Lizzy will be devastated! Tell her I am sorry not to be there to consoll her.*

*Your wife,*
*F. Bennet*

The astonishment was thoroughly felt by everyone in the room. The colonel immediately poured brandy. They drank to Mr. Chamberlayne's uncommonly fine aim—to have found a heart at all in his victim—and Wickham's health and safe journey into the fires of Hades.

*20 December 1811*

*My Mr. Charming must get himself back to Hertfordshire to court his heiress. He says she is a nasty little freckled thing. I must wonder what he says about me behind my back!*

*And I am full of consternation to learn Darcy knows Wickham is in the militia, for Darcy has lately been in Meryton, and I only now have been told their paths had crossed. It appears, so Mr. Charming says, that they came into little contact and avoided each other, but still, had I known it sooner, I would have bid Wickham transfer to another regiment at some removed place and not so far away from me. In fact, the more I think on it, the more vexed I become. I do not like to think of my purchased swain boasting of his conquest of Darcy's "betrothed" when in his cups where Darcy might hear of it.*

*It seems Mr. Charming's bouncy lady took a firm dislike to Darcy although he does not say why. Darcy and she met through various social engagements for, in a poor place, a daughter of a modest estate gains much importance. How very amusing to imagine Darcy in unknown company in some market town in an impoverished county. How he must suffer! But presumably he was there to visit friends, and the rest of it was a burden he bore grudgingly.*

*I feel bloated and anxious, and I am hoping these are symptoms of being with child, for I desire nothing more than for my liaison to end. —A de B*

# CHAPTER 18
## Pleasant Conversations

*1 March 1812*

*I have proof that the world grows more complicated, for what do you think? I do believe the friend coming to visit Mrs. Collins might be Mr. C's "Bouncing Bess!" She comes from a small estate near the Lucas family in Hertfordshire, and Mrs. Collins was a Lucas. Her friend is named Elizabeth Bennet, so she may be known as Bess, but no name is as mutable as Elizabeth.*

*Mama was boasting that the connections of the Collinses continue to grow since Darcy's arrival will throw them into the path of one of Derbyshire's wealthiest men. Mama's reaction to learning that everyone has already met him can be well imagined. I found it diverting and hard on me not to laugh. They will have to content themselves with the novelty of meeting the second son of the Earl of Matlock, Cousin Alex.*

*I have tried to remember all Mr. C has said of "Bouncing Bess" other than her pleasing physical attributes. I recall lively manners, self-confidence, a pretty face, good conversation, and she likes books rather more than does Mr. C. It all makes perfect sense; it must be her.*

*And if these clues were not enough, I heard Charlotte Collins whisper to her husband that she hoped "Eliza" would tolerate Darcy's company well enough since they did not get on at all in Hertfordshire. How intriguing! I shall not have to exert myself to like her, I imagine.*

*I am feeling quite well tonight though my breasts continue tender—but I own I am rather agitated by this news. It may take a little something more than chamomile tea to induce sleep tonight! —A de B*

*Saturday, 25 April 1812, the Hunsford vicarage*

"Lizzy, I would speak to you." Mr. Bennet waved his daughter into his late cousin's book room. Once she was seated next to him, Mr. Bennet took her hand. "Dearest girl, you are not yourself." He held up his other hand against her protest. "No, I shall hear no denial. The present tragedies are unfortunate but hardly the sort of events to put *you* in low spirits. What is it that weighs on you?"

Elizabeth briefly met her father's eyes before looking down at her hand in his and making a decision. *I shall tell him. He might as well be entertained by this. I am sure that someday I shall also be amused when I am healed by hindsight.*

She licked her lips and met his gaze fully. "I am sorry to report such a folly of myself, Papa, but I seem to have, quite accidentally I assure you, fallen in love. The gentleman I admire is someone I previously misjudged. Indeed, we all did."

"Yes?"

"Mr. Wickham was a dissembler of great skill, as Mr. Darcy has confessed to you, but I learned the truth of his character and his slanders of Mr. Darcy some weeks ago. In addition to having the particulars explained by that gentleman, Colonel Fitzwilliam has offered verification of every part."

Mr. Bennet spoke without thinking. "It is *Mr. Darcy* who has captured your heart?"

Elizabeth nodded.

"Are you out of your senses to be in love with this man, Lizzy? His family will never approve. You will never be welcomed. It is too great a leap."

"No, Papa, you must allow me to explain."

Mr. Bennet stood and began to pace, much as his second eldest daughter did when she was agitated. "Very well. You will get none of my usual mild torment. This is a matter of no small importance. Proceed."

"We have all thought Mr. Darcy a proud, disagreeable sort of man. His pride raised my prejudice against him. For all his wealth and position, he is not comfortable in company, and we all met him when he was at a decided disadvantage. He was afraid of being judged, and so was misjudged. But, Papa, all the time we thought he was looking at me to find fault"—she paused for breath before saying—"he was falling in love with me."

Mr. Bennet stopped and stared at her. She was serious!

"I admire his choice," he said, trying to lighten her heaviness. As he considered further, his aspect became graver. "*Was* he in love with you? May I ask how you learned of this?"

"On the Thursday after Easter, he proposed to me, and I refused him in the harshest possible terms."

"Say on, Lizzy, you have my fullest attention."

"His offer was ill-timed and, to be frank, rather inept. He was more eloquent of the degradation his position would suffer than of love, but his regard for me overcame his scruples. On the day he proposed, I had learnt he was, in part, behind the removal of Mr. Bingley from Netherfield, and once knowing that, I could never have accepted him, even had I liked him. He never dreamt I felt naught but contempt, but once I had started my refusal, I became unrelenting. I brought forth his dealings with Wickham. I dared him to defend himself…"

Mr. Bennet could see she was agitated and working herself into a state. He again sat beside her and took her hand.

Now it was Elizabeth who was too exercised in spirit to remain still, and she jumped up to resume the pacing her father had quit. "The next morning he found me on my walk and presented me with a letter. I know you will not approve, but he was adamant that I read it. He wrote to explain his actions as they affected Jane and to defend his character from Wickham's slurs. I know I should have refused it, but my curiosity was too aroused to behave otherwise than to read every word."

"Do you still have it, Lizzy?"

"I do."

"And who knows of this proposal?"

"Charlotte, Jane, and Colonel Fitzwilliam. Of them, I am certain. Mr. Darcy may have told Mr. Bingley once he arrived hither, but I can detect no such knowledge in his behaviour. He may have told his sister too, but she would never dare speak of it."

"They all know of the letter?"

"No, not Charlotte or Mr. Bingley, and likely not Georgiana. And no one knows every part."

"May *I* read it?"

Elizabeth looked alarmed.

"If a man has written you such a letter as to change your opinion entirely, I would like to see it."

"The letter did not wholly change my view of him. It is his recent actions that have occasioned his earning my good opinion. Every fault I found in him, he has attempted to improve. He wrote Mr. Bingley to invite him to Rosings once Jane had arrived. He has shown such depths of compassion, and although I know he can no longer love me, his forgiveness has humbled me and, sadly, inspired my affection. He is a good man. Intelligent. Forthright.

"Imagine it, Papa. He held me in the deepest affection. He would have made me mistress of all that is his; such was his confidence in me. Now that I return his regard, his cannot possibly be the same."

Mr. Bennet shook his head in wonder. "You must produce the letter, Lizzy. I would read it."

"Yes, Papa." Elizabeth believed he was right, and she hoped it would begin to change her father's opinion, as it had so effectively moved hers. "But there are parts that speak of his sister and must remain private."

'You have my word."

Elizabeth arose and in a few moments returned with Darcy's letter. "Please have a care, Papa. It has become fragile with my near constant perusal." Mr. Bennet smiled, and she withdrew, closing the door behind her.

Charlotte was in her sitting room toiling at her embroidery when Elizabeth entered and took up her own work. Elizabeth had only completed six stitches when the front bell was heard and Mr. Bingley duly announced. They wondered that he was alone, for he had called earlier for a walk with Jane.

"Oh, Mrs. Collins!" He bowed. "Miss Elizabeth! Is your father in residence?"

"He is reading a letter, and cannot be disturbed at present. It will not take long, and then he may see you." Elizabeth noticed that Bingley was nervous, and a light sheen appeared on his forehead. He smiled. *He smiles too much,* she thought. And then another more pleasurable idea intruded.

"Mr. Bingley..." Elizabeth met his eyes. "*Why* must you see my father?"

He looked down, and his cheeks coloured. "Your sister has accepted my offer of marriage!"

Charlotte laughed, and Elizabeth exclaimed as she bounced to her feet, "Jane! Oh, how delightful! Where is she?"

"I left her at Rosings. She returned to the packing in Anne de Bourgh's room and hopes you will join her."

Elizabeth scampered into the hall, laughing unguardedly for the first time in weeks. As she gathered her bonnet and gloves to rush to Rosings, her father emerged from the book room. In her joy and haste to share the triumph of love with Jane, Elizabeth had, for several moments, forgotten her own tenuous situation. She turned to join her father, gathering herself to defend her feelings and Darcy's character.

Mr. Bennet folded the letter by its worn creases and returned it to his daughter. "Elizabeth, my love. If Mr. Darcy regards you with this depth of admiration and *respect*, you may depend upon it; he cannot halt his feelings, much as he may wish to. In spite of any unkind and ungraceful sentiments you have expressed to him, this letter makes clear he requires your good opinion. And after observing his continued observation of *you*, I now surmise that he loves you still. If you persist in moping, he will, perhaps, assume you have not noticed his improvements. My dear, be of better cheer. Return to your lively manners. Tease him. Do those things that stirred his attentions. Show him your feelings are the opposite of what they were a month ago. You will not regret it, I think."

"Thank you, Papa."

Father and daughter gazed frankly into each other's eyes. Then Elizabeth remembered there was a guest in the house. "Mr. Bingley has called and awaits you. Shall I send him in?"

"Oh, yes, please. I have been expecting this." Mr. Bennet folded his hands over his belly and looked over his pince-nez at Elizabeth. "This is becoming a vastly illuminating and diverting day."

Elizabeth found Bingley and admitted him to her father. She felt Darcy's letter in her gown pocket. It was strange to think other eyes had seen it, but she was relieved in her heart; the whole truth was known by someone as dear to her, in his way, as the man who wrote it. After tying it with her ring and returning it to her reticule, she turned her steps to Jane and Rosings.

*Meanwhile, at Rosings*

Darcy was settled into a comfortable chair in the Rosings library in such deep consideration of the Shakespeare he was reading that he did not hear Jane Bennet's quiet approach.

"Mr. Darcy?"

Hearing his name spoken by a lady, Darcy jumped to his feet. "Miss Bennet!"

"I am sorry to interrupt your reading, but might I have a word?" Jane advanced a few more steps. "There has been a conversation to which you were not a party but that I fear might have been misrepresented to you."

"Oh?" He was bemused and turned to face her as Jane walked past him and selected a nearby chair. Once she was settled, he resumed his seat.

Jane cleared her throat. "Are you aware of a conversation between Mr. Bingley, Colonel Fitzwilliam, Miss Darcy, Lizzy, and myself?"

"Er...no. Should I be?"

Jane appeared surprised and perhaps a bit confused. "Oh, dear. Perhaps I ought not speak." She smiled gently.

*She smiles over the oddest things. I am glad Bingley finds it charming; I would find it irksome.* "But you *have* begun. Was I a topic?"

"No, sir. Pemberley was the topic. Lizzy realised afterwards that her words could be seriously misconstrued, and might be reported to you, casting her in an ill light. But it is not my intention to betray her heart, rather to explain it. She does not know of my intention and would surely stop me if she did, but she is with our father at present."

At her mention of Elizabeth's heart, Darcy's own leapt to his throat.

"I see...I think...that her opinion of you is changing, sir. I hope you have observed it?"

She had his fullest attention, but he could not respond to her question by anything other than a curt nod.

"We were discussing Pemberley as we had tea in Miss de Bourgh's sitting room. You are aware there is a magnificent painting of Pemberley over the mantle? Lady Catherine had it hung there, I was told."

This, at last, produced a brief smile from Darcy. *Poor Anne. I am certain her mother meant it as an inducement, a reminder of Anne's prize should she secure me. My poor cousin.*

Jane continued, "Your home is most impressive, and of course Lizzy has never been, thus she asked most particularly for details from the colonel and your sister. She was quite taken with its situation in the landscape and asked whether it was a true likeness.

"Lizzy was, I could see, quite agitated—very moved. I understood her even without the explanation she made to me later. We comprehend each other closely as I am sure you are well aware."

Jane stopped smiling and fixed Darcy with a most serious and knowing expression. This was the first time Darcy had ever seen a resemblance between the sisters, and he understood her meaning. Here, more apparent than ever, was additional proof of his grave mistake in dragging Bingley from Hertfordshire in November. Jane might not have the lively manners and ready wit of her sister, but she was intelligent and obviously observant with some accuracy.

"When Lizzy reflected upon that conversation, she feared that Miss Darcy and the colonel, who do not know her as well as I, might perceive her interest as mercenary—that she was regretting the loss of the opportunity to be mistress of so fine a home and such beautiful country."

"The conversation was not repeated to me. You need not fear, Miss Bennet. By the very nature of your sister's refusal, I know she is not mercenary." In spite of the heartache expressed with his words, Darcy held Jane's candid gaze. "But what do *you* intend by this telling?"

Jane's eyes dropped as did the volume of her voice. Darcy leaned closer as she began again at just above a murmur.

"That you were prepared to bestow all of it... all you own upon her... You loved her—perhaps you still do—enough to have made her mistress of such a grand place, a place she thinks beautiful, if only in a painting." Jane's eyes filled with tears as she expressed her sister's thoughts. "Until she saw that painting, sir, she did not quite believe...or comprehend...the depth of your admiration, of your confidence in her.

"But now she does." Jane's tears spilled down her cheeks, and she produced a handkerchief from her sleeve. "She *knows*."

Darcy's heart was so full—*Elizabeth thought Pemberley beautiful, and an image of it was more eloquent of my affection than my paltry words*—that he could not form a response.

After a moment of sniffles and eye dabbing with a handkerchief initialled "CB," Jane finished her belief. "I know her heart, Mr. Darcy. *I know it all.* Lizzy is generous and forgiving, and she feels her mistakes keenly. She is not as stubborn in her opinions as an impartial observer might think."

Darcy coaxed a direct look from Jane. "Let me assure you, Miss Bennet, that excepting at our very first meeting, I have *never* observed your sister impartially." *You, Jane, yes, but Elizabeth, never.*

Jane smiled a grudging smile, one she obviously did not want to make and rather different from her habitual serenity. *At last, a singularly genuine smile,* Darcy thought. *If Bingley has seen such a smile, then I understand him entirely.*

"Yes, so we have all seen," she replied, one eyebrow rising, completing an expression that made her look as much like her sister as she ever could.

Jane stood, and Darcy did likewise. "I have said all I came to say, sir. Probably enough to earn a set-down from Lizzy should she learn of it."

"I must thank you a dozen times over, Miss Bennet. You may be assured of my discretion. You have given me much to ponder. But I must ask, has your sister another suitor?"

"Why would you think so?" Jane asked with evident surprise.

"She has been seen by both Bingley and my cousin reading letters in the woods. Alexander said she wore a ring and was embarrassed to be discovered. Bingley said she hid a letter in a most secretive manner when he disturbed her."

Jane seemed confused and hesitated a moment before replying, "I know nothing of any letters. To whom would she write excepting our father? And he is here!"

"Perhaps the gentlemen are mistaken…?" Darcy asked hopefully.

"Perhaps. She has spoken of no one." Jane curtsied and Darcy bowed. When Jane reached the open hall door, she stopped.

"Mr. Bingley has walked to Hunsford just now, Mr. Darcy. He will speak to my father." She looked knowingly over her shoulder.

"Miss Bennet!" A warm smile over spread his countenance. "I am truly delighted. This calls for champagne."

Jane smiled widely. "No, sir. You must appear to be hearing it for the first time when Charles tells you."

Darcy laughed. "Of course. You are quite right. I shall attempt surprise."

"You may call me Jane now, Mr. Darcy. You are Charles's best friend and as close to a true brother as I am ever likely to have."

At Jane's departure, Darcy returned to his chair but did not take up *A Midsummer Night's Dream.* Rather, he sat and yet again contemplated his hasty and ill-spoken proposal. He had spoken too briefly of desire and passion, but being a maiden, perhaps Elizabeth would not have approved of his saying more. Knowing her now for another few weeks, he quite acknowledged the truth of Jane's words. If his praise had been needed, as was clearly the case, it was of her intelligence and abilities that he should have spoken. She might not trust his admiration of her beauty, given his altogether stupid comments in Meryton, but she could have no doubt of her capability to play the part of mistress of Pemberley with grace and vigour. She would learn any necessary skill she did not already possess with readiness and good humour. The tenants would love her and know they could depend upon her good sense as they depended upon his.

If circumstances ever presented him with another opportunity, he now understood what to say. Assuming Jane was as correct about Elizabeth as Elizabeth had been about Jane, and there were no letters from another gentleman, perhaps fate would grant him a reprieve from the dull ache that was his bosom companion since returning to Rosings.

After the space of a quarter of an hour, for such was the length of his musings, Darcy heard a noisy yet breathless Bingley burst through the front doors, loudly and happily calling for Jane—not Miss Bennet—simply Jane. A glimmer of happiness took root in Darcy's heart. Jane and her Charles: there would be a great marriage, just as Mrs. Bennet had so artlessly announced months ago. And, as she had also said, it would throw her other daughters into the paths of rich men. *Well,* one *daughter certainly—into* my *path.*

AFTER A JOYFUL CELEBRATION OF THE NEWLY BETROTHED COUPLE, JANE and Elizabeth sorted through Anne's gowns and personal effects, accompanied by Charlotte, who assisted in advising which younger Bennet sister might be flattered by which colour. Georgiana was able to comment on some of the gowns, identifying unusual fabrics and sharing shivering tales of shopping excursions with her aunt. Even with much movement to and fro, Elizabeth could not become accustomed to Darcy's portrait still hanging in the hall. She blushed each time she passed it.

After selecting clothing enough to fill four trunks bound for Longbourn and two poor boxes for Charlotte to distribute within the parish, there was nothing to be done but deciding the fate of the de Bourgh jewels. The pile of gems had not been moved from the careless heap upon the tea table in the bedchamber.

Elizabeth opened the velvet cloth. The multiple sparkling colours and gleaming gold danced before her, but she was unmoved. "Jane, is there any of this you would care to keep for yourself? Should we select some small thing for each of my sisters and our mother? Charlotte? Georgiana?" Elizabeth sighed with distaste. "Take anything you wish."

The four women stared at the pile and were of one mind.

"You are most kind, Lizzy, but I think not," said Charlotte.

"Indeed, Lizzy. It is yours to keep or sell. I have my memories of my cousin. I do not need a jewel for remembrance." Georgiana smiled and turned back to watch the packing of the trunks. She espoused a method of folding gowns that she considered much more efficient than the dictates of her late aunt.

Jane spoke quietly yet with great conviction. "I could never wear any of it, Lizzy, knowing how near these brought us to losing you forever. And I should not like to think of you remembering that day whenever you saw a broach or ring upon me, our sisters, or our mother."

"I want none of it either." She thought of her pink diamond ring. *It will suffice.* "We shall take it all to London and sell it at the jewellers to whom our Uncle Gardiner extends his custom."

*Sunday, 26 April 1812, Rosings*

"My cousin Darcy is an awful object, is he not, Miss Elizabeth?"

The Hunsford crowd dined at Rosings and was now spending the gentle spring evening together. Mr. Bennet had been left alone in the library, and the ladies and younger men were in the larger drawing room. At Georgiana's suggestion, all the ladies brought handiwork to occupy them for an evening of conversation.

The topic at dinner had been the travel many expected to be undertaking in the near future. In the morning, Bingley would send word to open Netherfield. Mr. Bennet would write to his wife with Jane's happy news, and he was feeling rather complaisant that he would not yet be at Longbourn when Mrs. Bennet received it. Mr. Bennet and his two eldest daughters would stop in London to visit Mr. and Mrs. Gardiner for a few days and see to the disposal of the de Bourgh jewels.

Darcy had silently vowed to remain in London as long as Elizabeth was in town before travelling with his sister and cousin to Pemberley for the planting. They would return to Hertfordshire for the wedding, for Charles had made an elaborate toast to Darcy during the betrothal celebration, insisting Darcy stand up with him.

Charlotte had promised Jane she would go to Meryton for the wedding before deciding where to settle. Colonel Fitzwilliam had almost immediately stated his hope that, although he had not such intimacy with Bingley as Darcy had, he might be invited to the wedding.

Elizabeth now considered what the colonel was saying of his cousin but did not raise her eyes from her work. "I would not say so, Colonel Fitzwilliam. Neither awful nor awesome, though at present, mightily bored." At last, she looked at Darcy and said merrily, "If you would care for it, sir, I shall shoulder the burden of instructing you in embroidery. Once the fingers take up the pattern, it frees the mind wonderfully to wander where it will."

Darcy studied her, basking in her gay countenance. *I know where my mind would wander…* Darcy thought, coveting the exposed skin at the base of her throat. Was there an enticing little mole upon the point of one collarbone? He licked his lips before realising he was staring at Elizabeth in a most impolite manner.

The colonel smiled at her. "I see you still use comedy as a defence, Miss Elizabeth."

Darcy was moved to her protection. "And more apt and clever satires are rarely created."

Elizabeth felt all the force of the compliment. "Indeed, sir, I would not wish to be considered a miracle of learning. I have no desire to be astonishing."

Darcy's head bobbed with a chuckle. "Again, madam, you express sentiments which are not your own. You astonish me rather constantly, and I begin to wonder whether it is by design."

Elizabeth turned away to hide a smile from him, only to have it beheld by her sister.

Jane cleared her throat daintily. "Are we teasing Lizzy? Surely that sport would ease anyone's boredom of a Sunday evening, Mr. Darcy!"

The idea of spending each and every one of his future Sunday afternoons, evenings and nights, pestering, annoying, and generally making a nuisance of himself to Elizabeth Bennet robbed Darcy of a response. It was his turn to blush and look away.

# CHAPTER 19
## Highly Satisfactory Explanations

*24 March 1812*

*I have eavesdropped upon a most instructional conversation between my cousins Darcy and Alexander. Mama grouses that they spend too much time in the billiard room, but I adore it as a place where they quite mistakenly assume themselves sub rosa. I position myself at the hinges, and the gaps allow me, upon occasion, to see the countenance of one or the other, a further amusement.*

*Upon their arrival yesterday, they were, as one would expect, almost immediately beset upon by the vicar, and Darcy, in a most interesting contrivance that gave the appearance of nonchalance while pushing Alex into motion, made to return Mr. Collins's call instantly.*

*When they returned, they adjourned to the billiards room, where their sole topic was EB. I was not surprised to hear Alex singing her praises as quite the most likely marriage prospect either had seen in an age. Darcy was quick to cry him off with the recitation, rather well practiced, I thought, of her poor connections and lack of dowry. This reduced Alex to an exaggeration of sighing and fussing, all the while teasing Darcy that he need have no such scruples, at least as to dowry. The following exchange proved the most intriguing:*

*"She describes you as her severest critic."*

*"If the lady has a fault, it is putting excessive faith in her first impressions. She takes delight in misreading me."*

*"Oh? She seemed to know the mention of her elder sister's presence in London would silence you, Darcy, when you finally condescended to speak. Are you and the sister at outs?"*

*"No! No, indeed. I hardly know the sisters except by observation. But I can never be in company with Miss Elizabeth without being grieved to the soul by a thousand fond recollections."*

*I was able to see Alex stare outright at our cousin, astonished at the revelation, I am sure. I know I was. Fitzwilliam Darcy of Pemberley, a charming boy now grown conceited, arrogant, disdainful, and burdened, has developed a tender regard for a poorly connected gentleman's daughter from a middling estate in a backward county—a clever, spirited, well-mannered lady with nothing to recommended her but herself. Were I a man, I would find her wit, face, and figure irresistible.*

*My breast fills with hope. Please, Darcy, fall in love with her, so blind in love you will not overthink yourself. You need a lady such as she to make a proper man of you. And if your affections are known to be fixed elsewhere, my freedom will be that much easier to obtain. —A de B*

*Monday, 27 April 1812*

DARCY WANDERED THE WOODS OF ROSINGS, LOST IN THOUGHT. ELIZABETH seemed to be friendlier of late with no ill effects from her near courtship by Colonel Fitzwilliam or from his defection to Jane. She watched the star-crossed machinations of Jane, Bingley, the colonel, and Charlotte Collins with the same detached amusement as did Darcy.

And yet, Bingley would persist on opining Elizabeth was lovelorn, and Alexander said the same. The two men, his dearest companions, were sure of what they saw. Charlotte Collins perhaps knew the truth, for her looks and manner often implied so if Darcy could muster the courage to ask her. No one could or would give an accurate accounting of the heart of Elizabeth

Bennet. *Perhaps I should speak to Mr. Bennet. I should ask permission to court her before they take their leave.*

Although he knew Georgiana to be healing from Ramsgate, the violence of so many deaths was simply too much for her gentle nature to bear, and it was time to withdraw to the safety and serenity of Pemberley. At dinner the previous evening, Georgiana insisted they return to London instead for Darcy to partake in the last weeks of the Season, but he wanted none of it. The balls, receptions, and frivolous entertainments held even less allure than usual, for he realised the events at Rosings would give others leave to slight him. He knew he would not meet a lady in town who would view with enjoyment the absurdities to be witnessed therein. He knew he would not find the next mistress of Pemberley in London. She was here in Hunsford. *Why pretend otherwise?*

Georgiana pleased him by requesting to commence a correspondence with Elizabeth, and Darcy was quick to allow it. Until Elizabeth revealed her heart's preferences, or she was truly betrothed to another, he would dream if not hope. Perhaps Georgiana could be persuaded to invite her new friend to Pemberley for a few weeks, or even a month, in the summer. Darcy shook his head. *Too much could happen between now and then; the past weeks are proof of that.*

He sighed. *Elizabeth Bennet*...had she come to care for him in a way that might develop into affection? He thought of Elizabeth's fine eyes at Anne's memorial as she silently asked him how he fared. He would take to his grave the smile she wore when Bingley arrived—a smile she had turned to him as they stood at their separate windows—enhanced by her shining tears of relief. Again, her tempting lips had formed a silent benediction, her thanks. After his aunt's burial, when he looked at all the players in the interlaced love triangles, only Elizabeth appeared surprisingly unconcerned. When he met her beautiful eyes, she was already gazing at him and asked in a whisper, "You will be my ally in this?" When her smile gained radiance as he nodded, he had turned away, fearful of revealing too much. He would be her ally in anything, forever.

Elizabeth sat on the beech stump reading, for perhaps the hundredth time, the letter Darcy had written her in the night after his proposal. She was in much the same position she had assumed when opening it for the first time, but her feelings were now completely the opposite. The letter, read first in anger and under the assumption it had been written with that same emotion, she now believed was as much a declaration of love as the words Darcy had spoken, and was, in most ways, much more eloquent.

*How could I have been so blind?* Only a man violently in love—a good man called upon to defend himself for love—could have written such a letter, which now, with the hindsight of multiple readings, she had come to regard as beseeching her to understand him, to bless him with kindness, to not think ill of him as her father had suggested. The letter confirmed the passion of which he had spoken in his proposal. This she now desired—a man who would feel a naturally flowing passion for her.

Her eyes stung, as they often did as she reread his heartfelt words, and she started to cry. She had squandered her chance and feared she would never stop mourning him, the Darcy who wrote this beloved letter, the Darcy who smiled so winningly in the Rosings portrait and had twice smiled in such a way at her. The little pink diamond winked at her, the token of a betrothal that did not and might never exist. Still and all, she was his.

The grove where Darcy and Elizabeth had walked several times prior to his misbegotten proposal was a place Darcy assiduously avoided. He now understood his presence had been a source of annoyance. He confined his riding to the east side of the park and, if on foot, stayed at the fringes of the meadows and pastures where he could be seen by any lady fond of walking who might wish to avoid him. Today he was distracted by his debate—should he pay a call on Mr. Bennet this morning?—and did not notice he was walking towards the bowered lane until he heard a woman softly crying.

Darcy approached the sound of tears, the mossy ground muffling his advance. He wondered who it could be. He knew well the sound of his sister's tears, and it was not Georgiana. And although he believed he should avoid the heartrending sound, he could not. When he was close enough to see the back of Elizabeth Bennet bending over a letter, her other hand dabbing at her eyes with a handkerchief, he was arrested.

Clearly, the unworthy cur—whoever he was—had jilted her, and she was crying over his betrayal. Darcy was instantly livid with the bastard who would cast her hard-won love so incautiously aside. *To earn her love would be a grand thing indeed. What scoundrel would have the temerity to disregard her affection?* He noticed the twinkle of the ring upon her finger, just as Colonel Fitzwilliam and Bingley had said. They were not mistaken. His heart sank into his Hessians.

Elizabeth stuffed her handkerchief into her pocket, not noticing she had dropped a page of the letter. It wafted silently to the ground. She sighed and sat upright, straightening her shoulders. She must accept he was leaving for Pemberley, and she was unlikely to ever see him this intimately, and for such an extended a period of time, ever again. *How he must be champing at the bit to escape so callused a harridan as myself.* She shook her head. *I was pitiless, cruel. He has done everything he could to make his wrongs right. What have I done to correct mine? Nothing...exactly nothing.*

"This poor letter is all of him I am ever likely to possess—proof I am the most ungrateful girl under God's creation," she castigated herself vociferously. "To make such a good man defend himself...and I called *him* arrogant!" She carefully folded the pages, drew out a ribbon, removed her ring, and slid it in place. When binding the letter, she realised the first page was missing.

Elizabeth stood, looking around fretfully. She picked up her bonnet, but she was turned away from the sheet lying in the grass.

Unthinkingly, Darcy rushed forward. "Miss Bennet! You have dropped a page of your letter." He swept it up and held it out to her. Now that he had overheard her pain, he would offer any comfort she might allow.

She looked discomposed. "Mr. Darcy!" When she reached for the page, she saw her hand was trembling but could not control herself. *Here I have always thought trembling an affectation, but I seem to be doing so, and I cannot stop. Did he hear me speak?*

As Darcy held out the page, he glanced at the writing. It was narrowly written with even lettering. *That is* my *hand!* He pulled the sheet away as Elizabeth grabbed for it. He read his words with amazement. *"Be not alarmed, madam, on receiving this letter, by the apprehension of its containing any repetition of those sentiments, or renewal of those offers, which were last night so disgusting to you."* He looked at her distressed face. His mind was whirling.

Elizabeth dropped her hand and looked down. Never had she felt more exposed.

"My letter..." Darcy whispered. "Why have you kept it? You should burn it." He turned the page over, noticing the paper showed evidence of being much handled and well creased.

"No!" She snatched it from his hand in a panic. "How else…" She stopped herself from saying more. *How else am I to know you once loved me? What other proof do I have that it was not just a dream?*

"How else…?" Darcy stepped closer, encouraging her to finish her query.

Tears reappeared in her eyes, and she looked over his shoulder into the trees, eyelids fluttering impatiently to halt the flow. She was determined not to speak as she believed it would only lead to further embarrassment.

*Is this the letter she has been seen to be reading? My letter? Has she regrets of me? Am I the cad who does not see she loves him? Does she cry over me?*

"Miss Bennet…" He produced a handkerchief from his frock coat under his linen duster. "Please." He offered it to her, assuming the one stuffed into her pocket was sodden.

When she did not take it, even though fat tears were sliding down each side of her nose, he turned mischievous. "You may certainly have this one to keep with the letter, something more of me…"

"Oh!" She looked at his spreading smile, which was so rarely bestowed on anyone. It was the countenance of a man looking with fondness upon someone he loved. He *had* heard. Would the smile turn mocking? She was cross and nervous and suddenly dizzy. She dropped her bonnet and turned abruptly away, sitting without grace upon the stump. "Wretched man!"

Elizabeth realised with a jolt that she had spoken the same words about the same man and had sat on the same stump once before, only now the man could hear her. "Are you happy to know that my feelings for you make me miserable? That we are now equals? We have, quite separately it seems, managed to hold each other in an affectionate regard just when the other could not reciprocate."

"Miss Elizabeth?" Darcy's smile turned inquisitive.

"Must I say it?" She stood from the stump, facing away from him. "I love Fitzwilliam Darcy," she said in a forthright voice. Then more loudly, "I love Fitzwilliam Darcy!" She gathered a deeper breath and stood to shout with great force and anger, "I love Fitzwilliam Darcy!" She cried to the heavens as if it would cast the feelings from her heart and soul.

Darcy stood behind her, his bare hands clutching her upper arms. To provide counterpoint to her frustrated exclamations, he whispered, with his lips at her ear, "I love Elizabeth Bennet."

She crossed her arms over her chest, resting a hand on each of his as he pulled her back against his coat, and she sobbed in disbelief. When she could manage it, she murmured, "But how can you?"

He kissed the crown of her head. "I know not. There is no earthly reason why I would still love a vexing, cruel, heartless vixen, a creature who has never shown a moment's kindness to anyone, least of all me, but there it is."

He was teasing her! It all became too funny, and she began to laugh through her tears.

"Since the death of your poor cousin, does it not seem, Mr. Darcy, as if you and I, and our families and friends, are trapped somehow in a particularly amateurish and rather ghoulish production of *A Midsummer Night's Dream*?"

Darcy laughed. It was a release of enormous tension, and the sound of his unrestrained mirth added to hers.

"Georgiana would heartily agree. You are always astute in your observations, Miss Elizabeth."

Elizabeth considered his words and stopped chuckling. She stepped away from his embrace and turned to face him, her chin high in defiance. "No, sir, with that I cannot agree. When *you* are the topic, I cannot get on at all. In taking your measure, I have been a great deal less than astute."

"Is *that* why you have kept my letter? To remind yourself I am a wretched man?" His eyes grew solemn.

"No, that is *not* the reason." She could feel the colour rising in her moist cheeks.

"I once said I would not flatter you, but I find I must. You are not like other ladies. You are quite lovely when you cry. How is it you prevent your face from crumpling? And when you blush, as I see you doing now...well, what man could resist you?"

"You could, quite easily, one night in Meryton."

"Very early in our acquaintance, I lost any ability to resist you. Since returning to Rosings when Anne died, I have fought every minute to regulate myself."

She turned away to hide a smile of relief. He *was* teasing her. Was he similar to her in teasing only those he loved? Dare she accept his whispered confession?

She drew herself to her full height and nodded her head. There was nothing for it but to be as truthful as she would wish him to be. "Mr. Darcy, there is something you have done for which I owe you my gratitude."

Darcy's eyes widened a little. "Gratitude for flattery?" He could not follow her thoughts.

"Gratitude for saving my life. Your portrait, sir—"

"I do not comprehend you," Darcy interrupted.

"The morning I first viewed the de Bourgh jewels, when your aunt meant to..." She stopped, took a breath, and continued. "What I am about to tell you lays me bare, Mr. Darcy. You will know it all, for you will soon leave, and I must explain why I fainted the morning of the murders."

He thought it odd... He remembered Jane Bennet saying something similar: ...*knowing it all*. Perhaps it was a family affectation. Darcy looked away, confused.

"When Lady Catherine was called away, she insisted I take tea and see the jewels without her... I would have too. I would have had a cup of tea and a slice of cake. But I saw your portrait, and it distracted me. In that moment, seeing your smile, it was as if you were smiling at *me*. I admitted to your image that my feelings for you had materially changed. I cried for all I had so wantonly, stupidly, thrown away. Your smile...I lost my appetite." She paused. "Oh! That does not sound as I intended it to! I mean, rather, um... I was very taken with your smile. Very. And then I knew myself."

They each made a particular study of the grass at their feet, suddenly too awkward to speak further.

It was Darcy who next gathered his courage. "Miss Bennet, it seems to me, in these last few moments, you have used some sort of arts or allurement to cause me to reveal that the desire and love I have previously expressed to you are undiminished. If you think better of me, enough to consider courtship and eventual marriage, if you have not yelled away all your feelings, tell me so at once. If you do *not* think you love me enough to tolerate me day upon day for the rest of our lives, then I shall never speak of this again."

"I...I cannot believe it. You *do* love me? Your whisper was not a tease?"

Darcy only nodded, his eyes pleading.

"That is why I kept your letter. I never had a love letter before. I did not know it for that when I first read it, but now I appreciate what you were trying to say. I was unjust—so needlessly spiteful. It was wrong of me. I was wholly mistaken in you. Yet you still love me?"

"I shall always love you." He was earnest.

"So I shall always love *you*, Mr. Darcy. I own I have come late to the fight, but now I know my heart."

He blinked a moment and held out his hand. "You are accepting me? Miss Elizabeth Bennet will marry me?"

"I have already accepted you. You will think me unforgivably forward." Elizabeth pulled the letter from her pocket, untied the ring, and held it in her palm. "That morning, when I was so enamoured of your portrait, this one little pink stone, of all the de Bourgh treasure, sparkled at me. It is the only piece to be saved." She took in a deep breath for strength. "As I left the hallway, I stopped before your picture and pledged myself to you with this.

"Is it possible for a lady to select her own betrothal ring, or must the gentleman always provide it?" She placed the ring in Darcy's open hand. She was astonished and breathless at the change in his countenance. His eyes were warm and his aspect thoroughly sincere. "Mr. Darcy," she whispered, "you are an irresistibly handsome man when you smile."

"Now that you have consented to have me, I shall always smile if it pleases my wife." He spoke softly, slipping the ring onto her finger. "Will you have me, Elizabeth?"

"Yes, I shall have you. Name the day." She felt a heat spread from his gentle fingers up and across her chest. She beamed as he kissed her hand.

"May I ask: what made you smile in the portrait?"

"Georgiana was there, tweaking me. Before Wickham's advances to her, she was a typical younger sister. She was no doubt calling me her 'bugly-rother'."

"I knew you would reserve such a smile only for someone you truly love."

Darcy kept hold of her hand, which he had raised to his face, and smiled against her palm. "She lost her confidence, but since meeting you, she seems to be…unfolding again. She is following your lead as I had hoped she would when I proposed in April."

Elizabeth inhaled. "Why did you not tell me so? I would not have thought so ill of you had I known you considered me a good example for Georgiana."

"I did not practice those addresses as I am sure was abundantly clear."

"Did you practice for today?" Her eyes were merry, and she was enjoying the way he held her hand against his cheek and lips.

Still smiling, he murmured, "No, Elizabeth, this all comes very much as a surprise." Darcy lowered his face to hers and drew her into an embrace.

Elizabeth's fingers on his cheek instinctively guided his lips to hers. She had wanted him to kiss her since seeing his portrait.

Darcy's hands caressed her neck, his thumbs rubbing her earlobes. He feared alarming her but did not hesitate to turn his mouth on hers, forcing her lips further apart and tentatively running his tongue along the length of her upper lip. After allowing himself the heavenly miracle of kissing her, he gently slid one hand to the middle of her back. He revelled in the sensation of her bosom pressing into his chest before giving her mouth a final taste and pulling away.

It was everything Elizabeth hoped a first kiss would be. He was gentle but insistent. When he pulled her tightly against his coat, she felt her knees weaken.

Their eyes opened and met. Silently, Darcy tilted his head with a devilish half smile.

Elizabeth nodded her understanding.

Darcy tossed away his hat, and they enjoyed several much longer and more thorough kisses as she moulded her body to his and, at long last, tousled his curls.

Colonel Fitzwilliam stood at a window in the drawing room at Rosings, absently sipping coffee and gazing down the long view of a sheep-filled pasture. Georgiana was plinking at the pianoforte in an irresolute manner, which complimented her cousin's mood. As he pondered sending the Rosings sheep to Pemberley—where the colder Derbyshire winters would increase their wool yield—and giving the meadows over to a herd of charmingly grouped cows, Darcy emerged from the west side of the park with Elizabeth Bennet on his arm. And not only was she on his arm, Darcy's hand was over hers, stroking it. They looked to be quite happily engaged in conversation and appeared more than friendly.

"Georgie?"

"Yes, Cousin?"

"I think I might be witnessing the solution to the mystery of the formerly lively Miss Elizabeth brooding so around your brother, and I believe her sadness is ended."

Georgiana crossed the room to join him at the window. As they watched, Darcy bent to plant a series of kisses upon Elizabeth's upturned face: first on her closed eyes, lowering to her nose, and then lingering on her lips.

"What can this mean?" Georgiana asked in surprise. "I knew he continued his regard for her, but he told me yesterday that he thought her to be lovelorn over someone who did not return her affection."

"Clearly your brother grew a… er." The colonel stilled himself from using a crude military phrase before his sheltered ward. "Darcy has developed the courage to pay his addresses again, and knowing Miss Elizabeth as I do, we can safely assume that this time he has been accepted."

"Wait. What are you saying? My brother had proposed to Miss Elizabeth *before*? And he said nothing to me?" She looked at her cousin in confused query.

"It is true, Georgie. During the week after Easter, just before we left Rosings, Darcy proposed and was summarily refused."

"But for the duration of our stay, she has always looked at him in unguarded moments with what I would call fondness," Georgiana protested. "And the day we had our tea in Anne's rooms and spoke of Pemberley, I would have said she felt more."

"Would you?"

"Well, yes. I am sorry to pain you, Cousin, but even as you were shilly-shallying about deciding whether or not to court her, she would constantly look to my brother with the utmost concern. Her first thoughts were not of you, but rather, she was afraid of giving pain to him."

"I know you are right. The night before her sister arrived, I had determined to talk to her about Darcy. I could never have married her once I believed she was falling in love with him. When Jane Bennet arrived and I had the chance to make a shameless fool of myself"—the colonel sighed, remembering how Charlotte Collins had frowned at him—"well, other problems arose, and Miss Elizabeth released any claim on me."

They continued to watch the couple in the park. "Darcy was furious with me and wrote immediately to Bingley."

As the colonel spoke, Darcy looked up at the house and saw the two figures in the window. He waved boyishly, took Elizabeth by the hand, and began running.

Georgiana smiled. "It does seem Miss Elizabeth is disposed to laugh at my brother as I have been told she used to do."

Rather than entering the house, Darcy and Elizabeth approached the window, and Darcy motioned for Colonel Fitzwilliam to open the glass. "She has accepted me!" he announced when his cousin and sister could hear.

Darcy showed her hand with its shining pink diamond.

Elizabeth was blushing with the knowledge that the colonel and Georgiana had most likely observed Darcy kissing her.

"Cousin, send a phaeton to Hunsford to fetch Mrs. Collins and Miss Bennet. Go find Bingley and bring Mr. Bennet. I am of a mind to celebrate!"

"Bit early in the day, is it not?" the colonel asked. He was surprised to find his inclination was to confer privately with Charlotte Collins about Darcy's intentions and Elizabeth's inclinations—what she knew and when she knew it. There was a no-nonsense precision about the mind of Charlotte Collins, which the colonel had come to appreciate nearly as much as his memory of her shapely posterior. The woman could be positively military in her manner.

Darcy objected. "It is never too early for champagne!"

# CHAPTER 20
## Preparing for Two Weddings

*5 April 1812*

*What can have happened? I still know no more than I did when Darcy and Alex left yesterday morning. That Mama is saddened and somewhat subdued by the loss of male company to lord over is no great mystery, but I cannot think why EB should be so. Yes, she still stands on her hind legs to Mama, but her eyes were not merry as she explained her travel plans, which seem so brave! But EB is anxious to leave our little corner of Kent as she had planned. The luxury of the conveyance that removes her matters little.*

*It would come as a surprise to EB, but I should very much wish to correspond with her. I sense a kindred spirit. I am certain her view of the world is not far from mine. To marry is not her first object, for I think very little encouragement on her part would have secured Cousin Darcy.*

*This is why I would correspond with her: she might make an excellent companion for me when I allow my little scandal to be known. It would soothe me to hear that her preference is for a single life, and she will need employment. It is difficult for a woman with no income of her own.*

*No, I must not allow her to depart next Saturday without managing some future means of communicating with her. I like her company, and if she will not have Darcy or Alex, I cannot suppose she wishes for any man.*

*I must finish my wine. My pains come and go but worsen when I lie flat. Perhaps I should pass the night partially reclined upon my chaise lounge. Or there is that divine tincture of opium from London. I am sure Dr. Roberts would not approve. As I float away, I shall pretend Mr. C is at me again as he was at our last tryst, for that always calms my nerves. —A de B*

*Friday, 1 May 1812, Gracechurch Street, London*

Darcy pondered being unsettled by the prospect of meeting Elizabeth's relations in trade. Was not the Bingley family a mere generation removed from their business? He imagined tradespeople grovelling after and discussing nothing but money. Further, it was generally supposed by his acquaintance that the merchant class constantly pushed themselves and their wares—whatever such might be—forward to increase revenues. And yet, his honesty must admit that every marriageable woman in the *ton* behaved the same.

However, today was Elizabeth's birthday. She was now one and twenty, legally independent of her father. Mr. Bennet encouraged him to take her to Gretna Green, and Darcy was not certain it was in jest. For her part, Elizabeth insisted she wanted no gift other than his attendance at the party in her honour hosted by the Gardiners. He decided, given the lengths of praise Elizabeth heaped upon this aunt and uncle, that it was better he stand aside and observe.

The Darcy carriage stopped in front of a lovely home that took up half the length of the street from a mews entry to a lane. It could be lifted and transported to any address in Mayfair and not be found wanting. Darcy stood next to his carriage as the Bingley barouche arrived.

"Darcy!" Bingley emerged from his equipage. "Allow me a moment before we go inside."

"Here, on the street?"

"We must be united as bridegrooms. Jane has had a letter from her mother, and she fears Mrs. Bennet will draw out setting any date for our wedding. As Mrs. Bennet has not yet responded to Miss Elizabeth's letter announcing your betrothal, I say we prevent any delay with a double ceremony. Jane is keen for it. My sisters think the idea indelicate. 'Country manners,' they call it, but I believe Mr. Bennet will agree. I would like to be married in a month's time."

Darcy clapped Bingley on the back. "Excellent plan."

*May 1812, Hertfordshire*

Netherfield Park was duly opened, and Bingley and Darcy were ensconced therein. Georgiana made quick friends with Kitty Bennet. Lydia was put out, and Kitty was delighted to at last be someone's particular friend rather than waning in her younger sister's boisterous shadow. Mary committed the deadly sin of envy when she heard Georgiana at the pianoforte, but with the influence of a book of sermons for young ladies and Georgiana's eager offer to play duets, Mary's misplaced pride in her own playing was gentled.

Darcy did, with great reluctance, depart for a week to the north for the planting. Georgiana removed to Longbourn for the time he was away. The travel to Pemberley was not so easy, and he was away nearer a fortnight than not. Still, he did not stay as long as was his custom. His steward, Mr. Belper, and his housekeeper, Mrs. Reynolds, completely understood his leaving almost as soon as he had arrived. They were pleased beyond measure to know a new mistress was on her way to them, and their master's light heart told them the future of Pemberley was to be a happy one. Darcy set in motion the restoration and improvement of the master and mistress's suite of rooms, which he had not done since inheriting. If the work was not complete in the three weeks before his return with Elizabeth, they would camp in a guest suite.

A mere ten days before the double ceremony was to take place on Wednesday, 10 June, Colonel Fitzwilliam arrived unannounced at Netherfield in a Rosings chaise and four. It was no hardship, as Bingley's family would not arrive until two days before the wedding, but the colonel's agitated manner led Darcy to suspect something was afoot.

That afternoon, Darcy called at Longbourn to take tea with Elizabeth and was surprised to find Charlotte Collins with her in the drawing room. Mrs. Collins wore a gown of pink and pale blue, and both ladies were beaming.

"Mr. Darcy!" Elizabeth hastened to him and he took her hand to kiss. She whispered, "Charlotte has told me the most splendid news! She and Colonel Fitzwilliam are to marry!"

The lady was blushing furiously as Darcy bowed over her hand saying, "My congratulations! Why are we whispering?"

Elizabeth told the tale in a low voice. "Charlotte is afraid my mother will accuse her of stealing our thunder, but she and your cousin wish for us to stand up with them."

Darcy could not recall ever seeing Charlotte so nearly undone.

"Will you, sir?" she hissed happily.

Darcy looked back and forth between the two women. Elizabeth appeared glad of the notion. He could not deny her even though he thought Mrs. Collins coming so soon out of mourning was at least *slightly* improper. Could it be that his cousin had done something to necessitate the expedited ceremony? *That scoundrel! I shall never let him live it down.*

"I would be honoured, Mrs. Collins," Darcy whispered.

Elizabeth understood the look in Darcy's eye. "It is not what you think, sir! Charlotte's parents are alarmed that she has overset her mourning, and they would challenge the reading of the banns. They believe she should wait six months complete. And to think they were so quick to marry her off to Mr. Collins! Now she will make a much better connection, yet they demand she wait. The colonel has acquired a special license, and they are to be married early in the morning on the same day as we are."

"How is it to be managed?" Darcy asked.

"I shall take one more walk to settle my nerves, and you will take an early ride, as you so often do," Elizabeth replied.

Darcy chuckled. "You plan to be nervous?"

"Oh, indeed," Elizabeth said with a low giggle.

Darcy laughed aloud. "Well! It seems all is in order, then!"

*Monday, 8 June 1812, the path to Therfield Heath*

All plans were in readiness, all gowns and other trousseau items had arrived, and Mrs. Bennet was growing tired of having so much family underfoot. Mr. Bennet had said nothing to her for a fortnight excepting, "No lace, Mrs. Bennet! I shall hear no more about lace!" But he winked at Elizabeth each time he said it.

Jane had gone to Netherfield to await the arrival of Bingley's sisters, leaving Elizabeth idle and fidgety, much to Mrs. Bennet's annoyance. "Lizzy! Have pity on my poor nerves and take yourself for a walk. You are a wretched creature when you are bored. Perhaps one last circuit of Oakham Mount?"

Elizabeth welcomed the idea. She had not been long on her way when

Mr. Darcy called for her at Longbourn, as he had not felt obliged to await Bingley's family. Mrs. Bennet explained where Elizabeth had gone, and Darcy was quickly after her.

As he was on horseback, it was but a few moments before Darcy found her. He could see by her determined stride that Elizabeth was exorcising her "wedding demons," as she called them. She turned at the sound of hooves and smiled with open delight.

"Mr. Darcy! Will you join me, sir?"

He slid from his horse, and before she knew what she was about, she was in his arms and being kissed in a most pleasantly ardent manner. "Oh! Oh, my!"

"Mmm..." Darcy made his usual sound of approbation before exercising due restraint. "Promise me you will always allow me to greet you thus?" His chest, amongst other things, swelled to know his kisses left her gasping for breath.

"When we are alone, most assuredly," she chuckled.

Darcy took the reins of his horse in one hand and Elizabeth's gloved hand in the other, and began walking down a different path. "We cannot go to Oakham Mount."

"No?"

Darcy gave her a sidelong glance. "My cousin is taking Mrs. Collins there." He wiggled his eyebrows.

"Ah. Well, no then." Elizabeth shook her head knowingly.

"Is there another pretty place you would see once more before I steal you away to London and then northward for a very long time?"

They walked quietly for a moment before Elizabeth brightened. "I know. I must visit Therfield Heath. We have missed the pasqueflowers in their abundance, but the heath is always covered with *some* manner of flowers. Perhaps we might go as far as Church Hill."

"Ideal."

It was a pleasant but lengthy stroll, during which Elizabeth was rather quiet. When they reached the heath, she led Darcy to several places where the prospect up the slopes was very fine.

"This is a beautiful place, Elizabeth, the loveliest you have brought me to yet."

She looked up at him with some question in her eyes. "Mr. Darcy..."

He tilted his head, curious about what she was going to say.

"Do you think…is it possible…"

"Hmm…?"

He dropped the reins of the horse and was now holding her face between his hands. Even though he had not removed his gloves, she found it difficult to remember her point. "Do you suppose your cousin and Charlotte have…?"

"Have?" Darcy fought appearing too amused. It had crossed his mind that, having already been married, Mrs. Collins would not be overly strict in waiting for her wedding. The colonel had intimated certain liberties were allowed, but despite the prior experience of both parties, they were still, by any definition, chaste.

Elizabeth sighed impatiently. "Come, sir, you know my meaning perfectly well. You do delight in luring me to say something daring."

Darcy chuckled but did not admit the truth of her observation. He did find titillation in seeing her innocent lips form words of passion. Since his ploy had failed this time, he settled for stealing a light kiss.

"Would you prefer to be *doing* something daring?" His voice had grown husky. They wandered into a copse of large shrubs, and the near privacy made him bold. He removed his gloves into his pockets.

"Mr. Darcy," she scolded. Still, she did not pull away when he held her again.

Darcy accepted her remonstrance as pro forma. He kissed her more thoroughly and allowed his hands to slide down her hair to her neck. She moaned when he pulled away, and there was nothing to be done but kiss her again. He knew he was allowing himself more arousal than he should, but her gloved hands were around his waist under his coats. If she was not ready to release him, what was he to do but continue? He knew she would stop him, and if she did not, he would stop himself…eventually.

But as it was, he opened his eyes and searched for the little mole on her collarbone. The dappled light of a greying afternoon made it a challenge, but at last, he touched it with his finger, gently rubbing a little repeated circle.

"I saw this little spot the other evening. It has rather obsessed me, the longing to touch it," he confessed.

The air had grown heavy, for the morning was warm. Elizabeth felt constricted as Darcy kissed her, as if her chest could not expand to breathe. She longed to open her spencer but feared he would see it as a willingness she did not intend. *Or do I?*

Darcy's kisses could not distract his finger from finding and minutely caressing the spot Jane called her sister's "beauty mark." Elizabeth was nearly mad with her body's response. She removed one hand from Darcy's warm waistcoat, and pulled away just enough to release the top frog closure of her spencer.

His kiss moved from her mouth to the corner of her jaw, and finally he nipped her earlobe. She shivered, and without a thought, placed her hand over his enticing finger, flattened his palm, and moved his hand over her left breast inside her spencer.

"Can you feel my heart?" she murmured.

"Elizabeth. Dearest Elizabeth." Darcy started to lift his hand. There was nothing he longed for more than to bare her skin, but he must not let things go so far as that.

"Please, oh please. This once. Do not stop." Elizabeth pressed his hand back to her breast, and he clasped her in a firmer caress. *How could he not feel the pounding? It will burst from my chest.*

There was a flash of lightning, followed almost instantly by thunder. Elizabeth heard the scream of the horse, and felt its front hooves stamping the ground before it bolted.

"Damn it!" Darcy cried.

They pulled apart. "I'll follow it; you go that way," Darcy ordered, indicating the opposite direction.

"What is its name?"

"Withers."

She choked back a laugh. "That is its name? It is named after a part of itself?"

Darcy shrugged. "Bingley…need I say more? He had a gelding named Fetlock when we met."

Darcy ran out of the copse as more thunder and lightning announced the heavy rain that began to fall a few moments later. He cursed aloud, and suggested to his God that the stable master at Netherfield be gelded too. Perhaps the horse would run itself into a wide circle and return. Darcy turned back to the copse, and in a moment, the horse reappeared.

"I should not have let her go," he muttered. He tied the horse to a branch and went to the edge of the copse in the direction Elizabeth had run. He could see her on the heath, hair falling in heavy locks, calling for the horse.

"Elizabeth!" He shouted and waved. At last, she saw him and began to return. He ran to her and covered her with his greatcoat. "Elizabeth, are you well?"

She did not speak but nodded emphatically.

"You are drenched, and we have come a long way. Let me sit you on the horse, and we shall ride back."

"Together?"

"That is the fastest way, and you must not become chilled."

Elizabeth said nothing more, and she made no resistance when he stood her near the horse with his hands upon her waist, bidding her to jump as he lifted her. He settled her sideways upon the saddle, and swung himself up to sit astride behind her. After adjusting the greatcoat to cover them both as best he could, he urged the horse to a canter. To go any faster was impossible.

She sat in his warm embrace feeling utterly bereft. Now he knew. He was marrying a wanton. She had lost herself to sensation. How she had ached for him. In truth, his hand over her heart had offered her feelings little release. She wanted more touching, more kisses, more untoward whispers in her ears. Elizabeth thought he would not notice her tears in the rain, forgetting he could feel her sobs against his chest.

He held her tighter. "I love you." He had to shout it over the rain.

*He is being polite. I have invoked his honour. How could he say otherwise? I do wish he would reproach me and be done with it.*

She said no more even when they rode into the paddock at Longbourn. Her mother and Mrs. Gardiner had been watching for them, and they came outside to assist Mr. Darcy.

Mrs. Bennet saw the look of apology from her daughter to Darcy, the fallen hair, the unclasped spencer. She gave a little snort under her breath.

"Elizabeth! Are you well?" he asked as Elizabeth was led inside.

"She will be, *Mr. Darcy*, she will be," Mrs. Bennet said with a knowing glare as the door closed to Longbourn.

*Tuesday, 9 June 1812, Longbourn and Netherfield Park*

The day before the wedding began uneventfully enough until Mrs. Bennet took it into her head to perform an inventory of Jane and Elizabeth's wedding clothes. Much of Elizabeth's clothing had been sent on to London or directly to Pemberley, as she would only stay in London for little more than a se'nnight.

In Jane's case, Mrs. Bennet had sent Jane's older clothing to Netherfield but kept the new garments under her roof. She did not quite trust Bingley's sisters—who were not so pleasing in their manners now that Jane was to supersede them in Bingley's household—not to take an unhealthy interest in Jane's trousseau. Mrs. Bennet was also uncertain of the loyalty of the Netherfield servants to their new mistress. She was wholly unaware of how thoroughly the amiable and unassuming Miss Bennet would be welcomed by the staff as Mrs. Bingley.

Had Mrs. Bennet considered the previous three and twenty years of Jane's life, she would have realised the real danger to any wedding finery lay within Longbourn's walls. Thus, by noon, the house was in an uproar over missing shoe roses.

"Lizzy!" Lydia burst into Elizabeth's room with a stage whisper. "Please! You are so good at hiding things. Put these away for me." Lydia imposed a pair of shoe roses of the finest, creamiest kid leather into her sister's hands.

Elizabeth stood, thrusting them back into Lydia's possession. "I shall do no such thing, and you will return them to Jane immediately." Although Lizzy was shorter than Lydia, she was a little hardier, and she turned her youngest sister by the arm.

Lydia stomped her foot. "I shall not! Why are you and Jane to have all the pretty new things? It is not fair!"

"Lydia!" Mrs. Bennet had heard the girls quarrelling and swooped into the room. "What has fairness to do with it? You have made Jane cry! When *you* are betrothed to a man worth five or even ten thousand a year"—Mrs. Bennet beamed at Elizabeth before landing a stern eye upon her youngest daughter —"you will have all the shoe roses you want. But until that time, you will stand by me and learn from the example Jane and Lizzy are setting for you."

Mrs. Bennet then took Lydia by the ear and dragged her away, squalling that she must apologise to Jane with Lydia loudly adamant that she would not. Lizzy sighed. The noise continued for an hour.

At Netherfield, the atmosphere was much the same. Caroline Bingley treated Darcy with as much deference as ever. It was to her brother that she applied to halt the proceedings.

"Caroline, have you taken leave of your senses?" Bingley cringed. They stood in the library, and she had just made the most ludicrous request she had ever expressed. "I shall not cancel my wedding to Jane Bennet. Why do you not apply to Darcy to halt his wedding to Miss Elizabeth? You needn't answer, I know why. Either he would laugh at you with that particularly derisive tone he sometimes has or he would be so provoked as to cut you forever. Do you think me so easily persuaded as to act against my own interests?"

"Charles, I would not attempt to persuade Mr. Darcy of anything if he is foolish enough to marry that little hussy. But your marrying her sister means I shall be constantly thrown into her company. Will you not spare me this torture?"

"No! I should have you fitted for Bedlam!"

Caroline followed her brother out of the library. She had not seen Darcy seated in a chair facing the window. The argument continued in the hallway, raising and lowering in vehemence until Bingley concluded he would send her to London immediately. Caroline burst into angry tears and said she would not go.

"How will that look, to be sent away from my brother's wedding?"

"How will it look for me to jilt Jane Bennet? You are lost to reason, Caroline. You must leave at once."

Darcy heard the whole of it and had a glass of brandy poured for his friend when Bingley strode back into the library after calling for his sister's carriage to be readied.

"I must make a confession to you, Bingley." He watched as his friend drained his portion in nearly one go. "When I so mistakenly warned you away from Miss Bennet, it was in part because of her family's want of propriety and connections. After your sister's exhibition, and having met the estimable Gardiner family, I see that I should have directed my warning to Miss Bennet, not you!"

Bingley laughed. "I appreciate your forbearance, Darcy. I believe the party for Miss Elizabeth's birthday was one of the most pleasant evenings I have ever spent in town. Did you notice the fond look she bestowed upon you when Mrs. Gardiner asked the nurse to remove the children and you would not hear of it?"

Darcy's countenance warmed into a smile. "No, I did not." His mooncalf expression changed to a tease. "Bingley, as my friend and future brother,

I expect you to alert me to any example of Elizabeth's affection I might perchance overlook."

"And I shall expect nothing less than the same service from you, although we know you are not so successful at reading my betrothed as I am at knowing yours."

The exchange quickly deteriorated into a cheerful squabble over which friend could more accurately sketch the character of the other's bride-to-be. It was nearly agreed they were both rather poor at it when Darcy revealed that the letter Bingley had seen Elizabeth hiding was from none other than himself!

"Now Darcy...how was I to know that?"

"True enough. To this extent you were correct: she *was* lovelorn, but she was pining for me!" Darcy puffed out his chest with pride.

Bingley laughed at him. "And thus Miss Elizabeth is shown to be less sensible than I thought!"

Their amiable dispute continued from there.

It was half an hour after dawn when Darcy saw Elizabeth from a distance, stealing into the church in Longbourn village. They had not spoken alone the day before, and he had grown agitated in the night that she might be cross with him for the debacle on Therfield Heath.

They stood together at the altar, equally nervous. Elizabeth was wearing a cape Darcy recognised as belonging to Jane, and she held it closed. Her hair was pinned to the back of her head in simple loops.

The vicar, whom Elizabeth had known all of her life, cleared his throat as he entered from the rectory door. "Miss Bennet, Mr. Darcy! Perhaps you might wish to marry now and save yourselves the effort of formal dress?"

Elizabeth blushed. "I *am* wearing my wedding gown under this cape."

Darcy laughed. "Alas then, for I have not brought the license."

"I have a license, but you may not have it!" Colonel Fitzwilliam entered wearing his dress uniform, ablaze in red with gold braid.

The foursome gathered in wait for Charlotte, and they were just beginning to grow uneasy when she peeked into the church.

Darcy and Elizabeth listened solemnly to the very words they would exchange later in the morning. After witnessing the wedding vows of Colonel Alexander Richard Fitzwilliam and Mrs. Charlotte Collins, they both felt much more at ease with making the same statements to each other. Elizabeth smiled sweetly into Darcy's eyes as she handed him the pen after signing the registry. His fingers touched hers and Darcy smiled in return.

"Now? Or shall we wait?" Darcy asked with a chuckle.

Elizabeth took his arm and turned him for the door. "You must wait, sir. Three more hours is not so very long, and I must have my hair seen to." She squeezed his arm before releasing him and hurried away on the footpath to the manor house.

Darcy saw the flash of eau-de-nil silk under the cape as she went.

"Eternity," he mused aloud.

Darcy and Bingley stood at the front of the little church in their best frock coats. The perturbation of one fed that of the other, and the two friends fell silent.

*It is not like Darcy to be so discomposed*, Bingley thought as he watched his friend twist his neck to and fro. He failed to notice his own bouncing from heel to toe.

"Bingley, be still!" Darcy whispered.

"Ahem, gentlemen…" The usually jovial vicar was censorious. "I believe your brides have arrived."

The grooms turned and lost all rational thought. They would only remember the details later, when in private conference with their wives.

# CHAPTER 23
## Two Gentleman and a Lady Are Surprised

*5 January 1812*

*A new year starts with a new experience. Yesterday, and again today, I had assignations with Mr. C of a very different nature than the stilted cold matings previously shared. When I arrived yesterday, he was already at the cottage and had taken the risk of starting a fire in the grate. I informed him it would be our last attempt. I explained that perhaps something within me was barren—of course the fault could just as easily be with him, but a lady must be politic, as I have learnt—and I was unwilling to expend further cash with nothing to show for it.*

*He quite surprised me by saying he had consulted a midwife in Hertfordshire about the getting of children. She explained to him, so he said, that women who could find it within themselves to take some pleasure from the act proved more fertile as a rule. We stared each other down for many minutes before he said, with smirking charm, "Dear Anne. I do not wish to make you love me. I do not think you want to or will. But I can make what we do more enjoyable if you will allow me certain liberties."*

*I could not resist replying, "More than I have already granted?"*

*"Yes."*

*I set about preparing myself for the act as I usually do, but before I could remove my stockings, he knelt between my legs. "Allow me."*

*With the practiced hand of a French maid, Mr. C had me mostly disrobed before I knew what I was about. He loosened my corset, and my meagre diddies bounced loose in a way that quite enthralled him, though I do say so myself. He kissed them, and I am ashamed to say, I nearly swooned. He caught me and carried me to the bed.*

*His subsequent ministrations were masterly. I shall not attempt to explain what I felt, or rather, the sensations he raised, and raised again and again, but it was as though physical congress, as we enacted it yesterday, was a totally different assemblage of actions than he and I had ever accomplished before. When I think what I allowed him to do… No, I shall not think of it. Except to say that, as I left him yesterday, I insisted he return today. I should blush.*

*When I parted from Mr. C today, I handed him 100£ as a gift. If what we did in the last day and a half does not get me with child, it is better I never see him again. To take pleasure from the act—oh, and I have—causes the arousal of certain affections that I shall not encourage. With enough of what I experienced at his bidding, any woman could fall in love with any man, were he to care enough to entice her thus.*

*I have no doubt he will use the money for the seduction of someone else. If my little extra capital allows him to make a better showing, I am happy for him.*

*And as for me? I cannot help but think the midwife he consulted is a scholar amongst her profession and a credit to her sex. If I am not now with child, I shall at least know I tried my very best, and so did Mr. C. —A de B*

*10 June 1812, Rosings, Kent*

A naked Alexander Fitzwilliam stood agape, staring at his new wife.

How he had enjoyed teasing Darcy and Bingley over the billiards table at Netherfield! He, at least, would be spared the torment of initiating a maiden. He laughed as Darcy and Bingley fretted, and imagined giving Charlotte such pleasurable sensations as she could not have felt with Collins but of which she would have read in Anne's journal.

"You are a *virgin*? Unfledged?" he sputtered. She looked so sheepish in her lovely, revealing nightgown that his alarm turned to amusement. "But how…"

Charlotte was trying not to laugh, and she tilted her head and pushed out her lips, looking at Alexander from under her lashes. It was an expression her late husband had never seen, but then, he had never, ever, caused her to feel coy. "Mr. Collins was a man of weak knowledge, easily confused. He came to the marriage bed with no understanding at all of the female… um, uh…" Charlotte at last had the decency to blush at her deception of her late husband.

"Whereas I…" The colonel raised his eyebrows, smiling provocatively. "Dearest Charlotte. I fear you will find me a good deal less easy to fool."

She returned his smile ruefully and stepped towards him. She held out a hand, which he took gently, watching her eyes as he bent to kiss her fingers.

*She has the prettiest hands.* He was pleased to think they would touch him in ways they had never touched Collins. As she drew closer, he could better discern the detail of her nightgown, the delicate floral embroidery at the low neckline drawing his attention to a bosom of greater ampleness than her usual mode of dress led him to expect. His tumescence increased.

"Then Collins dithered about your person to no great effect for you but sufficient to his own needs?"

"It seemed so. He was—God rest his soul—a man of small parts. He thought he was effecting a union when he was not, and I did nothing to correct him." Charlotte's delicate blush deepened. She caught sight of Alexander's manly organ and came to think she had committed a grave tactical error, unforgivable in a military man's spouse. Had she instructed Mr. Collins to the whys and wherefores of deflowering her, she would not be faced with having the task performed by a virile husband with much less modest equipage.

The colonel arose from bending over her hand. He stood next to her; she had to look up at him. "I shall be attentive to your comfort." Her straight hair caught the firelight as it fell about her shoulders. He brushed the strands, fine as silk, from one side, and slowly slid his hand over her breast, caressing it. She sighed. "My charming Charlotte, did you never take pleasure in his attempts to conceive?"

"I dared not dwell upon it."

"He never touched you like this?" her new husband whispered as he rolled a puckering nipple between his fingers.

"Never," she inhaled, finally remembering to breathe.

"But you did not wear nightgowns such as this, I would wager." The colonel's breath was in her ear, inspiring her shiver of excitement.

"No, I did not."

Alexander drew a tender earlobe into his mouth and applied both hands expertly to her breasts. In mere moments, Charlotte was writhing against him. In another minute, her breath grew ragged, and she tried in vain to speak his name, managing only, "Al...Alex..." Her knees gave way, and her full weight straddled his leg, her ardent parts pressing her husband's muscular thigh. He caught her by the waist as a storm of desire raged through her, leaving her wishing for something further.

He quietly chuckled. *This should not be difficult if her capacity for sensation is so easily engaged.* He sighed contentedly, pleased to recognise Charlotte would only ever be his. "Do you see the potential for pleasure in marital relations *now*, Mrs. Fitzwilliam?"

"Indeed, I am all astonishment. I never dreamt I would marry for love."

"Nor did I, my beloved Charlotte. Nor did I."

*Meanwhile, at Netherfield Park, Meryton*

CHARLES BINGLEY STOOD OUTSIDE THE DOOR TO HIS BRIDE'S BEDCHAMBER, bouncing on his toes and rocking back on his heels. Bingley was not a pacing sort of man when perplexed. Nor was he given to running his hands through his hair in the face of frustration. He was not aware of the motion he made, for his attention was fixed upon the woman awaiting him on the other side of the door.

Bingley had not the least idea what Jane had been told of marital relations. *Has she seen animals? Does she comprehend the gist of it?* For all the talk he had heard and overheard, for all of the reading and gazing at pictures, and even after once spending a few hours with a harlot on his grand tour three years earlier, he still did not know quite what to do with the wholly inexperienced Jane Bennet.

Bingley closed his eyes, still rocking on his feet. He wore soft breeches and a thin shirt untied at the neck, garments upon which no little consideration was given. He bathed and shaved, saying not a word to his valet through the entire proceedings. It was as if time crawled as he crossed his bedroom to the door of the mistress of Netherfield's bedchamber. The expanse of twenty feet seemed more like a mile. He heard no movement. Perhaps she was not yet there although he tried to sound masterful when he informed her after their evening meal that he would meet her there in an hour. That hour was well past as he stood at the door, quiet but not still.

Inside the lids of his closed eyes, he envisioned Jane's angelic face as he kissed her—not the innumerable pecks on the cheek or delicate meetings of puckered lips, but when he had ardently kissed her. After luring her to part her lips for his tongue, she responded in a passionate manner, embracing him and wriggling her fingers into his collar. She admitted in a whisper to wanting to touch his neck, which she was sad to see always too tightly bound. The memory made him smile, and encouraged, he knocked.

"Come in, Charles," came the immediate reply.

Bingley stepped inside the fire-lit room and turned to the bed. The bedclothes were folded down, but the bed was empty. He turned towards the fire, and he was met by fleeting impressions: waves of wild blond hair, soft breasts with firm points pressed into his hands, a wet mouth nibbling his neck, a whispered "Charles, at last..." The force of her naked haunch winding around his waist pushed him back, and they slammed the door. He returned her embrace if only to keep them from stumbling. The next sound Bingley heard was his own relieved laughter, which was soon silenced by his wife's kisses and her throaty chuckle.

"I hope you are not laughing at me, sir." Her blue eyes were merry in a different way than he had ever seen before.

"No, dear Jane. As usual, I laugh at myself." It was beyond his power of reasoning to have intuited Jane might want him, to have felt her longing for him in the same way he had dreamt of her. His fears had been for nothing. Somehow, she was more than well prepared for this night, this moment.

Supporting the thigh already encircling him, Bingley touched her other leg, and this she lifted, climbing him and opening herself with a giggled yelp of excitement. Thus enrobed by his formerly serene and unflappable Jane, Bingley carried her to the bed and gently leaned forward until her back was upon the mattress and pillows. He stood, and before he could fully take in her nakedness, she was up on her knees, struggling to remove his shirt, tugging at the buttons of his breeches, and bending him to her face for feverish kisses.

Only when he, too, was naked did she sit back upon her calves, and in the dim fluid firelight, they gazed upon each other. She reached for his aroused member but just stopped from touching it, instead stroking his firm abdomen with a mew of pleasure. Bingley wanted to speak—he needed to tell her how beautiful she was—but her finger stilled his lips.

"Nay, Charles, let us keep silent this first time…at least, no words."

He smiled, kissed her fingers, and pulled them away. "May I not laugh for joy, Mrs. Bingley?"

Jane giggled and nodded, pulling him down into the bedclothes. She wrapped around him, and their eyes met in smiles as he felt her beneath him, warm, compliant, and sufficiently padded to be supremely inviting. Her breast against his cheek felt like the velvet squabs of Darcy's landau.

"We must order a finer carriage," he murmured.

Jane's laugh was so robust that she snorted for the first time in her life. "This is precisely why we must be silent, love."

He rose on an elbow, one hand caressing a hank of her hair, his other hand exploring every inch of her within reach. She set no limits and observed no boundaries. Whatever he wished to do, she would enthusiastically allow. Bingley could not look away from her face. He had seen Jane appear pleased with him but never like this. *Perhaps I do not know her as well as I thought. She is much more enchanting than I could even anticipate…*

Jane's delight at his every movement granted Bingley a masterly confidence. His fingers took possession of her secret places. She writhed with approval, encouraging him to exert his ultimate right as a husband, and when he entered her, she relaxed against him. They paused for a moment, and when she met his quizzical eyes with giddy encouragement, Bingley completed their act of union with the aplomb of a man who had been pleasing a willing and responsive wife for many months, not for mere minutes.

When she at last lay at his side with her head on his chest, he asked, "You were not hurt, sweetest Jane?"

"No, just a very little at the first."

"How…?"

"I have spent some portion of each of the past ten days secretly riding astride my father's horse. I wished to spare you fearing you had hurt me."

"You are the most considerate woman that ever was."

"Charles, I do not wish to always be an angel."

"Duly noted, madam. There is a mystery to you, Mrs. Bingley, which I shall enjoy solving."

They smiled at the notion of such a thing, and continued smiling well into the night.

# CHAPTER 22
## Fitzwilliam Darcy is Surprised

*1 September 1811*

*Ugh! Well, tis done, and let us hope the consummation enacted today need not be repeated much more often. What a ghastly business! How do women bear it? And why? Is the urge to procreate so strong that the ridiculousness of the act is forgiven?*

*Wickham arrived expecting to enact a seduction, ever ready to charm. I quickly informed him charm was not necessary. After lying on the cot, I lifted my skirts and asked if the smallness of the bed was insufficient for our needs, and gave him the opportunity to suggest otherwise. He was in a mood to acquiesce, and knelt between my legs, leering. He made to touch between my legs, saying some nonsense about preparing me, but I could easily see, what with the bulge in his trousers, that no encouragement was needed for him. I informed him that, if he was ready, I was likewise. He would have argued, so I moved his hand away and spread my legs further. This was enough encouragement. He unbuttoned his breeches as I looked anywhere else.*

*He asked if we might loosen my bodice, but I could not see the use of that, my chest having no orifice that would effect conception. I shook my head no. He chuckled and stroked my thighs. "You will give me no joy, madam?"*

*"Taking a wealthy virgin is insufficient inducement? I would not have thought so," I replied.*

*"Saucy!" he said, the scoundrel.*

*Rather suddenly, he bent over and pushed his apparatus at me, I suppose thinking the decidedly unpleasant sensation of his rubbing it on my thighs was somehow necessary for my willingness. I said nothing, which was enough, and just as he was to commit the act, it all became ticklish, and I wriggled against my will. This displaced his aim, and he bashed his member against the bend of my leg, spending himself in my short hairs with a curse.*

*"You moved," he said in what was a decidedly accusatory tone.*

*"You were tickling me. Begin again. I shall be still."*

*He informed me it would take some minutes, which vexed me greatly. The fluid already emitted oozed around on me, a waste. I asked after the possibility of somehow getting what was already done into the proper place, which elicited an annoying, indeed disparaging, laugh. Were I not already lying there compromised, yet not quite, I would have left him to amuse himself.*

*"Hurry up, then."*

*He huffed. "It would help if you would touch it."*

*Now it was my place to laugh. "No, Wickham, that will never happen. Do what you must, but you will have no such assistance from me."*

*He cursed once more, arose, and stood with his back to me. I soon surmised, given his actions, that he was touching himself, and vigorously too. After a time, he turned back to me and flung himself down. With a jerk and a groan, his hands held my hips, the weight of his body drained the breath from my chest, and I was no longer a virgin. He thrashed about, causing me all of the discomfort I had been led to expect, and did finally spend himself in the proper place.*

*"There, madam. I would ask if you are satisfied, but that is not your intention."*

*This sentence I did not at all comprehend, so I replied, "Let us hope you were successful."*

*We both stood. He buttoned himself and put on his rather worn frock coat. Seating his hat with a nod, he enquired, "Tomorrow?"*

*"At the same time," I said. I was arranging my skirts. The substance dripping from between my legs felt disgusting.*

*He was gone. I took up the towelling I had brought, and cleaned myself thoroughly. There was some blood. I inexplicably stood trembling for some moments.*

*I suppose I would never do it again had I not my present goal in mind. But I must continue until my courses stop coming. I am told that is the first sign.*

*It is all too arduous. When I returned home, after finding the bench of the phaeton most cruel, I gave my usual excuses and made for my bed. It was all too revolting and outrageously silly. Once alone, I laughed—A de B*

*10 June 1812, Darcy House, London*

Darcy entered the bedroom to find Elizabeth under the bedclothes. Only her head, shoulders, and arms were visible. She wore a rough raw muslin nightgown with long sleeves. Of all his hopes for this night, Darcy had not prepared himself for this, that she of all women would be reticent.

As he stood watching from just inside the doorway, Elizabeth turned but did not seem inclined to meet his gaze. Her countenance was solemn. She drew in a deep breath and stated in a flat voice, "I am ready for you, husband." She pushed away the counterpane and pulled her hem to her waist, revealing shapely white legs joined at a lush mound of dark, short curls.

At first, Darcy was stunned to see, so suddenly and artlessly displayed, the shiny triangle of hair and curve of alabaster thighs, but this was not as he had dreamt. Her legs were stiff and the hands holding her nightgown showed fisted knuckles.

Darcy studied Elizabeth's face. Her eyes were closed, her expression an indication that she expected something unpleasant to be visited upon her.

*What in heaven's name has she been told? Did she not read Anne's journal?* His staring wonder turned to amusement, and against his better judgment, a chuckle escaped him.

At the sound of his rumbling chortle, one of Elizabeth's eyes opened suspiciously then closed again as he approached.

"Elizabeth," Darcy said with mirthful exasperation, "this will not do." He took the nightgown from her hands and smoothed the coarse fabric down below her knees. "Indeed, madam…I can only wonder what you have been led to expect."

As he covered her, Elizabeth's eyes flew open. She was confused. "I was told to welcome you."

Darcy snorted once more into a chuckle. "Were you? And this is your manner of welcome? Your beautiful face looking as if you expect a brutish husband?"

She blinked as he sat at the opposite end of the bed, leaning against the curtained post and stretching his long legs next to her, his bare feet reaching her hip. He was a study in nonchalance. He took care to keep his robe closed, but she could see he must be naked under it, for his calves were as bare as his feet, and the deep collar displayed his neck and a glimpse of skin at his chest.

"I…" she stammered, "…I was not welcoming?"

Darcy was still smiling with his hands folded to hide his lap. His manly organ was not as daunted by her countenance as were his thoughts. "No, wife, I am afraid you have fallen shy of the mark. A grimace of distaste is not welcoming. Neither are thighs clamped tight. No, I am sorry to say it, but a chastity belt could not have served you better."

Elizabeth looked chagrined and began to blush. *He is not Wickham, nor am I Anne. This is another matter entirely. Blasted Mama, and foolish, foolish Lizzy.* She sighed. *I do not know what I am about.* Had she been standing, she would have stomped her foot at her stupidity.

Darcy's quiet voice interrupted her fretfulness. "May I ask, my love, how you came to choose such a modest nightgown? This is not what I would have expected from the woman who told me not to stop two days ago."

"Oh! A gentleman would not remind a lady of her misbehaviour!" Her eyes were wide with alarm.

"You were not misbehaving then, and there is nothing you can do to misbehave now. In our bedchamber as husband and wife, notions of proper behaviour are likely to get…confused if not dispensed with entirely. Or so I had hoped."

Elizabeth took a thorough reading of Darcy's countenance. His face was kind—he was not angry—but there was an expression of disappointment (the cast of his eyes, the droop of his shoulders), and it gave her heart a painful tug. "Oh dear, I…oh. I have already failed you." She drew in a ragged breath. "My mother said a wife should welcome her husband, but she ought not feel pleasure. Kindness is to be hoped for but not expected."

"And was *that* the sum total of her advice?" He was incredulous.

"That was the upshot, yes." Elizabeth nodded in affirmation. Impulsively she drew herself forward and knelt by his knees. "And your cousin's journal was not encouraging." When Darcy frowned, she blundered on, "I felt pleasure when we were alone. I wanted…" Words failed her.

"What did you want?" Darcy matched her seriousness.

"…I wanted what I have since been told I ought not to want." Her eyes searched his, willing him to explain the sensations and emotions her mother had only acknowledged as inappropriate for a lady. *But how would he know? He is but a man.*

"When did your mother speak to you?"

"That evening. Monday. With Aunt Gardiner. When we returned…they saw my agitation."

"Your Aunt Gardiner took part in your instruction?" Darcy was all astonishment. Mrs. Gardiner had seemed sensible and *happily* married.

"Well, she was there, and she *wanted* to speak but Mama hushed her—repeatedly. Aunt Gardiner became annoyed and quit the room, saying she was not needed."

Darcy chuckled again, imagining the scene. *It seems this will be a slow endeavour, but not, perhaps, impossible. I am not Wickham and she is not Anne, and she most assuredly did not read Anne's last assignations. How can I raise her confidence in this?* He sighed. "Elizabeth…is it logical that I would treat you with tenderness and passion on Therfield Heath, only to become a savage beast when we are in our marriage bed for the first time?

"Your mother is not here. She will never know you have met my advances with equal ardour. Have I ever made a secret of my desire for you? On

Therfield Heath, I believe you desired me. *That* is what you felt, and I was captivated. We were betrothed, and we expressed our affection. There has been no chance to tell you that, had the thunder not startled the horse, I would *not* have tried your virtue nor found you wanting for surprising me with your forwardness. My feelings were quite the contrary."

"You did not disapprove? You seemed displeased."

"I was! With Bingley's stable master! That man cannot train a horse to ignore the weather? I cursed him and all his relations."

"But the horse came back directly!"

"Whereas you did not."

"I was searching for the horse!"

"Yes, I mean, it gave you time to fret and assume my disapprobation. You chastised yourself for your actions and told yourself I know not what about how you thought *my* feelings must be. When you returned, you were changed."

"But I had…I-I put your hand on my…" She could not say it.

"On your breast. Yes. It was not the sort of thing I am likely to forget, I promise you. You must understand…it made me happy that you did so. *Very* happy."

Blushing, Elizabeth looked down at her hands. She was absently twisting her betrothal ring. "What a fool I am," she murmured.

Darcy reached to still her hands then pulled one to his chest as he sat forward. "You are only misinformed. Let me teach you." He placed her hand on his bare skin. "Can you feel my heart?" He softly repeated her question from their morning on the heath.

Elizabeth looked into his eyes. He saw some sparkle ignite in her gaze.

"Mr. Darcy, I humbly request your leave to begin this night anew. If you would be so kind as to excuse me, I shall search my dressing room for a more suitable nightgown." She pulled her tingling hand away.

Relinquishing her nearness seemed counter to furthering their progress. Darcy leaned to kiss her nose. "You make an excellent suggestion, Elizabeth, but it is not necessary. We can make do."

Elizabeth laughed, which brought Darcy much relief, and he laughed too.

"I am glad to know you are willing to cope with a difficult garment, sir."

"Always."

"But allow me this."

As Darcy watched, Elizabeth untied the narrow ribbon at the end of her plait and unbound her hair. She shook her head.

"Let me," Darcy murmured. Almost timidly, he stroked her tresses smooth over her shoulders.

"An improvement?" One impertinent eyebrow lifted, challenging him.

He was too enchanted to speak.

"Not improved?" She smiled.

"M-much better," he stuttered. He captured her hand and kissed her palm. "But you are anxious?"

"Uncertain, yes. Other than to sit here and attempt to summon a more sincere come hither expression, I know not what to do."

"But you have been told what will happen, you have read of it...what we will do?"

She met his eyes earnestly. "Like all male creatures, you have a...a part. And...and...I, I have a place. Your part must join with my place. My...?"

Darcy pursed his lips. He tried biting the insides of his cheeks, but his mouth uncontrollably widened to a broad smile. "Yes. Precisely. My part in your place—if only 'twere so simply done, the first time."

Elizabeth smiled crookedly, displaying her trepidation while watching him fight his laughter. "At the very least, you cannot doubt your bride's innocence."

He pulled her into an embrace that warmed her from scalp to toenail. She savoured being in his arms and feeling the reverberation of lying against him as he laughed, even if she was certain he was entertained at her expense. She began to laugh at herself. "Such a fool, your wife."

Her giggling incited him. Pressing her more firmly breast to chest, he drew in his breath, mastering his laughter and giving way to passion. He gazed into her eyes and was vastly relieved to see, in the candle glow and firelight, some return of the intoxicating countenance he had witnessed two days before.

Elizabeth was astonished at the heat of him. *What need have we for a fire once we are abed?* She shook her head vaguely as he looked into her eyes as if to pull forth her soul. Her thoughts surprised her. "Oh!"

Darcy kissed her with everything he had. The only way he knew to calm her was to show her that she would be protected and cherished. He must leave her in no suspense. He was cross with himself for allowing her, even fleetingly, to suspect his disappointment. When she made a slight moan as his tongue passed her lips, followed by a shiver that spoke nothing of chill, Darcy lifted a hand to carefully cup her breast through the nightgown. "Mmm...Lizzy."

"Ah!"

He pulled away only far enough to read her eyes. "Are we as we were on Therfield Heath?"

Elizabeth's heart raced as it had that day. She knew he would sense her palpitations and whispered, "I would not have granted you much more than this."

"Nor would I have tried you further."

Her eyebrows raised in disbelief.

His dimples betrayed his thoughts. "Well, not *much* further. But I would have certainly tried this."

He kissed her again as his hands worked the little buttons that began at the neck of her gown. His lips moved to her jaw, her throat, and, once it was exposed, to the tiny mole at her collarbone. He opened the placket further, his lips following his hands as they pushed her garment aside, lighting a trail of fire ending at the nipple of the breast under which her heart fluttered. He kissed it reverently before drawing her into his mouth with a groan.

The sensations he unleashed, first of anticipation followed by dizzying desire, caused Elizabeth to push against him, cradling his head to her bosom. "You would have done *this* on our walk?" Speaking was nearly beyond her.

"Yes," he replied against her seductive skin. "You said not to stop. Do you approve?"

She hesitated. Approve seemed a weak word. Torment for more was warring with appreciation for his current ministrations. Wholly the opposite of what she had expected, she now wanted nothing more than to lift her gown again and let him touch or kiss any part of her, if it felt as wonderful as this. He was a gentle gentleman, and she ought not to have doubted him. Unsure, she fell back onto her habit of teasing. "You would not have found it so easy then, although I often do not wear a corset when I walk out early."

He straightened. "Why was I not told of this?" His eyes were alight with a mischievous glint.

"It is hardly proper information for a maiden to reveal!"

With a growl, he lifted her hair over one shoulder to bite her playfully, and she gave a little shriek of laughter. He rolled her away and spooned behind her, cupping both breasts—one freed from her nightgown—moving his lips over her exposed nape. "My Lizzy wanders the countryside half dressed?" He continued tasting her shoulders. He reached under her bosom, pushing away the fabric to take his purchase of both bared breasts. "Yet she greets me on her wedding night like a vestal virgin."

"We have established I am foolish; you need not belabour the point. Now I have a question for you of great importance. Mr. Darcy? Or Fitzwilliam? What would you...*have me*...call you?" She made little gasps as she spoke, responding to his touch.

Her sighs were setting him aflame. "*Have you*... Yes, call me whatever you like, only give me leave to *have you*," he whispered against her neck.

Unable to speak further, she pressed his hands over her bosom, encouraging him. She moaned, "My love...yes." She turned enough to lean her head against his chest.

Wishing for further progress, Darcy opened his robe. His hands returned gently to her breasts, pulling her against his nakedness. He shook his head to settle his wits. He was not successful.

"Is that...?" Elizabeth whispered when he rubbed against her rear end.

"Yes." He huffed an amused breath. "My part."

She studied the sensation of his potency's touch. His every motion and whisper let her know she was irresistible. Her confidence blossomed. "Do you desire me, my love?"

"More than anything."

Elizabeth turned in his arms, and she was enthralled by his bare chest with its scattering of dark hair. She brushed her lips against him, stealing tastes over the muscled, warm skin. Pushing his robe down his arms, she leaned into him, still marvelling at his heat.

Darcy began inching the rough muslin up her legs. Elizabeth smiled against his skin, thinking of her silly and altogether blunt exposure of herself when he first entered the room. *Yes, he wants to find his own way. It is part of the allure. I should have known him better.*

When he grasped half of her derriere in one hand, Elizabeth's throat released several low notes and she instinctively parted her legs.

Darcy's cheek leaned on the top of her head. He smiled dreamily when he felt her legs acquiesce. Smooth and lush as her backside felt, she was offering her body, her essence. She would join with him, and they would both be more together than each had ever been alone. His fingers crept between her soft thighs. He gently touched where he might unlock her passion. Her breath was rapid. He could feel it as she pushed against him, as if she would enter *him* by adhering her skin tight to his.

Elizabeth was amazed at what his hand was provoking in *that* place and wanted more of it. The bestirred feelings could not be contained. She cried out, "Ah! Mr. Darcy!"

His other hand stroked her shoulder then took a firm grip of her waist. "Shh… Lizzy, I shall cease if you would prefer it," he assured her.

He was mistaken.

"I most certainly *do not* prefer it."

Uncertain, he stopped the motions of his hand.

"You will continue," she whispered more insistently and then realised her incivility. "Please." She smiled when he laughed in her arms.

"You are still too ladylike, my love."

His fingers continued tracing circles between her thighs. Her instinct was to close her legs, to trap his hand and keep it forever there. She was alarmed upon hearing herself emit a guttural sound. Unconsciously her hips began to sway, adding to the sensation.

Elizabeth closed her eyes and rolled her forehead against his chest. Darcy's instrument was pressed between them. It made her light-headed, and she unthinkingly bit at the flat nipple nearest her mouth. He was salty, and the nub of his flesh firmed between her teeth. Like hers, Darcy's breathing was rapid.

His hands withdrew and forced the nightgown off her arms. He began kissing her fragrant skin inside her elbows, breastbone, and soft belly, deliciously lingering at her navel.

Her hands were in his hair, encouraging him with nonsense. She was dazed as she cried, "Darcy! Mr. Darcy! You should not. Oh! My love! Oh… please. Touch me."

Darcy rose to his knees abruptly and turned away. "Enough of virtue."

Her eyes tried to focus. She looked down his back as he pushed his robe away. She was charmed by the whiteness of his backside.

"I do not mean to be so loud," she whispered. "What will everyone think?"

Darcy smiled and with tender care lay next to her, supported by his elbows. "They know it is our wedding night."

He looked down at his bride. Her nightgown was bunched over that which she had exposed to him earlier. Now it was the only part of her covered. Elizabeth was beautiful beyond his imagining, and she was to be his.

Her gaze was confused and adoring. "Is this more welcoming?" With the hand wearing the betrothal ring, she stroked his face and stretched her other limbs like a cat. She then spread her legs and rubbed them against his.

"Infinitely." He slid against her, instantly setting his fingers to work, plying her. "Lizzy, oh, my Lizzy. Let me…"

She was in turmoil and had no words. Her hand reached down to touch his, urging him. She wriggled and gasped, sensible only of his fingers inside her. There was a whispered acknowledgement that he was not hurting her. He was being exceedingly slow and solicitous. Perhaps she might prefer it all happen a bit more swiftly.

He arose to resettle his knees between her legs, never withdrawing his hand. Arched over her, his mouth explored her bosom.

"Your hair…on my skin. I…want this…you…husband," she murmured.

His gaze met hers and he saw her come undone. Elizabeth's eyes faltered as if drugged. Her mouth opened, and he felt a moan begin in the middle of her body, rising through her throat. As her hands gripped his hair, her hips rolled sharply. Pushed by her surprisingly strong hands, his face was brought back against her chest, and after several moments, her inarticulate sounds and sighs lessened their feverish frequency.

There was the track of a tear on her cheek. "This is married love?"

"We can make of it whatever we wish." His eyes were warm and adoring.

She was incoherent—the lucid moment was gone—but she smiled, touching his chest, his shoulders, burying her hands in his hair, kissing him possessively when his mouth passed near hers.

He could wait no longer, and spoke at her ear. "Dearest, loveliest. It is time."

She nodded against his shoulder. "I want to," she whispered.

He guided his ardent member to begin his advance. There was no doubt she was willing, but would she be hurt? Darcy knew hesitation might be the worst offence. He affected their union deliberately, evenly, refusing to forge ahead recklessly. He recognised a constriction and slowly pushed through it. He felt more than heard Elizabeth's sudden sigh but she did not cry out or become tense. She continued to spread her legs.

"Lizzy?"

The little hands clinging to his back slid to his buttocks. One of her legs embraced his waist, the other wrapped over his thigh.

"This is better."

"Better?"

"Better than your hand."

Darcy had slightly withdrawn but her encouragement made him mindless, and he filled her again and again.

She held him fiercely. It was far different from what she had imagined. There would be no describing it. The act of accepting him flooded her with love. At each whispered, "Yes!" from her, his strength seemed to increase. Elizabeth found herself overwhelmed with heat spreading throughout her limbs from where they were joined.

One of his hands was at the top of her derriere, holding her steady as he buried himself inside the woman he loved. He met his release with a roar. "Elizabeth!"

"Love!" she cried with him, excited by his completion. When he was quieter she whispered, "I love you," over and over. She was relieved to not be the only one who was loudly indiscreet.

Darcy was unaware of his potent cry. He only knew their joining was profound, and Elizabeth Bennet, the one thing in his life that had ever been unattainable, was now and forever his. As she cooed delicate words of love in his ear, he could scarce believe he was living his dreams. It was as if the waning spasms of his completion were echoing his heartbeat and the rhythmic murmur of her name, "Elizabeth… Elizabeth…"

Moments or hours later, as he raised himself on one elbow, she looked up at him. "You were correct, my love," she whispered, returning his smile. "There was nothing gentlemanly or ladylike about that." She paused for breath. "I feel very sorry for Miss de Bourgh, to have never known this."

Rather than reveal he had read more of Anne's tales than his wife had, Darcy simply laughed. He looked around them and his laughter increased.

"What…?" Elizabeth grew apprehensive.

"We have been at this wrong way round. Our heads are at the foot! We are lucky I did not knock myself cold on the bedpost."

Elizabeth began to giggle but stopped when he started to move from the bed, and she clutched at his arm. "Do not go. Please! I know husbands and wives sleep apart, but *must* you go tonight?" Her panic was plain in her eyes.

"I have so rarely slept alone."

Darcy touched her hands. "I shall return directly, and I shall bring some towelling. I am…uh, sticky, and I think you might be too? But I intend to sleep with you—my head on the *pillows*. In that, at least, you will find me traditional." He took the candlestick from the nightstand.

He was gone just a moment, returning with pieces of moist cloth. He set the candle on the nightstand and stood with his back to her, washing.

Elizabeth had covered herself with his robe when he arose, and now opened it, freshening herself. She noticed the moistened towel was tinged with blood. She moved her place on the bed and saw the same on her trailing nightgown. Darcy turned at her movement, seeing the evidence of her first bedding.

"My love." He sat next to her impulsively. "Were you more hurt than you said?"

"No, truly I was not. It was a momentary stinging, and then…"

"Then?" He took her hands and helped her to stand. He pushed his robe from her shoulders, and her nightgown fell with it to the floor, leaving her as naked as he.

Elizabeth gave him a slow smile. "You know very well what happened then." In betrayal of her knowing expression, her sudden nakedness made her blush.

"That does not mean I do not wish to hear how you would say it…" He tried not to smile.

"You became…" She was searching for a word. "You became my lover. In error, I thought you my enemy once, and then you became my friend and ally. You progressed with exquisite stealth to being the man I love without my realising it until knowing it saved my life." She shook her head at him with merriment rather than censure. "Then you became my betrothed, and today my husband, but I think I prefer this above all else." Elizabeth became impish. "I have taken Fitzwilliam Darcy as my lover, whom everyone thinks *such* a gentleman." She looked in his eyes to see how he would respond to such an indecorous admission.

Darcy was delighted and chuckled deeply as he embraced her. "I have married a rascal! A far cry from the block of ice who invited me to this bed an hour ago."

"Then I must assume you *prefer* being married to a rascal?"

"Yes, Mrs. Darcy, I do. I most certainly do. Ah, Lizzy…"

They were properly under the bedclothes, still giddy. It took surprisingly little effort for Darcy to coax his new wife to couple with him again before they slept.

Elizabeth awoke in the night. They had rolled apart after the heat of their second joining, but she continued to hold the hand she had taken as fatigue consumed her. She raised his knuckles to her lips. It was everything a man's hand should be, and she held it up to appraise it in the moonlight. How was she ever to look at his hands in company again without blushing and wishing them to be at her for her pleasure?

Darcy awoke feeling soft lips upon the back of his hand. Elizabeth was so intent upon her study that she did not notice his eyes open as he smiled. Saying nothing, for he thought he understood her rightly enough, he wrapped his other hand over hers and settled his arm between her breasts as he rolled to his side and curled around her.

"This is far superior to sleeping with Jane," Elizabeth observed.

Darcy chuckled when he felt her laughing in his arms. "I am a success, then, as a husband?"

Her response was to wiggle herself against him, tucking her head under his chin, her cheek against his warm skin. Within moments, Elizabeth was asleep.

He was not accustomed to sleeping with anyone, but he fully intended to become so. Darcy lay awake for much longer, smiling into the moonlit night.

*30 March 1812*

*Darcy is much worse. His eyes follow her everywhere. He is as besotted and moonstruck as I have ever seen a man. Poor fellow! The lamb is completely lost, yet she is unaware, and he fights his inclination when he can.*

*She is just the sort of woman he needs. She is lively and intelligent. She has a conceited independence to match his, which I'd have thought impossible to find. Her pride glows from within yet does not overcome her charming manners. Darcy is quite the opposite, donning his haughtiness to conceal the warmth that now leaks from him like the breach of a dam when she is in our company. I fear he will not, yet hope he will crack apart like an egg and allow himself to be the man his father was.*

*In fact, I believe with a well-chosen wife, a wife of personal merit and quick wits, he could be a better man. Elizabeth Bennet is just the thing for him, and so healthy! One can only imagine what a passionate husband might draw out of her. But my cousin is no Wickham. Would he be troubled to make enquiries as Wickham did? Would he learn those delicate manoeuvres? I cannot imagine it of Darcy.*

*But how are Darcy and EB to manage it? How is such a match ever to be realised? I would manipulate and direct them if I could, but I cannot see how the thing is to be done —A de B*

THE END

# Acknowledgements

This story was born during the editing process for *The Red Chrysanthemum*, just a little aside that grew. Perhaps I enquired of Gail Warner, my editor-beyond-price, what-if Darcy had to return to Rosings while Elizabeth was still at Hunsford? Why would he? Perhaps someone had died and he returned for the funeral? Who was likely to have died? Anne is sickly; let's kill her off! And so, one thing led to another down a decidedly macabre lover's lane. I started collecting snippets of conversations that came to mind, reading Elizabeth's stay in Hunsford in *Pride and Prejudice, An Annotated Edition* (Patricia Meyer Spacks, editor) carefully, and making notes of Regency funeral customs.

Much to my amazement, Anne de Bourgh began to keep a journal, which added tremendously to what was initially a little trifle of a *Pride and Prejudice* meets *A Midsummer Night's Dream* mash-up. Dear wise, frail, flawed Anne, who accomplished much for her cousins with her determination and iron will but did not live to see it!

Once hearing of *A Will of Iron* (which started its life as "Death Comes to Rosings" but morphed into the present title for obvious reasons), my friend Jacqueline Mitzel began researching Regency funeral habits and customs, and to her I am greatly indebted for many of the arcane details she was able to exhume.

My best friends in the A Happy Assembly chat room were also invaluable for their often not too gentle reminders for me to give this story my attention when other temptations loomed. Thanks especially to redhead, beezie, and our chat chap, Chris Polk. Every, "Anything new in AWOI lately?" spurred me and kept me on task.

As ever, I thank the team at Meryton Press for their wholehearted support of this story, although now the cover artists run when they see me coming. I make them do things like stare at desserts, major gemstones, and Colin Firth's legs.

CPSIA information can be obtained at www.ICGtesting.com
Printed in the USA
BVOW08s1653250715

410101BV00004B/58/P